DETECTIVE DUFF UNRAVELS IT

DETECTIVE DUFF UNRAVELS IT

by

Harvey O'Higgins

RAMBLE HOUSE

Detective Duff Unravels It ©1925 by Harvey O'Higgins

ISBN 13: 978-1-60543-165-9

ISBN 10: 1-60543-165-6

Ramble House Edition: 2008
Cover Art: Gavin L. O'Keefe
Preparation: Fender Tucker and Gavin O'Keefe

CONTENTS

THE

MARSHALL

MURDER

THE MARSHALL MURDER

I

"THIS IS MR. DUFF," the lawyer introduced them. "Miss Marshall, Mr. Duff." And Duff shook hands with a very small, a very dark, a very alert and fashionable spinster-lady of middle age, who looked up at him with a sweet and ironical smile.

"Well," she said softly, "you're big enough."

He was huge. He was nearly six feet tall; he weighed some two hundred pounds; and he was solid with muscle.

"It's a disguise," he assured her. "I use it to deceive people— the same as you do." And he met her smile with a shrewd, appraising twinkle.

"The same as I do?"

"Yes," he said. "They never suspect me of being a detective, any more than they suspect you of being an autocrat."

Her smile became sweeter than ever. "What makes you think I'm an autocrat?"

"The same thing in me that makes me think I'm a detective. Won't you sit down?"

She accepted a chair by the fireplace with a tiny dignity that was not unimpressive. "I only hope," she murmured, "that you're not equally deceived in us both."

She and Westingate, her lawyer, had come to consult Duff in his rooms, instead of at his office, because they wished to keep their visit to him a careful secret. His rooms were on the second floor of an old brownstone house on Eleventh Street near Sixth Avenue, and the living-room in which they found him, typical of the decayed gentility of the district, had a high ceiling, an old black marble mantelpiece, tall windows, and a hardwood floor. He had furnished it chiefly with a law library, descended from the days when he had been an unsuccessful young attorney. As a living-room, it looked studious and celibate. The chairs were all fat bachelor chairs, upholstered in dark leather, as severe as they were comfortable; and they were so burly that Alicia Marshall, for all her furs, sat in hers like a little fairy godmother in a giant's seat.

The lawyer, Westingate, took a chair on the same side of the fireplace as she, and frowned at the blaze with a forehead that was permanently corrugated. A somber and bilious-looking bald man, he seemed always to be brooding over the obscurities of the law behind a set and worried countenance. "I suppose you've guessed," he said, "that we wanted to see you about this"—he coughed—"murder."

Duff raised his heavy eyebrows, deprecatingly. "No," he admitted. "I wasn't sure."

"Well," Alicia Marshall said, "we *did.*" She had unbuttoned her sealskin sacque. She threw it open, now, with a gesture of beginning the discussion. Duff sat down. The lawyer cleared his throat.

The murder—the Marshall murder—was one of those picturesque New Jersey murders that happen in the best-regulated families of a state that prides itself on its "swift Jersey justice"— murders of which no one is ever found guilty, so that they present the fascinating spectacle of an irresistible force meeting an insoluble mystery. The chief victim was a distinguished citizen, Senator Amos K. Marshall, a corporation lawyer and party politician; and his outrageous end may have been more shocking to the popular mind because, after all, the murder of a "big business" lawyer, who is also a machine senator, contains elements that do not wholly horrify, and it is necessary for many people to be volubly distressed at such a crime in order to overcome a contrary impulse, perhaps. In any case, the public outcry was tremendous, measured either by the amount of newspaper space that was filled with accounts of the Marshall murder, or by the amount of boxwood hedge that was carried away from the Marshall lawn by souvenir hunters.

There was killed with Senator Marshall, a young widow, named Mrs. Starrett, who was his housekeeper. When a man and a woman are murdered together, scandal seems inevitable; and in this case, the scandal traveled fast because no evidence was found to support it. It moved as freely as a flying column that lives off the countryside without any need for a base of supplies. And it was followed by the rumor that the man accused of the murder had been in love with the housekeeper, though there was no discoverable basis in fact for that report either.

The man accused was an ex-soldier named Andrew Pittling—a young veteran of the Argonne, suffering from shell-shock—whom Marshall had employed as general utility-man around his suburban home in Cold Brook. Pittling had been voluble in his support of President Wilson's League of Nations, and Marshall had conspicuously helped to defeat Wilson's policies. Hence, many arguments about the murder were warm with the animation of political sympathy.

Hence, also, Alicia Marshall—before her lawyer could get his cleared throat into action—broke out gently to Duff: "We've decided that there's no use leaving it to the local authorities any longer. They're a lot of Democratic politicians. I believe they're capable of protecting the man who killed Amos, if they knew who he was."

"You were not in the house, that night?" Duff asked, meaning the night of the murder.

"No, I was not."

She lived, she explained, in the original Marshall homestead, on Marshall Avenue, in Cold Brook. Her dead brother Amos, when he married, bought an estate in the hills behind the town; he rebuilt magnificently an old Dutch farmhouse on the property and he had lived there ever since. There had been no one in the house on the night of the murder except his daughter, Martha—so ill in bed with influenza that she was too weak to lift her head from the pillow, and a number of servants, all women except this one man, the ex-soldier, Pittling.

"What is the actual evidence against Pittling, do you know?" Duff asked the lawyer.

Well, to tell the truth, there was none. Senator Marshall had been killed, evidently with a hatchet, as he lay asleep in his bed. His housekeeper, Mrs. Starrett, had been struck down, apparently with the same hatchet, in the hall outside his door. In the morning, a bloody hatchet was found lying among some rose bushes under an open window that looked out from the dining-room on a side lawn. Either the murderer had dropped his weapon there, as he escaped out the window, or he had tossed it out the window and remained in the house himself. In neither case was there anything to cast suspicion on Pittling except the fact that the hatchet was his. He kept it in the furnace-room of the basement to use when he was building fires; and he had used it earlier in the day to split kindling for a fire in the bedroom of the daughter, Martha. The weather had turned suddenly colder that afternoon, and Martha had complained that her room was chilly even with the furnace on full draught. Pittling and the housemaid built a fire of cannel coal in her bedroom grate, to satisfy her; but neither of them could remember whether Pittling had brought the hatchet up out of the basement then, or whether if he *had* brought it up, he had failed to return it to the cellar. No distinguishable fingerprints were on it when it was found in the morning. There were no footprints outside the window, because the ground was frozen hard and bare of snow. And no one but the dead housekeeper knew whether the window had been left unlocked the night before, or whether it had been opened from the inside after she had locked it. It was her duty to make the rounds at night and see that all the doors and windows were closed and fastened before she went to bed.

"And no one," Duff asked, "heard any noise whatever during the night?"

No one. No one could be expected to, except Martha, the sick girl. Her room was next to her father's. The housekeeper was killed in the hall between her father's door and hers. But she had gone through the crisis of her fever that afternoon; she fell asleep, in a weak perspiration, late that evening; and she did not wake till the following dawn. Her door had been closed after she fell asleep, evidently by the housekeeper, to protect her slumber; and she heard nothing. The women servants—that is to say, the cook and the two maids—slept in the kitchen wing, out of hearing of anything that might happen in the main portion of the house. The chauffeur slept over the garage. Pittling, the ex-soldier, had fixed himself a room in the basement, where he lived as if he were in a cement dugout. He was peculiar.

"I see," Duff said. "And he heard nothing either?"

"Nothing," the lawyer replied, "of any importance."

"No? What was it?"

Westingate explained impatiently: "Senator Marshall's home is not supplied with water from the waterworks in Cold Brook. It's too far outside the town. It has its own pumping plant—an air pump, in a driven well, at some distance from the house. Compressed air is stored in a tank in the pumphouse, and the pump is quiet except when any of the faucets in the house are opened; then, as water flows out of the pipe, the mechanism of the pump trips off with an audible stroke. Pittling complains that he was wakened in the night by this sound of the pump working. The main supply pipe to the house runs through the basement just outside his room, and the sound of the pump travels quite loudly along that pipe. It prevented him from sleeping. For half an hour at least, he says, he was kept awake by it. Then it stopped."

"He doesn't know at what hour this was?"

"No. He thinks he'd been asleep for some time, but of course he can't be sure. It may have happened before all the others had gone to bed."

"Of course. And he heard nothing else?"

"Nothing until the housemaid screamed when she found Mrs. Starrett dead in the hall. Pittling had been up for some time. He'd dressed and tended the furnace——"

"Oh, never mind all that," Miss Marshall broke in, with a mild impatience. "You can't possibly suspect poor Pittling. He's the last man in the world to murder anyone. He had enough of that in France."

Duff had been listening, very much at his ease, his eyes on the fire, asking questions in a voice that was almost absent-minded, his big hands at rest on the massive arms of his comfortable chair. He already knew many of the details of the Marshall murder; he had pieced them together, with a professional interest, from the newspaper accounts. And he had been listening less to what Alicia Marshall and her lawyer said than to the state of mind about the murder which they unconsciously expressed.

Thus far, the most striking fact that he had learned was this: Alicia Marshall was not as deeply concerned about her brother's death as she was about "poor Pittling."

"He's been arrested, has he?—Pittling?"

"Yes. He's in the county jail."

"Has he a lawyer?"

"I'm his lawyer," Westingate replied.

"I see. I may have to get a talk with him, if you don't mind. And the other servants? Where are they?"

"They're with me," Miss Marshall said. "At my house."

"And the daughter, Martha?"

"She is, too. She's still in bed. We had her moved, the next day. It was impossible for anyone to remain in that house, with the crowds that gathered."

"Naturally. I suppose you've left some one there to see that they don't carry the house away piecemeal."

"Yes. The chauffeur has moved in from the garage."

Duff nodded. "I'll put in a caretaker and his wife—if you don't object—and relieve the chauffeur." He turned benignly to Miss Marshall. "And I'd like to send you a trained nurse, supposedly for your niece, so as to have some one in touch with those servants. They may know something they haven't reported because they don't realize that it's significant. If I tried to cross-examine them myself, I'd only frighten them. I'll not send a detective," he added, seeing her reluctance in her eyes. "I have a very nice girl who goes out for me, now and then, on confidential cases—a girl of good family. She's had training as a convalescent nurse. You'll like her."

"Have you any suspicion," she asked warily, "about who did it?"

"No," he said. "None. None whatever. If it were a murder of revenge, committed by some enemy from the outside, he'd have brought a weapon with him. He wouldn't've had to use that hatchet—whether he carried it up from the basement or found it somewhere upstairs. On the other hand, if it was a burglar whom Mrs. Starrett surprised, he might have killed her, naturally enough, but why should he kill your brother in his bed? And I understand that nothing was stolen?"

"Nothing whatever."

"If it were Pittling, he'd have taken the hatchet back downstairs and cleaned it off, probably, or concealed it. It's not likely that he'd direct suspicion against himself by leaving his hatchet, covered with blood, lying around where it would be found at once. No. That suggests, perhaps, an attempt to cast suspicion on Pittling."

"Exactly," Miss Marshall agreed.

"Or, the whole thing may be just an insane accident. Some madman may have broken in, and found the hatchet, and dropped it again as he ran away."

"That would be my theory," the lawyer said.

"I suppose this Mrs. Starrett has been looked up?—to see whether *she* had any enemies."

"Yes, thoroughly. They've found nothing."

"And Senator Marshall's relations with Mrs. Starrett? They've gone into that?"

He asked it casually, reflectively, looking at the fire. The lawyer did not reply. Duff turned to Miss Marshall and found her regarding her shoe tips with a sarcastic smile.

"Well," she said, "my brother was no fool. If there was anything going on between him and Mrs. Starrett, no one will ever find it out."

"You think there *was* something, then?"

"It's the last thing I should think. Senator Marshall had about as much private life as the Statue of Liberty."

"He was a very religious man," Westingate put in, "very strict with his family, a leader in the law-and-order movement, and most severe on all this modern—er—laxity."

"And the daughter? Is *she* religious?"

"Ah, poor Martha," Miss Marshall sighed. "She's a saint."

"I see. Well," Duff decided, "I'll start work on it at once. If I send a caretaker and his wife to you, to-morrow morning, you can install them in the house?"

"Certainly," the lawyer promised.

"And my nurse may come to you, Miss Marshall, to-morrow afternoon?"

"If you wish it."

"Thanks. I'll arrive in Cold Brook, probably, tomorrow evening, and stop for a few days with the caretaker. That'll make it easier for me to consult with you both the moment I get any sort of clew. If anyone notices me and asks questions, we can explain that Senator Marshall's estate is in the hands of a New York trust company, as his executors, and I'm their agent, appraising the property and making an inventory of the estate. My name is Duffield."

"Very good."

They all rose.

"You'll not tell the truth about me, or my operatives, to anyone—the servants, the chauffeur, nor even your niece?"

"Certainly not."

They shook hands on it.

"I'm beginning to think you really are a detective," Miss Marshall said.

"Then, at least, I'm not deceived in us *both.* " replied Duff.

II

Cold Brook did not remark the arrival, next day, of a new caretaker at the Marshall home, installed by order of the executors of the estate. The nurse whom Miss Marshall engaged, from New York, to take care of her invalid niece, came unnoticed, in the afternoon, and went silently to work. Duff drove out by automobile, after dark, spent the night in one of Senator Marshall's guest rooms, and appeared next morning, as the agent of the executors, to look over the other properties which Marshall had owned in Cold Brook, and to consult Alicia Marshall and her lawyer, Westingate. He ate dinner, that evening, with Westingate and the County Prosecutor at Westingate's home; and the following morning a tramp, arrested for drunkenness, was put in the cell that adjoined Pittling's in the county jail. Duff drove back to New York in the afternoon, and no one seemed any the wiser. Not even he.

Cold Brook, with its tree-lined residential avenues and its suburban homes, was a commuters' town that had no public opinion
of its own outside of its one business street of shopkeepers, lawyers, real estate and insurance agents, plumbers, barbers and such.
Its commuters read the New York papers and smiled with the New
York reporters at the provincial animosity of the local authorities
to the metropolitan newspaper men. The business district resented
those smiles. Duff might have walked the streets of Cold Brook
openly, for a week, and none of the reporters would have known
that he was a stranger in the town, because none of the real towns-
folk would have tipped them off. He was not recognized as a detective anywhere, except in those circles in which he found his
clients. He did not, as he said, "hunt criminals with a brass
band"—that is to say, he never advertised. He had served with
Military Intelligence during the war—especially around airplane
factories and shipyards—and some of his wartime friends had
urged him to set up a detective agency of his own when the war
ended, and one of those friends was an automobile manufacturer
who happened to be a client of Westingate's. The automobile man
advised Westingate to see Duff about the Marshall murder. That
was how he came into the case.

When, after two days of a peculiar dawdling sort of inconspicuous diligence in Cold Brook, he returned to his office near
Union Square, he telephoned to Westingate: "I'll have something
to report in about a week, I think. My operatives are busy. I believe we're on the trail of something."

"What's your theory?" the lawyer asked.

"Well," Duff said, "this murder, you understand, occurred in
two places."

"In two places?"

"Yes."

"How so?"

"It occurred in Cold Brook, in the home of ex-Senator Marshall, but before that, it occurred somewhere else."

"Somewhere else?"

"Yes. It occurred first in somebody's mind, because it was evidently a premeditated murder."

"Oh. I get you."

"And it left a trail in that mind."

"I suppose it did."

"And while the County Prosecutor is trying to find its actual
trail, I'm going after its mental trail."

"In whose mind?"

"I'm not yet sure, but I can tell you this much: I don't believe it was Pittling's."

"I'm glad of that. Then I may expect to hear something definite from you in a week?"

"Or two," Duff promised.

And it was two.

The tramp who had been shut up with Pittling wormed his way into the ex-soldier's confidence and obtained nothing but indications of innocence. The caretaker and his wife did as much for the chauffeur, with the same result. Mrs. Starrett, the murdered housekeeper, had had no enemies, apparently. She had been a respectable young widow who had lived all her life in Cold Brook. Her only surviving relative, an older sister, kept a boarding house; and an operative who went to live there found nothing on which to base a suspicion that there had been anything illicit in Mrs. Starrett's relations with her employer, or that there was anyone to resent such relations if they had existed. The nurse, at Miss Marshall's, made friends with the dead man's servants and discovered nothing startling from them. The county authorities were beginning to believe that the crime had been committed by some insane yeggman who had broken into the house to burglarize it and killed two people in a homicidal mania; and they were holding Pittling, merely as a matter of form, until the popular excitement passed. All these confessions of failure were received cheerfully by Duff in daily conversations over the telephone and in the daily reports which his operatives wrote for his office files. He motored out twice to Cold Brook and consulted with the members of his little field force at night, in Senator Marshall's library, looking blankly meditative and saying nothing. He called on Alicia Marshall to admit that he was making no progress, and he talked with her chiefly about her father, Jeremiah Marshall, with whom she had lived for years in the Marshall homestead. He had died of heart disease, in 1909, at the age of 71, in Senator Marshall's house, where he had gone to live after a quarrel with his spirited daughter. "My brother always gave way to him," she said. "I'm afraid I irritated him. At any rate, the doctor declared his heart was so weak that the excitement of living with me was too much for him. He was too old to live alone. So he went to Amos. And he died there in about a month." She smiled at Duff placidly. "You don't think *he* was in any way connected with Amos's death, do you?"

Duff returned the smile. "Yes," he said, "I'm beginning to suspect so."

She accepted the statement with an air of humorously resigning herself to the fantastic. "Well," she sighed, "I hope you can prove it—he's so safe from the police."

III

He proved it on the following Sunday night. He proved it to Alicia Marshall and to Westingate, in an after-dinner conversation that took place in the picture gallery which Miss Marshall had added to the old Marshall homestead, in Cold Brook. She had been much abroad after her father's death. She had brought back a collection of Italian primitives and housed them in a gallery that was furnished with medieval chairs, antique carved tables, Oriental rugs, bronzes of the Rodin school and church vestments. In this room that looked like the showroom of a Fifth Avenue picture-dealer, by the light of electric bulbs that had been wired into church candelabra and seven-branched candlesticks, Duff made his report to Miss Marshall and her lawyer, over their after-dinner coffee. And it was a report as grotesque as any utterance of the mind of man that Miss Marshall's curiosities had ever heard in their long association with human life and its dramatic emotions.

He locked the big carved door of the gallery. He looked around to see that there were no windows at which anyone could listen. He warned them: "I don't want you to worry over anything I tell you. It can't possibly make trouble for anyone, simply because it can't possibly be proved." He drew from his pocket a modern octavo volume bound in green boards. "This is my case," he said, and handed the book to Miss Marshall.

She was sitting, very erect and diminutive, in a pontifical carved chair beside the heavy library table on which their coffee had been served. She was in an evening gown of silver brocade and crimson, and she looked at the volume with the aid of a lorgnette. It was called "The Roosevelt Myth," a book published by the author, James Clair Billings, in 1908 and dedicated to "the enlightenment of all loyal subjects of Theodore, Rex." On the flyleaf was written, in a girlish hand: "In memory of my beloved Chester, Dec. 1909."

Miss Marshall said: "This is Martha's handwriting."

Duff replied: "Yes. It's her book."

Westingate drew up a Savonarola chair beside her and studied the inscription silently.

"Your father," Duff said to her, "your father, Jeremiah Marshall, was a great Roosevelt fan, you remember. This book is an attack on Roosevelt. It's the book that he was reading, the night he died."

Alicia Marshall turned to him with her sweetest smile. "Yes? And who was Chester?"

"Chester was a cat."

"A cat? Well! And that's your case?"

"That's the beginning of it." He indicated the book with a nod to her to go on. She turned over the pages till she came to a photograph, a snapshot that had been pasted into the book like an extra illustration. It was a faded picture of a young man and a girl in a canoe. "The girl," Duff said, "is your niece, Martha. The man is a young minister, named Keiser, who left Cold Brook some years ago."

"I'll have to take your word for it," Miss Marshall replied. "It's too dim for me to make out."

"She was in love with him, wasn't she?"

"I believe so."

"And Senator Marshall interfered."

"Yes. I'm afraid he did."

Duff nodded at the book again. She turned the pages to another insertion, a folded letter pasted in like a map—a letter from Senator Marshall to his daughter Martha, telling her that the household expenses were too high and that he intended to employ a housekeeper who was to oversee all expenditures in the future. Miss Marshall read it slowly. "Yes," she said, with a sigh, "it was very foolish. Very foolish." The letter was dated July of the previous year.

"There's one more exhibit," Duff said.

She went through the book without finding it. He turned to the inside of the back cover and showed them that something was concealed under the final page of paper that had been pasted down on the cover-lining. He drew out a typewritten note, unsigned, which read, "I shall arrive, my dear, for our anniversary." He handed it to Miss Marshall.

"That's my whole case," he concluded.

She gave the book and its contents to Westingate, with the air of resigning a puzzle to an expert. "That's your whole case?"

"Yes."

"But," she complained cheerfully, "I don't at all understand what it means."

"Well," he said, "let's take the first exhibit, the book itself. Jeremiah Marshall, your father—Martha's grandfather—died of heart disease in your brother's house on the fifteenth of December, 1909. Is that correct?"

"I believe it is."

"The doctor had warned you all that any excitement would be likely to kill him. That was the reason why he left your house. He was always quarreling with you."

"Always."

"When he went to live with your brother, your niece Martha was about seventeen years old. Her mother had been dead about ten years. She was a solitary, eccentric child, with a stern father and an irritable grandfather. The only living thing in the world for which she seemed to have any affection was a pet cat, named Chester. Do you remember that the grandfather had a great aversion to cats?"

"Yes, I do."

"Did you know that he had Martha's pet cat poisoned?"

"I didn't know. I vaguely remember something of the sort."

"That's the meaning of the inscription in the front of the book. In order to annoy him, to persecute him for killing her cat, she took into his sickroom and left on his bedside table at night, this attack on his idol, Roosevelt. She may have heard him arguing with Senator Marshall about Roosevelt. Or she may have known that Senator Marshall refused to argue with him about it, for fear of exciting him too much. At any rate, she knew that; if he read the book it might irritate him dangerously. And it did. He may have thought that his son had put it there to plague him. He was furious. He jumped out of bed, in a rage, and threw up the window, and flung the book out on the lawn. And the strain of that violent action killed him. They found him dead, next morning, on the floor, with the window open, and his reading lamp still burning at his bedside. One of the servants picked up the book, outside, later in the day, and no one knew where it had come from. When Martha finally got it back, she wrote in it: In memory of my beloved Chester, Dec. 1909.' "

Alicia Marshall spread her hands in an eloquent gesture which said, "Well, even so! Supposing it's true. What of it?"

Westingate asked suspiciously: "Who told you all this?"

"The girl told my nurse."

"You mean to say that she told the nurse, in so many words, that she had killed her grandfather?"

"No. She described a nightmare that's been persecuting her—a nightmare of a Cheshire cat that showed its teeth in a grin like Theodore Roosevelt's. My nurse asked her if she had ever had a cat, and she recalled a pet cat which her grandfather had poisoned. Subsequently, she asked the nurse to go to her father's house and get this book out of her room. The nurse pretended that she couldn't find it and sent it to me. Later we learned, from Senator Marshall's old cook, about how the grandfather had died in the night beside an open window. She's superstitious about the coincidence, in both cases, of an open window—and in one case a book, and in the other case a hatchet, flung outdoors."

Miss Marshall drew back in her chair, in an attitude of obstinate defensiveness. "Well, if Martha really did this to her grandfather," she said, "I, for one, can quite understand it. It was time that some one retaliated on him. He'd been making life impossible for everybody, for forty years, to *my* knowledge."

"Quite so," Duff agreed. "And you and I can understand how an angry child could give him that book, with no clear idea of killing him, though with a sort of furious hope that it might pay him back for killing her cat. Quite so. But do we realize what it would mean to her to succeed, and accept her success definitely, and inscribe a book with her triumph, as a Westerner cuts a notch in his gun?"

Alicia Marshall, for the first time, frowned at him. The lawyer rose and put the book on the table and pushed it away from him nervously, as if he were legally refusing any responsibility for its possession.

Duff went on: "Nothing's as satisfying to one's ego as the death of an enemy. Any soldier can tell you what a godlike feeling of power it gives you. You can't in a moment, and with a wave of the hand, create a human being, but you can destroy one, that way. And the effect on you is almost as great as an act of creation. This girl had already a very sturdy sense of her own importance. She was solitary and eccentric, but she was not timid and depressed. She was an only child. I judge that her mother had been devoted to her and proud of her. I understand that her father thought her spoiled and obstinate. Well, here was this old man, the grandfather, who had been persecuting her with his bad temper. And by a sort of magic act, she had simply wiped him out of the world. That is the sort of youthful experience that makes a unique personality.

From this time on, we have to reckon with a human being who has had an experience that may make her superhuman."

"That," Miss Marshall said flatly, "is all nonsense. Martha has never been anything but a devout and simple girl—"

"She became devout," Duff cut in, "she became religious, after the death of her grandfather."

"She became religious, as I did, when she should have been falling in love. If you knew anything about women, you'd know that half of us are like that."

"Naturally." Duff leaned forward on the arms of his chair, with a slowly genial smile. "But—did you ever notice how often religious fanatics are killers? It's my experience that whenever there's a mysterious murder in a decent, respectable family, it's a safe bet that the thing was done by the most religious member of the household. And why? A religious person hates himself. He knows that he's a hateful animal in the sight of heaven, full of low animal impulses that are sinful and nasty. He hates those things in himself, and so he hates himself. An emotion of that sort—an emotion of love or hatred—is almost like a charge of electricity in a person. It either gets drained off naturally in expressions of love or hatred for somebody else, or it stores up as if it were electricity in a storage battery until it's a tremendous charge of suppressed emotion. A religious person can't drain off his hatred freely on people around him, because hatred of others is a sin. So he goes on storing up hatred until he's charged full with it. And then—something happens. The hated person blunders into circumstances that make the electric connection, and there's a flash that's murderous, and the thing's done."

Westingate asked hoarsely: "Are you trying to prove that this girl killed her father—and the housekeeper—with a hatchet?"

"I'm not trying to prove anything," Duff smiled. "I'm trying to tell you privately how this case looks to me."

"I never heard anything more absurd in my life," Miss Marshall said.

"Good!" He seemed actually relieved. "I was afraid I might worry you. I appreciate how absurd it looks, and how safe the girl is from any charge of the kind, but I wasn't sure you'd feel that way about it. Now that you understand how ridiculous the whole thing sounds, I can go ahead with it, more frankly."

Neither of them replied. The lawyer, having seated himself with the table between them, was staring at Duff with eyes that saw only too clearly the possible implications of his charge. Alicia

Marshall, sitting as if her back were against a wall, watched him silently, intent and frowning.

"Let me go ahead," Duff proposed, "and tell you the whole story as I see it, without any reservations, or apologies, or anything like that. This girl, Martha, after the grandfather's death was at first defiant, as her inscription in that book shows. Then she began to feel guilty and remorseful, and she fell ill. When she recovered, she became religious, and that annoyed her father. You've spoken of him as a religious man. He wasn't religious. He attended church. And for many years he helped to take up the collection, I know. But that was merely part of his routine of life as a respectable citizen, a leader in the community who had to set a good example to the ungodly and keep himself high in the estimation of his clients and his constituents. He had no patience with his daughter's excess of piety. And when she fell in love with the minister—this young Keiser—he objected to the match. He refused to settle any money on her—so as to keep her from marrying. He used his influence to get Keiser transferred. He told her that Keiser only wanted to marry her for her money. And when Keiser went away, and stopped writing to her, she blamed her father.

"As far as my nurse has been able to find out, this was her only love affair. She was taken ill again after Keiser left, and when she recovered she was more religious than ever, but now her religion began to take a bitter turn. She read mostly the Old Testament, and that's bad reading for anyone who's full of hate; there's too much revenge and murder in it. She became an active worker in all the leagues and associations for the enforcement of Sunday observance laws and prohibition and such—or, at least, she contributed to them every cent she could get from her father or save out of the money he gave her for household expenses. I find that she made herself conspicuous by her opposition to the war and by her refusal to help the Red Cross or the Liberty Loans or anything of the sort. That's significant."

"Of what?" Westingate asked.

"War," Duff replied, "is murder."

Miss Marshall dropped her eyes, and she did not raise them again. She continued looking at the floor, without a word, her head up obstinately, grasping the arms of her chair.

"Her father quarreled with her about her attitude to the war. He quarreled with her about scrimping on the household expenses so as to give money to the societies in which she was so active. He stopped her allowance, and allowed her to purchase only on charge accounts, paying the monthly bills by check, himself. That was a serious matter for her. She was a proud young woman, silent, repellent in her manner, with none of the magnetism that makes friends. Her ability to contribute money to the causes in which she was interested—that brought people to her, made her important, won her praise. Without that power, she was cut off from everybody. She knew it. She shut herself up in the house. She gave up all her committees, her meetings, her outside work. Then in desperation, she attempted to jockey her accounts, and he found it out. And he wrote her that letter in which he announced that he was putting in a housekeeper who was to have charge of all her expenditures. Did you know that she had to have even her personal accounts—for clothes and books—endorsed by Mrs. Starrett?"

Miss Marshall did not answer. She did not look up.

"This long struggle between her and her father was carried on, you understand, in silence. She never spoke to anyone about it. She never remonstrated with him. She set her will against his, obstinately, and never bent to him once. He had deprived her of her lover, of her friends, of her station in life, of everything that a human being—Well, there you are. She began to have these long periods of illness, headaches, attacks of nervous exhaustion. She kept herself shut up in her room, with her thoughts. She expressed them, as far as I've been able to learn, to no one. The servants report of her exactly what you report, Miss Marshall—that she was a saint."

Miss Marshall raised her hand from the chair arm and dropped it despairingly. "I had no idea," she said, "and my brother could have had no idea. I merely thought her—a peculiar girl. She never told me—"

"Quite so. She never told anyone. And I have no means of knowing what her relations with Mrs. Starrett were, or whether she suspected that there was anything going on between Mrs. Starrett and her father. I believe she did. I believe that when she got hold of that letter to Mrs. Starrett, about their 'anniversary,' it only confirmed a suspicion that needed no confirmation."

"You mean," Westingate asked, "that this note is from Senator Marshall to Mrs. Starrett?"

"Yes. Senator Marshall wrote it on a typewriter himself and left it unsigned, in case it went astray. He addressed the envelope himself on a typewriter, but he made a mistake, absent-mindedly, in the address. He addressed it to 'Mrs. Agnes Starrett, Brook Farm,

New York City.' He didn't notice the mistake until he was about to drop the envelope in a mail box, I presume. It was evidently then too late to type another envelope. He struck out the 'New York City' with lead pencil and wrote in 'Cold Brook, N. J.' as you see." Duff had taken an envelope from his pocket and passed it to Westingate. "That's Senator Marshall's handwriting. The note was still in its envelope when I found it concealed in the back cover of the book."

The lawyer offered the envelope to Miss Marshall. She shook her head without looking at it, her eyes averted.

Duff rose from his chair and began to pace slowly up and down the room, as if he were dictating a report. "The postmark on that envelope shows that it probably arrived at Senator Marshall's home some thirty-six hours before the murder. I judge that the girl intercepted it. She recognized her father's writing in lead pencil and read the note. The fact that it was typewritten and unsigned was sufficient indication that it was a guilty note of assignation. She hid it in the back of the book in which she kept her case against her father, and then she went to bed, ostensibly ill with the grippe, and remained there brooding, in a state of mind that you can imagine. Her father returned on the following forenoon, and found her, as usual, ill in her room. She had been pleading illness, whenever he was in the house, to avoid seeing him. So far, there was nothing unusual.

"But now the circumstance occurred that brought the deadly flash. She complained of being cold. She was probably shaking with a chill of hate and despair. And Pittling was ordered to build a fire in her bedroom fireplace. He brought up a basket of kindling, and in it, I believe, he brought the hatchet that he'd used to split the kindling. It's my theory that he put the hatchet aside as he took the kindling out of the basket and he forgot the hatchet when he returned with the basket to the basement.

"Have you seen that hatchet? It's a real woodsman's broad 'razor-blade' of forged steel. I believe that the girl saw it, standing against the fender, after her fire was lit, when she turned in her bed to stare at the blaze. And I believe that when the housemaid came back into her room, she had concealed the hatchet between the mattresses of the bed on which she was pretending to be sleeping in a weak exhaustion."

Westingate asked, in a shaken whisper, "Did Pittling tell you—"

"No," Duff said. "Pittling won't admit that the hatchet was ever in the girl's room. All he'll admit is the business about the pump.

It wakened him, in the middle of the night, and he heard it working slowly, with long intervals between the strokes, as if some one were drawing water in a very small flow. But that flow continued for a long time—for so long that he thought some one must have risen to get a drink and left a faucet running. Then it stopped. The faucet had been turned off. I believe that this water was used by the murderer to wash in. And I'm sure that Pittling suspects it. In the morning when the hatchet was found, outside the open window, he was sure that some one in the house had committed the murder, and this secret suspicion gave him the guilty manner that led the police to arrest him. I don't believe that he suspects the daughter. He doesn't know what to think, so he keeps his mouth shut, and pretends that he doesn't remember whether or not he carried the hatchet upstairs. Or perhaps he doesn't really remember now. He's in a bad state mentally.

"I have no evidence of how the murders actually occurred. I believe that the girl intended to lie in wait for Mrs. Starrett and her father and confront them together and threaten them with exposure and disgrace, unless her father gave in to her and discharged Mrs. Starrett and ceased to tyrannize over her. She probably seized on the hatchet as a weapon of defense, or perhaps she intended to threaten them with it. While she was waiting to waylay them, she heard Mrs. Starrett tiptoeing past her door, and she darted out, under an ungovernable impulse of rage and hatred, and struck the woman from behind. I don't believe she knew the blow was fatal, but her murderous frenzy was now beyond her control. She rushed into her father—"

Miss Marshall suddenly reached forward to the table and caught up the Roosevelt book. "It's impossible," she said, harshly. "Impossible! I don't believe a word of it. I'll never believe it. Never."

"Quite so," Duff said. "However, you'd better burn that book."

"Burn it," she defied him. "You may be sure I'll burn it."

He turned to Westingate. "There's nothing here for the prosecution to base a case on—even if they knew about it. And they'll never find out anything from her. When my nurse first asked her about her cat, she seemed really to have forgotten about it. I believe she'll forget all this in the same way. She'll probably behave about it as if she had a double personality. She'll become, perhaps, even more fanatically religious than she's been in the past. She'll be more proud and inaccessible than ever, with this secret buried in the back of her mind, but she'll bury it, and she'll keep her thoughts away from its grave. She's a very tough-minded young woman, with a Napoleonic ego, and she may break down physically, and become an invalid, but I don't believe she'll ever break down mentally, and though she may be peculiar, I don't believe she'll go insane."

Westingate asked: "Do your detectives—? Does your nurse—?"

"No," Duff assured him. "The nurse may suspect, but she knows nothing."

Miss Marshall rose, to end the interview. "I don't believe a word of it."

"Good," Duff congratulated her. "Then nobody else will. As a matter of fact, so many people kill their parents, in one way or another, that there's a natural resistance to believing a girl like this guilty. If wishes could have killed *your* father, for instance, Miss Marshall—"

"Stop!" She confronted him, in a sort of frightened rage, her head held high but trembling. "You're a fiend!"

Duff bowed, ponderously. "I'm a detective."

She turned and unlocked the door and flung it open. "You're a monster. I'll not hear another word against my niece."

"No," Duff agreed. "You probably never will."

And as far as anyone knows she never did. She heard nothing, certainly, from Duff, who closed the case then and there—nor from his nurse who left her charge next morning and never mentioned her again—nor from Pittling who was released from custody a few weeks later and went back to his home in Ohio, discreetly silent. By that time, Miss Marshall had taken her invalid niece to the south of France, and though she herself returned to Cold Brook at various times to attend to selling Senator Marshall's property and storing his goods, her niece has never come back. It is understood that she has joined some sort of lay sisterhood and devoted her fortune to works of piety. And the Marshall murder remains still a mystery.

THE

GOLD

FRAMES

THE GOLD FRAMES

I

DUFF HAD WORKED for Boadman before. He had investigated graft in the management of the G. P. & Q. railway, under cover, after Boadman bought control of that road. And they had liked each other. Julius K. Boadman was far from amiable, but he knew his business, and he did not try to lord it over Duff when he found that Duff knew *his*. They had worked together efficiently, and they had parted on terms of unwilling admiration not complicated by any envy. "You must lead a hell of a life," Boadman said, as they shook hands finally. And Duff replied, "I've been feeling the same way about you."

It seemed to him that Boadman was not so much a man as a human power-plant that supplied drive and energy to nobody knew how many railroads, steamship lines, steel mills, construction companies, automobile factories and industrial organizations whose boards he controlled even when he did not own their properties. If he had any life outside of his work, it was not apparent. He appeared to live on private cars and private yachts, in suites of offices and hotel rooms, at board meetings and conferences and directors' tables and office desks—perpetually on tours of inspection or driving like a rotary snow plow through a drift of letters and reports—incessantly active, issuing orders, making decisions, directing subordinates, vetoing projects or o.k.'ing plans, all day and most of the night, with no more rest than a dynamo that never carried less than its peak load.

"You think mine's a hell of a life, too, do you?" he asked, amused.

He was a small man, of what is called an insignificant appearance, too quick and nervous to give any impression of solid power. He worked a good deal on his feet, even in his office, walking up and down as he talked, running his fingers through the thinning disorder of his gray hair, flinging about restlessly in clothes that looked as if they had been carelessly chosen and hurriedly put on. His impatience was extreme. And he made no attempt to conceal it. He cut in on anybody's sentence without waiting for the end of it, as soon as he foresaw what the end would be. The moment that he made up his mind on a matter, he ceased to listen to any further argument about it; his sunken, eager eyes suddenly went blank. If the arguer persisted, he caught up some paper that needed attention, or turned anxiously to his telephone, or remembered a detail that he had overlooked and dashed into another office to attend to it. It was useless to wait for his return. He had three private offices, and he dodged from one to another as he worked.

This manner of his gave all his subordinates nervous breakdown. It wasted everybody's time but his own. It promoted an appearance of anxious speed that was more worried than efficient. And it quite failed to impress Duff. Large, slow, calm, the detective reported his findings at his own pace, ignored interruptions, made no answer to impatient questions, and preserved an impressive appearance of sitting thoughtfully undisturbed on the quiet sidelines of whatever bustle Boadman stirred up around him.

Now, turning to leave Boadman's office with his work there finished, he paused on Boadman's challenge ("You think mine's a hell of a life, too, do you?") and looked from Boadman to the pictures on his walls—framed photographs not of men but of locomotives, bridges, steamships, and factories that had some sentimental association with Boadman's past. "You ought to have your own picture framed and hung up there," he said. "You're the busiest machine that you own."

Boadman was interested. "Well, why not?" He glanced at the pictures and frowned at Duff. "Some one has to run things. They won't go by themselves."

"No," Duff agreed, "but where are you running them to?"

Boadman regarded that question a moment and then shook his head impatiently. *"I* don't know. I'm not God Almighty." He clicked a switch on his office phone. "Tell Judson I'll see him now."

Duff went on out. He was finished. He was paid. And he never expected to do any more work for Boadman. His detective agency had not the facilities for handling such large investigations as Boadman chiefly needed. "I'm just running a little corner grocery," Duff explained, "not a department store. My output's all handmade, if you know what I mean. To tell the truth, I don't believe any other sort of detective work's any good. It's an art. It can't be turned out by factory methods."

II

He never expected to do any more work for Boadman, and nearly two years elapsed before Boadman called on him again. Then he telephoned Duff, one November morning, to say: "I'll come by your office at five o'clock, this afternoon, if you'll be in. I don't want anyone to know I'm consulting you. If I send my secretary to bring you down, will you see me in my motor a minute?"

Duff replied that he would. "But don't send up your secretary," he said. "I'll have a lookout for you."

His office was on a side street, off Union Square—a dingy office that had once belonged to an unsuccessful lawyer from whom Duff had bought the furniture, as he might have bought a disguise of old clothes. On the floors above and below him, his staff of clerks and operatives were housed efficiently, in a modern equipment of desks and filing cabinets and typewriters and private rooms, but Duff had no desire to appear either modern or efficient. He continually used his office as a "plant," representing himself as a shyster lawyer, or a fake promoter, for the benefit of suspects whom he lured there in order to investigate them at his leisure, in the confidential relation of one crook to another. Any appearance of modern efficiency would have frightened them away before they came within talking distance.

At five minutes past five, a heavy motor drew up at the curb before the old red-brick house of five stories in which Duff's public office occupied the second floor. There were two men on the box, but before either of them could descend to open the door of the car, a newsboy jumped on the running board and offered Boadman a paper through the open window. "The Boss'll be right down," he said, officially.

The chauffeur came around the back of the auto and drove him away.

"Pappee!" he screamed. "Extra pappee!" as he went off down the street. It was a signal to Duff's office.

"All right, Petty," Boadman told the chauffeur. "We'll wait here a minute. Go back to your wheel."

The car was a landaulet, and it was Boadman's secretary who rode with the chauffeur. Boadman was alone, inside, a clutter of papers filling the seat beside him. He made no attempt to clear a place for Duff, and as soon as the detective put his head in the door, he said curtly: "Listen. I've only a minute. Something's going on in my home—something I don't understand—and I want you to make an investigation without letting anyone know that you're making it. I can't put detectives on my household, you understand. That would be an insult to everybody. At the same time, I have to know what's what." He was impatient, contemptuous, annoyed at having to confess so much of his private affairs to a detective. He asked gruffly, "Was that newsboy one of your staff?"

"Yes," Duff said. "We use him to tail people where a regular detective couldn't find cover. What makes you suspicious about your household?"

"Things are disappearing." He admitted it as if he were consulting a physician about a disease of which he was ashamed.

"You mean, stolen?"

"I don't know."

"What sort of things?"

He pulled his hat down on his forehead, his eyes averted. "Well, some photographs in gold frames, for instance. They've always stood on the piano in the drawing-room. I asked my wife what had become of them, and I could see that she was shielding some one. I'm not home enough to know what's going on. There's something wrong—that's all I can tell you." He waved the whole thing aside suddenly. "Don't ask me any questions. I haven't time to answer them." He took up the phone that connected him with the chauffeur. "And don't come to me for any information. I don't want to see you again till you make your report." He said, into the phone, "Go ahead, Petty."

Duff shut the door. He restrained an impulse to slam it. He was angry.

He was angry at being treated as if he were a butler. He was angry at being told that it would be an insult to everybody in Boadman's household to put detectives on them. And he was angry at Boadman's manner of speaking of the trouble in his home as if it were something beneath his notice, which Duff would naturally be interested in and glad to be employed upon. He said to himself, as he returned upstairs to his desk: "He needs a lesson. He's getting too vainglorious for this little old world. Some one'll have to bring him back to earth. He's too important, now, to know what's going on in his own home. Idiot! What does he think life *is?*"

In this mood, he telephoned a newspaper man who worked for him occasionally. "Bob," he said, "turn up Julius K. Boadman in your morgue, there—will you?—and give me anything you've got on his private life and his wife and family. I don't need anything about his business career. Just his private life, you understand. Yes. As soon as you can? Thanks."

Then he called in an operative named Carson—James ("Lucky") Carson—a sedate, fat man who specialized in financial "plants," legislative investigations, jury fixing, and the current methods of bribery and corruption. "Jim," he said, "I want to get a line into the home life of Julius K. Boadman, and I have to be damn careful about it. There's one of his sons, a Julius Junior in town, here. You might be able to rope him. I don't know where you'll find him except around his club, and I don't want you to make that approach. I thought perhaps you might get up an investment that he'd be interested in, and go after him as a son of his father, with an offer of a big block of stock for the use of his name or something like that. Rope him some way, and see if you can find out about the old man's home life, his relations with his family, and what his wife thinks about him. Take it easy. There's no rush. Keep your cover, even if you don't find out anything at all. Don't drop this other business you're on. Just take Boadman on the side, for a while, and let me know what you're doing."

Carson smoothed down the black broadcloth over the tight protrusion of his middle. "Julius K. Boadman, Jr.," he said, and pursed his lips appreciatively, and closed one eye. "Yes. I think I know a line on him." He looked like a successful lobbyist; that is to say, he looked political but too careful of his clothes to be a politician, and not shrewd enough in his bland rotundity. He passed a hand over his bald forehead and said, "All right, Chief. I'll look him up."

"There's another son," Duff continued, "a J. Spencer Boadman who lives on the old man's country place near Tarrytown. Get anything you can about him and we'll develop it later. Take this Julius Junior first, and be cagey. I don't want the old man to smell anything. He'd raise hell with us."

"Don't worry, Chief," Carson said. "No one's going to smell *me.*"

"All right, Jim," Duff dismissed him. "Leave word for Bilkey that I want to see him when he comes in."

Bilkey specialized in confidence men, wire-tappers, experts in the badger game, high-class blackmailers and sporting adventurers of various sorts. His official beat was Broadway and its side streets from Thirty-fourth to Fifty-ninth, and he knew that district, its crooks, its Central Office men, its hotel detectives and its Red

Light Ladies, as a wardheeler knows his political district. He also knew his theater, but there he figured as an enthusiastic amateur, a devoted first-nighter who "bought a piece of a show" occasionally.

He came into Duff's office with his stick and his gloves and his hat in his hand. "You want to see me, Major?"

"Yes," Duff said. "I want you to help me get a line on the domestic life of Julius K. Boadman, and we have to do it in our stocking feet. He has a son Rodney around town here—a sort of lounge lizard and jazz hound. He was at Yale last year, but I understand he never studied anything but the saxophone, and I think they sent him home. Anyway, he's on the town now. You can probably pick him up around some of the night clubs. I want you to rope him, if you can, and use him to find out what's going on at home. I'll give you more definite details as we work along. It's going to be a slow job. There's no hurry. Just land this Rodney Boadman, and see what he sounds like, and then we can make a plant of some sort for him, and feel our way into things."

Bilkey slapped his trouser leg with his stick, looking down at his spats. "I'm pretty busy on that Stanton case."

"Yes, I know. Just take this Boadman business on the side. Don't shove it. The important thing is not to tip anybody off."

Bilkey nodded, put on his hat, and loitered out as if he were going for a sunny stroll up the avenue. Duff returned to his deskwork.

And, finally, he sent for Mickey—Mickey McQueen, "the Boy Scout," as the office called him—a hungry-eyed, wistful-looking street waif whose chief stock in trade was this appearance of hungry wistfulness. Under it he was a precocious youth of fifteen with a plaintive mischievousness that enjoyed the part he had to play.

"Want to see me, Mr. Duff?"

"Yes, Mr. McQueen. Sit down here."

He was washed and dressed to go home, in the clothes of a neat office boy, his red hair sleeked back from his pale face, his shoes shined and his nose shiny. He sat down with a tentative smile that moved his lips sadly but did not last long enough to reach his eyes.

"Did you notice the old lad in the motor you spotted?"

"Yes, sir."

"That was Julius K. Boadman. He lives uptown on Fifty-sixth Street, near the corner of Park Avenue. You'll find the number in the phone book."

"Yes, sir."

"I want to squeeze you into that house, some way, and I don't know how we're going to do it. There's no one inside to help us. We've got to con them all, and get you set in there, so you can do an inside job without anyone getting wise to you. You'd better go up and watch things for a few days first. You can keep an eye on the house from the Park Avenue corner. I don't know whether you could work as a newsboy up there or not. I'm afraid not. Look it over to-morrow morning, and see if you can find any cover. Go slow, and don't stub your toe. I'll give you the details of the job later."

III

The first attempts to rope Julius Junior failed. He was living alone in a little bachelor flat on the fifteenth floor of one of the newer apartment hotels on Murray Hill, and he refused every bait to an interview that "Lucky" Carson offered him, either by phone or letter. He left the letters unanswered. He replied on the phone "I don't know you," and when Carson persisted, he added peevishly "And I don't want to." The doorman, the elevator boys, and the girl at the switchboard all had their orders, and no one could get upstairs unannounced. It began to be apparent that Boadman never received callers in his flat. He arrived there in the early hours of the morning, solemnly befuddled, and slept till after luncheon every day. At about three o'clock in the afternoon, he sauntered up to Fifty-eighth Street, where he drank a few slugs of gin in a speakeasy, without a word to anyone but the bartender, and then strolled back to his club for the afternoon. At dinner time, he returned to his flat to dress, and disappeared, in a taxi, to spend his evening among his friends. That was his almost invariable routine. He never went near his father's house.

He was a big, hardy blond—with a physique that remained to him from the days when he had been an amateur boxer in his youth—a sulky, self-sufficient drinker, idle, silent, suspicious. "Hell," Carson said to Duff, "you might as well send me out with a bag of peanuts to con some old yellow jungle-cat in the Congo. I can't get near him. And if I did, he looks as if he'd eat my leg off."

J. Spencer Boadman was worse. He lived isolated among the servants on the Boadman country estate near Tarrytown; he came to New York only to sit as a dummy director and "Yes man" for his father on various boards which his father controlled; and he functioned for himself chiefly as one of the governors of a neighboring country club whose ideals of fashionable formality delighted his soul. He was younger than Julius Junior but more arid. A small, sprightly, withered man of thirty-five, bald and fussy, he was quite unapproachable in any way that detectives could devise.

Rodney Boadman gave them their only opening. Bilkey got an easy introduction to him through a gold-digger who ran with his mob, and he and Bilkey came away together from their first bottle party, speechless friends. Rodney Boadman was musical. He played the piano and the violin, as well as the saxophone. His mother had intended him to be a composer; she had seen that he got a good musical education; and the result was that he could vamp up a jazz tune as readily as any hack in Tin Pan Alley. "He's all right," Bilkey reported. "He's a nice kid. I've fed him the idea that I'll back him to write the music for a summer show, if we can get some one to do the lyrics, and he's keen about it."

Rodney Boadman was only twenty-five years old, as big as a sloth bear in his coonskin coat, and as loose-jointed, and as slow-footed, and as shyly amiable. He had little to say for himself when he was sober, but after a few drinks he was talkative in a slow rambling fashion, and his favorite topic of conversation was his father, whom he admired and laughed at. Bilkey got from him a lot of disconnected information about Julius K. Boadman's private life. He also got some illuminating details of the lives of Boadman's three sons. And ultimately he got an introduction to Julius Junior for "Lucky" Carson, and Carson landed the eldest son with a Florida land scheme.

It was a perfectly honest scheme—to hear Carson tell it. A number of promoters had pooled their holdings on the West Coast, and they were ready to sell acreage to the public. They needed a big name to give class to their project. They were willing to endow Julius Junior with a substantial interest in the company if he would come in as president of their incorporation and let them call their properties "The Boadman Estates." These were the boom days in Florida. Carson had facts and figures to prove that Julius Junior would probably make a million dollars on his holdings.

The name of Boadman would sell the company like Standard Oil.

"It'll give the old man apoplexy," Julius said, and he said it with a glint of vengeance in his bloodshot eyes.

He was reluctant, of course, to do it, and his reluctance had been counted on. It gave Carson an excuse for numerous interviews in which he insisted on being vague about his backers until Boadman should be less vague about joining them. In the meantime, with dinners and drinks, he drew out Julius Junior about himself and his father and the family history and the present state of the family's affairs.

All this was done very slowly, in an idle-minded way that could not possibly arouse anyone's suspicion. It took the better part of a month, and during that month Mickey scouted around the neighborhood of the Boadman house, hunting for cover like a duck shooter.

There was no excuse for a newsboy on the corner; he would not sell a paper a day, and his presence there would be conspicuous. As a shoeblack, he would be even more noticeable. He put on his best clothes and sat on a bench in one of the grass plots that decorated the center of Park Avenue in those days, and he watched the goings and comings of the Boadman automobiles from afar, and he identified Boadman and Mrs. Boadman and young Rodney as they came and left, but he was uncomfortable because no one loitered there in cold weather, and the nursemaids and the children who came out to get the sun at midday stared at him too much.

With the first snowfall, he appeared in the clothes of poverty again, carrying a snow shovel, and solicited the work of cleaning sidewalks near the Boadman home. He had luck in one house where the furnace man was ill with the grippe. A tipsy caretaker across the street from Boadman's—enjoying his leisure while the family was in the South—found it more leisurely to employ Mickey for a quarter of a dollar than to work on the snow himself. Also, it appeared that the drivers of the coal wagons had struck against shoveling their cargoes into the coal holes; they dumped the coal on the sidewalk and left it for the household servants to stow away, and all the household servants fought against being employed as coal heavers. Mickey got work on a coal heap next door to the Boadmans'. He made a friendly contact with the drunken caretaker, across the way, and he called daily to see if there was anything for him to do. He looked in, for orders, every morning, at the office before he went on his beat, left his written report for Duff, and waited patiently for developments.

Nothing developed. The Boadman house remained inaccessible—an old brownstone house of five stories that had been converted into an "American basement," years before. The front door opened, from the basement area, into a bare reception hall of black-and-white marble squares. On the first floor, curtains of red damask hung in what was evidently a drawing-room. On the floor above, Mickey could see blue silk showing behind sash curtains of lace; it might be a sitting-room.

The windows of the next floor were evidently Rodney's; he looked out, one morning, in his pajamas. The top floor was probably the servants'. And there were enough servants to fill the house.

A butler and a footman answered the door. A furnace man came in and out of the basement stairs that went down from the areaway into the cellar. A fat man, mustached like a Turk, was obviously the chef. A precise young man in black was either a secretary or a valet. There were six women—parlor maids, chambermaids, personal maids, cook's helpers, scrubwomen, laundresses—Mickey could not tell what. And besides these, there were two chauffeurs, one for Boadman and another for Mrs. Boadman.

Mickey thought to himself: "The Boss might's well try to slip me into a beehive without gettin' stung."

He was careful to keep himself unnoticed by any of these people, and the day that he shoveled coal, next door, he smudged his face with his dirty hands as he worked, so as to be unrecognizable if he were seen by anyone, later, in any other role. He rather overdid the smudging. Rodney Boadman passed him while he was at work, and smiled at the sight of such a small boy laboring with such a large shovel. Mickey looked up at him shyly. "Say, kid," Rodney said, "you shouldn't try to move coal with your face." Mickey grinned in silence, and silently ducked back to his job. He had learned that when one of his elders joked with him, a tongue-tied bashfulness was more ingratiating than any pert reply.

Rodney went on about his business, and that was as near as Mickey came to getting into touch with the Boadman household. He was not worried by his failure. He had been a detective ever since he got his working papers at the end of his course in the public school, and he knew that a detective's life was like nothing the Nick Carter stories had led him to believe. He knew that it was mostly waiting and watching, following unknown people to unknown destinations, and reporting movements that had no meaning, for him, as a part of a record which he never saw. He waited for Duff to notify him if he were to move out of his trenches and go over the top. Meantime, keeping his head down most of the time, he peeped out occasionally across No Man's Land at the enemy's lines and reported any movement that he saw there.

IV

It was December, drawing on to Christmas, before Duff sent for him. "Mickey," he said, "we've been watching the wrong hole. The trouble that we want to locate's a couple of blocks further down, near the corner of Lexington Avenue. There's a little old white-brick house down there. It's painted yellow now, with green shutters. Near the corner of Fifty-third and Lexington. We've got to slip you inside it, and it won't be hard."

Mickey looked intelligently relieved.

"To begin with, I'll have to tell you something about the house. It's where the Boadmans lived when they first came to New York, about twenty-five years ago. Rodney was born there—the lad that spoke to you when you were shoveling that coal. They weren't so rich then, and when Boadman bought the house he put it in his wife's name, for safety's sake, I guess. Then he began to make a lot of money, and they moved, but this house still belongs to his wife, see? She rented it, at first, and then she had a couple of old servants she wanted to take care of, pensioners, too feeble to work—and not swell enough, I guess, to suit Boadman, after he had made his first million—so she gave them the basement of this place to live in and paid them as caretakers. One of them's dead. The other's still there, with a granddaughter that does all the work. There isn't much work because the house's practically empty, now. See?"

"Yes, sir." Mickey saw.

"Mrs. Boadman's furnished all the upstairs rooms with the furniture that used to be in the house when they lived there—things that got to be too shabby for Boadman, or not swell enough for a millionaire's home. Instead of selling them, you understand, she moved them down there, when he wouldn't give them house room any longer, and there they are still. This has been going on for years. In the meantime, she's had various people occupying floors in the house, rent-free, people that she's been taking care of— chiefly poor artists and writers apparently, and young singers and people she's wanted to help. She's artistic, you know. Remember that."

Mickey nodded brightly. He'd remember.

"Boadman doesn't seem to know a thing about this. He hasn't paid any attention to his family for years. Too busy, you understand. But recently he noticed there was something wrong about his home. Things were disappearing out of it, he says. Especially some photographs in gold frames that used to stand on the piano. Silver frames weren't good enough, see? They were old family photographs of her father and his mother, and he'd had them framed in solid gold. The darn fool thought some one'd stolen them for the frames, and he asked his wife about them, and she acted as if she were shielding the thief, so he came to us to find out what's really happening, see? Well, I figure, if we can get you into that house, we can find out all Boadman needs to know about what's happening."

He had been talking at his desk, with Mickey sitting in a client's chair to face him. He rose, now, and began to pace heavily around the room, standing a moment to look out a window, pausing to straighten an engraving of Daniel Webster on the wall, hitching a chair into position with his foot as he passed it.

"Are you musical, Mickey?"

"I can play the mouth organ."

"Well, that's something. You've been on the streets—see?— selling papers and shining shoes and playing the mouth organ, when the cops weren't watching. You're an orphan."

That was true enough. His mother had died when he was a baby. His father had gone West and forgotten him. He was living with an aunt—his mother's sister—whose husband was a truck-driver.

"You're an orphan, and you were raised by an aunt, and she died, and you ran away,—now you're just living on the street. Make up any story you like, to that effect, but refuse to tell them any names or addresses, because you're afraid you'll be sent back to your uncle, who was cruel to you, see? Your name's 'Crawford.' Remember that. It's important. Your name's 'Crawford,' 'Jimmy Crawford,' let's say. This Mrs. Boadman's name was Crawford before she married, and she called her first boy Crawford, as his Christian name. He died when he was about ten years old, and you don't look much more than twelve."

He stopped a moment, to smile down at Mickey quizzically. Then he roughed up the boy's shock of red hair with a jovial hand and strode off again. "We've got a piece of luck on our side. That first boy of hers was red-headed. So was Boadman before he turned gray. And if we can get you next to her, in any way that's more than half pathetic, you ought to be able to make a hit—with *your* youth and beauty."

Mickey smiled in his most plaintive expression of mischief. "How do I get to her, Mr. Duff?"

"Go to the basement door of that little house, about nine o'clock to-night, and ring the bell and ask the girl for a hand-out. There's a blizzard due here from the West late this afternoon. You'll have to be looking pretty blue from the cold, and you'd better be good and hungry. Have your papers under your arm and your mouth organ in your pocket. It's all you can do to stand up. Be sure there's no cop in sight, and then, while the girl's parleying with you through the wire grating of that outside door, you just naturally do a flop on the doorstep. Faint, see?"

Mickey thought it over, staring wide-eyed. "Will that get me next to her?"

"To Mrs. Boadman? Yes, if you don't trip up on it. It ought to get you inside the house. It's up to you, then, to stick till you get to *her*. She's been going around there a good deal lately, in the evenings, while Boadman's away. She's fixed up a sort of studio for herself, apparently, on the top floor. I don't know what she does up there. That's for you to find out."

Mickey rose. "I guess I better phone Auntie I'll not be home for a few days."

"Better tell her you're going out of town on a job. We don't know how long this's going to take."

V

It took, in fact, a week—during which time Mickey was as busy as a mouse that is gnawing out runways in a new suburban bunga-low—a pet mouse in a miraculous sort of household where they were all as eager to make friends with him as so many prisoners for life, in solitary confinement, delighted to see him in their cells. Mary Healy, in the basement, got him first. He did not have to faint. As soon as he said weakly, "I'm hungry," she threw open the door and caught him by the arm as he swayed, and drew him in out of the snow-storm. He staggered, convincingly, and she all but carried him in, to a fire in the basement sitting-room where she had been sewing all alone—her grandmother in bed in the room beyond, and not even a cat to keep her company, because her grandmother had a phobia for cats and Mary was a timid slave to her grandmother.

"Kee' quiet now," she whispered as she sneaked him in. She took his cap from him and his papers, and helped him to the rock-ing-chair in which she had been sitting, and tiptoed back to close the door to her grandmother's bedroom, as guiltily excited as if he were a lover that she was concealing.

She was a big, fat woman of about thirty-five, in a housemaid's cap and a black uniform, with a permanent expression of staring simplicity, and she showed her excitement less in the expression of her face than in the perspiration with which it shone. "I'll get y'a bowl o' soup," she said, "an' a bite o' cold chicken." Mickey stifled a sneeze. "Oh Lorrd! ye're catchin' cold. Get off them wet shoes an' stockings. Are yer clothes damp? They are that. Get 'em off now an' I'll find a blanket to wrap y' in. What're yer people doin', lettin' y' out a night like this, with no overcoat?"

Mickey answered feebly from his chair by the fire, "I got no people. They's all dead."

She cried, in a hoarse whisper, "Heaven help us! What's the wurrld comin' to!" and went down on her knees and began to take off his shoes and stockings, feverishly. "Ye poor boy! Ye're 'n orphan, are ye? Whur're ye livin'?"

"On the streets."

"Ain't it turrible," she said, "the way some people has too much an' other people nothin' at all! What a wurrld!"

Not for a moment did she suspect him; and certainly his cold and his hunger were above suspicion; and when she had him wrapped in blankets and filled with hot soup and three helpings of chicken and several cups of warmed-over coffee, his story of himself so blinded her with compassion that she could not have seen any holes in it if it had been full of them.

"Whur've ye been sleepin'?" she asked finally.

"Anywhere I could crawl in," he told her.

She threw up her hands. "Ye'll stay here then. I'll have to tell Miss Walling, but if she makes trouble about it, I'll phone to Mrs. Boadman—I'll do *that*—and she'd not turn y' out, this night, ner any other. Not her! Make yer mind easy to that."

Miss Walling, it appeared, was Mrs. Boadman's secretary, living on the parlor floor of the house. "Don't ye mind her if she scowls at ye, now," Mary encouraged him. "She's all bark and no bite. She's just a kind-hearted woman that's ashamed to be so. Make yerself easy here, an' don't worry whatever."

Mickey was not worrying. The room was comfortable with furnace heat and the open coal fire. It smelled stuffily of cooking and upholstery and human occupation. It was softly lit with a shaded lamp on the center table and another standing by the chair in which Mary had been sewing. He looked around him at his ease, sniffling experimentally in his blankets, depending on that sniffle to win his way for him, and planning—if Miss Walling tried to put him out—to find himself in a high fever, with a headache and a hoarse cold. He would even faint.

He need not have given it a thought. Mary Healy so eloquently pleaded his pathetic case for him, upstairs, that when she returned with Miss Alice Cuyp Walling, she carried a quilted dressing-gown of black satin that belonged to Miss Walling, and Miss Walling brought a pair of black satin mules to match. There was no question of turning him out. After one look at his wistful smile—and another at his poverty-stricken underclothes when he rose from his blanket to put on the dressing-gown—Miss Walling's only question was whether he should remain downstairs and sleep on a sofa by the fire, where Mary could watch over him, or go upstairs to a proper bed in one of Miss Walling's rooms and be in her care.

She was like nothing that Mickey had ever seen in the shape of a secretary. She limped in, with a walking stick, gray and elderly, squat and stout, her heavy masculine head set low between broad shoulders on a short neck; and fixing him with a sternly amiable eye, she said: "Well, young man, this is a nice story you have to tell of yourself. How is it that some of these children's aid societies don't get hold of you and lock you up? I thought they had jails for all helpless young innocents like you."

Mickey sniffled and looked shy. "I'm not so innocent," he admitted. "I allus see them first."

She smiled grimly. "I can very well believe it. You probably know your way about in the world a great deal better than I do." She gave her mules to Mary. "Put those on him, if they'll *go* on him." Mary knelt down before him to slip them on his feet. "He ought to have a hot bath and a drink of hot toddy. You'd better put a match to the fire in my room, Mary, and let him get into a comfortable bed. We don't want him developing pneumonia on our hands."

"There's no need o' turnin' y' out o' yer bed, Miss Walling," Mary objected. "He'll do well enough down here. I'll fix him up a snug bed on the sofy there—"

"He can't be running up and down those cold stairs from the bathroom. Do as I tell you, now. Take him up there, and give him a good scrubbing. He probably needs it. And put him right to bed between blankets before he catches more cold. I'll sleep on the couch in the front room."

Mary had to take her orders, and there was obviously something in the prospect of giving him a bath that pleased her as much
as if he were a baby. Fortunately for them all, Mickey was used to
less than complete privacy in his bath. There was no proper bathroom in the basement flat in which his aunt lived in Greenwich
Village, and he washed himself on Saturday nights in a laundry
tub in the kitchen, under her vigilant eye.

Consequently, he yielded to Mary's ministrations with an unembarrassed absent-mindedness, busy with his own thoughts; and
when Miss Walling came in to see that his head was washed—and
to contribute a bottle of her own special shampoo mixture for the
purpose—he accepted her superintendence of his scrubbing without resentment. He was small for his age, but well built in a minia-
ture of boyhood that was delicate and smooth-skinned.

One lobe of his brain was kept busy with such purely physical
facts as the soap in his eyes and the slipperiness of the porcelain
bath tub. The other half of his mind was plotting how and when he
was to reach Mrs. Boadman. Between these two activities of
thought he remained as unconscious of his nurses as a solemn
child, but when they had him wrapped in blankets and tucked him
in Miss Walling's bed, he came out of his abstraction to find that
he had won them both completely. Mary looked flushed and
happy. Miss Walling was tender and amused. "Fill a hot water bottle," she ordered Mary, "and put it at his feet, and get him a hot
lemonade, with a stick in it." He objected that he did not want to
turn her out of her bed. She patted his cheek. "You're a sweet
child!" she said. "I'm glad to have you in it. What's your name?"

"Jimmy."

"Jimmy what?" She had her hand in his hair, feeling whether it
was dry.

"Jimmy Crawford."

The hand remained pressing on his head. "Crawford?" She
looked almost frightened.

"Yes'm, Crawford."

"That's a strange thing!"

"What's the matter with it?" Mickey asked, though he knew
well enough.

She did not answer. She straightened up thoughtfully. She studied him in silence. "Well," she said, at last, "you've certainly
come to the right house."

And he certainly had. To Mary Healy, it was a miracle. She
was awed. Miss Walling admitted that it was a remarkable coinci-

dence which might have miraculous consequences for Mickey, and she went into the other room, to telephone to Mrs. Boadman, in a state of suppressed excitement that gave him a qualm of shame. He covered it by devoting himself to his hot lemonade. Mary continued to stare at him as if she saw a ghost. He snuggled down in his blankets and turned his back to her. "I'm goin' asleep," he said.

She tiptoed out of the room.

He was warm. He was luxuriously comfortable. The whisky in the hot lemonade made him feel dizzy and heavy-headed and relaxed. He shut his eyes for a drowsy moment and instantly he was asleep.

He slept for hours, but it seemed to him only a minute later that he was roused by the sound of whispers. He opened his eyes to see a strange woman, with Miss Walling, watching him from the foot of the bed. He blinked at her, only half awake. "Don't be frightened," she said, coming to lean over him. "Miss Walling has told me all about you." She tucked the coverlet in, around his shoulders—a motherly-looking tall woman, with a subdued and gentle voice. "I'm Mrs. Boadman. You're to stay here as long as you like. There are two rooms upstairs that you can have for your very own, to-morrow. We're all so glad to have a nice boy living with us. You need never be cold or hungry again." She was crying. "I once had a son named Crawford. We think you have been sent to us, dear boy. We're all so glad."

Mickey answered drowsily: " 'S all right. This job won't take me long."

He turned over and relapsed at once into unconsciousness, and they decided that he had been talking in his sleep.

VI

It was just a week later that Duff heard from Boadman—an excited Boadman who telephoned to say, "Come down here, right away. I want to see you."

"What's wrong?" Duff asked.

"Everything's wrong. I can't talk about it on the telephone. Get down here right away."

He was as peremptory as usual, but Duff was not offended. He was amused. He knew what was wrong, and he knew how he intended to handle it, and he hoped to handle it in a way that would considerably alter Boadman's tone. He put on his hat and overcoat with an air of pleasant expectation. "I'll be back in an hour or two," he told his secretary in the outer office. He did not intend to be hurried in his return.

If he had been Julius K. Boadman, he would have dashed to his motor car and taken an hour to arrive at his destination because of the congested traffic in the snow-heaped streets. Being a man of a large and leisurely celerity, he walked to the subway at Fourteenth Street, caught an express, and came out on Boadman's street ten minutes later. He strolled to Boadman's building at the same comfortable pace, indifferent to the impatient rush of people who were impeded by his huge bulk. He came placidly into Boadman's outer office and said, "Mr. Boadman wants to see me. Name's Duff." And he did not quicken his pace when the clerk replied anxiously, "Yes, Mr. Duff. You're to go right in," and hurried ahead of him to open doors and usher him down corridors, with such a faithful and doglike eagerness that Duff thought to himself, "It's a wonder he don't bark."

Boadman usually sat at an empty desk, proud of the efficiency with which he cleared it of correspondence and reports as fast as they accumulated. This morning, it was cluttered with papers and he was busy reading them. At the sight of Duff, he threw them aside and sprang to his feet. "What've you been doing?" he demanded. "I haven't heard a word from you for weeks, and all the time, things going from bad to worse—from bad to worse!—till it seems to me the whole damn family's *mad!* Mad! Crazy! Insane!"

Duff seated himself meekly. "What—specifically—is wrong?"

"Everything! Everything!" He was threshing around the room, evidently relieving at last a rage and resentment that had been too long controlled. "The whole family's gone crazy, I tell you. One of my boys—mixed up with a crooked gang of land sharks down in Florida—"

"You don't need to worry about that," Duff cut in. "I've been watching that. I can stop it any minute."

Boadman turned furiously. "Stop it? Stop it! How?"

"I have the records of those men. They'll quit the moment they know I'm watching them."

"Why didn't you stop them long ago? Do you think I want my name—'Boadman Estates'!—"

"No danger of that," Duff assured him. "You don't need to worry. It's perfectly safe. The whole thing'll drop the moment I pull the string on it. I was only waiting till I got them in deep enough to scare them good. Is that all that's wrong?"

Boadman swallowed and boiled up again. "No! This other boy! Here's this other boy! Some theatrical crooks have got hold of him, and they propose to put on a show of some fool sort—with his name on it! For the advertising, of course! And they've persuaded him that he can write the music—"

"You mean Rodney?"

Boadman wheeled on him. "I suppose you've been watching that, too, have you?"

"Yes," Duff said, "but that's not so crooked—except that the man who's proposing it has no money to back a show, and he's really counting on getting you to put up for it—"

"I thought so! I thought so!" Boadman began to show relief. "The damn fool! I thought there was something like that at the bottom of it. Well, you can tell him, I'll see him boiled first—him and his whole crooked outfit—"

"That's all right. I'll attend to that. Is that everything?"

Boadman sat down at his desk. "No," he said. He hesitated. He threw aside some papers, impatiently. "No . . . No, it isn't. My wife has picked up a young ragamuffin—"

"You mean this Crawford boy?"

He was silenced. He looked at Duff, uneasily, as if he were trying to guess how much Duff knew, and feeling, uncomfortably, that he knew too much. He asked, at last: "What do you know about *him?*"

Duff countered: "What does she want to do with him?"

"Adopt him."

Duff shook his head. "Not a chance. You don't need to worry about that. That kid has the wanderlust. He runs away from home regularly twice a year. He's liable to light out any minute. He'll go as soon as we let him know the game's up."

Boadman drew a long, relieved breath and sat back in his chair. "You've been busy, haven't you?"

"Yes," Duff said, "but not with these things. These are on the surface. They're not at the root of the trouble. They're only symptoms."

"Symptoms?"

"Yes. Do you know that your wife wants to leave you? That's what it amounts to. That's what the whole case amounts to—gold frames and all."

It was here that Boadman justified his success as an executive. He put aside instantly all his emotion, all his rage, all his resentment. He concentrated, on Duff, an impersonal attention, a watchful scrutiny, that was as cold as if the whole matter were a purely material problem of dollars and cents. "That sounds impossible," he said. "How do you know?"

"I'll tell you." Duff leaned forward, heavy-shouldered, his elbows on the padded arms of the leather chair. "When you married her, out in Milton, you were twenty-one and she was nineteen. She was musical. She had a voice, and her father hadn't any sympathy with her ambitions to get her voice trained and make a career for herself. Consequently, she was in revolt against her home—against her family—and that made it possible for her to resist them when they tried to prevent her from marrying *you*—a boy from across the tracks, almost a day laborer, on a construction job—although you saw yourself as a contractor, because you no longer shoveled dirt yourself—you hired men to shovel it and teams to haul it away. Of course, you were beginning to make money, and she believed in you, but if she hadn't been on the outs with her family she'd have taken their point of view."

Boadman nodded. "I appreciate that."

"Yes," Duff said, "but perhaps you don't appreciate that when she married you, she saw herself escaping from her father and starting out with some one who was going to help her realize her own ambitions. She may not have had that very clearly in her mind, but it was there. She's a woman of a good deal of character and considerable egotism. She didn't see herself submerging her identity in yours and devoting herself entirely to your career. She had a personality of her own and plans of her own, and she thought you were going to help her with them."

"Well?"

"Well, you didn't. You weren't interested in *her* ambitions, really. You were only interested in *yours*. You expected her to be satisfied with *your* success—a sort of silent partner in it, busy with the household end of your joint lives, as absorbed in your home as your mother had been. You forgot that you were marrying a wife, not a mother. And, in a little while, she was as much in revolt against you as she'd been against her father."

Boadman had begun to look skeptical. "It's the first I ever heard of it. Where did you get this?"

"I got it from her conduct and your sons' conduct."

"I don't follow you."

"Your sons have all disappointed you, haven't they? They've none of them done what you wanted with their lives. They've all of them refused to follow in your footsteps. The first one I don't know about, and anyway he died too young to develop any resistance to you, but the second boy, Julius Junior, has fought you from the start. He ran away from home, as soon as he could, with the waitress in the railway restaurant. He took to drinking, and now he's a wreck, kept afloat only by the money he gets from his mother . . . The third boy, Spencer, was too timid to revolt. He hid behind his mother, whom he adored, and he day-dreamed and wrote minor poetry, till you snapped him out of it and put him to work. Now he's a sort of frustrated amateur in everything. All he's got is a strong critical sense that shows as snobbishness. He has no virility, and he's as fussily incompetent as an old hen. He's peevish and unfriendly with his mother, and he's no use whatever to you. The best you can do with him is to make him a dummy director. He's a total loss. . . . The youngest, Rodney, is his mother's boy. She kept him entirely to herself and you let her do it. She tried to make him musical and she succeeded at first and then he turned willful and took to jazz. Now, he's a big lounge lizard with a mind that hasn't jelled and probably never will. . . . You don't suppose—do you?—that all this is just accidental. You know there's a reason for it, don't you?"

Boadman eyed him coldly. "If *you* know, I'd like you to tell me."

"All right. I will. This oldest boy, Julius Junior—some one gave him the ideals of a gentleman of leisure, and you had no sympathy with them. Never mind that. Who gave him those ideals and why? The next boy, Spencer—some one gave him artistic ideals. Who did that and why? You know who did it to Rodney. It was your wife. Why did she do it? Why did she give every one of these boys ideals that you've fought against? She's very fond of you. I don't suppose she's ever quarreled with you, openly, in her life. But, unconsciously, she's started all these boys on paths that brought you into conflict with them eventually, one after the other. And the conflict has destroyed them."

Boadman thought it over. "I don't find it convincing."

"Well," Duff continued, "what's she doing now? For years she's been furnishing that old home of yours, on Fifty-third Street, with the things that you discarded as you went along. Everything that you've been missing recently is there, including the portraits in the gold frames—only she's taken off the gold frames and put the pictures back into old-fashioned mahogany frames—as they were originally, I suppose. She's reassembled the background of your earlier and less successful days in New York, and she's been living in that background as much as possible. She's had her secretary living there, and now she's fixed up a studio for herself on the top floor, where she's been writing verses and trying to set them to music. All this has been a more or less unconscious revolt against you and your success. I don't suppose she's known what she was doing. But she's on the verge of knowing. Or, at least, she's on the verge of consciously revolting. She wants to adopt this Crawford boy. She's discovered that he's musical. She wants to adopt him and to educate him. She's been disappointed in her other boys and she feels it's because you've interfered with them. This boy isn't yours. She wants to take him abroad to study—to Munich. She doesn't know it, but what she really wants to do is to leave you and realize her ambitions, at last, in this boy—after she failed to realize them in the other boys."

Boadman had risen. He was walking silently up and down the room, his hands clasped behind him, his eyes on the floor.

"It's not going to be easy to stop this," Duff went on. "It's going to take a lot of maneuvering, a lot of finessing. You'll have to start with Julius Junior. If you want my advice, you'll get one of your own men secretly to take over this 'Boadman Estates' idea, put some real money in it, get some real land in Florida, and have him offer your boy the presidency of it. Then you write to Julius, tell him you hear he's been offered the position, and advise him to take it. He'd never take it without your permission. He acts as if he hated you, but that's because he admires you and resents the way you've behaved to him. As a boy, he wanted your affection and he never got it. His hate, you'll find, is just a reverse English on his frustrated affection for you. You've never given him anything but orders, and you've never asked anything from him but obedience. You've got to start in and win him. After he's in the company, you can tell him that you've put money in it, and ask him to come and discuss it with you. Never let him know that you planted the scheme on him. Show confidence in him. Keep your own man in charge of the business, but have him let Julius think *he's* a real power in it."

Boadman said sourly, "He'll get drunk and walk out some day."

"No harm done, if he does, but I think you've got the cart before the horse in this drinking business. It isn't his drinking that's made him a failure. It's his failure that's made him drink. He's frustrated, and his chief frustration's been in his affection for you. Get that straightened out and the rest's a cinch."

Boadman grunted.

"You can't do anything for Spencer. He's sterile. He's blocked. But you can do the same thing for Rodney that you do for Julius. Get behind him on this theater project. Con him. Take hold of a real producer, give him some real money, and tell him to dicker with the boy. Then tell the boy you're with him. Tell your wife. Tell her you hear that she's been writing verses and music and you think she ought to go in with Rodney and help him with the libretto. Tell them you'll invest some money in the show privately. Put one of your confidential men in charge of the whole thing and you can easily manage so that neither you nor your boy is made ridiculous. Beat these crooks at their own game—the same as you do with 'The Boadman Estates.' "

Boadman cursed. "Waste time! Waste money! A lot of damn foolishness!"

Duff went on serenely. "If you can win those two boys back, you can win your wife back. She'll never leave you if you have *them* with you. Give her Rodney to help and work with, instead of this Crawford boy, and she'll forget all about that little fakir. Help her to project her own ambitions into Rodney instead of adopting a substitute for a son, and you'll never have a moment's trouble with her."

"Where am I going to find the time for this sort of thing? I'm a busy man—"

"You've given nearly forty years to getting yourself into this situation, Mr. Boadman. It won't take as long as that to get out of it."

Boadman glared at him, miserably. "I don't know how to go about it. 'Con' this man! 'Con' that man! I don't know how to 'con' people."

"I'll help if you want me to. Introduce me to some one in your office capable of working up a land development scheme in Florida—an honest one. Put the money behind him and let him locate a good proposition. I'll introduce him to this fellow that's dickering with your son—"

"To that crook! Do you think I'd touch—"

"He's not a crook," Duff said. "He's one of my operatives."

"What?" Boadman blinked at him, stupidly. "One of your what?"

"One of my detectives. When I saw what the situation was, I worked out this solution of it. As a detective, it isn't enough for me to find out who took your gold frames. I have to return them to you. I worked out this way of returning your son."

"Then this whole 'Boadman Estates' business is an invention of yours!"

"Yes, but the conditions that produced it are no invention of mine. I only invented the cure for them."

"Is the musical comedy man one of your operatives, too?"

"Yes."

"And the Crawford boy?"

"Yes. He's the newsboy you asked me about, that day you drove to my office."

Boadman set his jaw. His hands tightened threateningly on the arms of his swivel chair. "Well, by God, Duff," he said, "you've certainly made a monkey of *me!*"

Duff shrugged his shoulders. "I saw no other way to show you the dangers you were in—and at the same time show you a way out of them."

"Go away," he said hoarsely. "I'm in no state—Go away. I'll send for you later."

~ ~ ~

When a New York syndicate bought Balk's Island, near Sorolla, Fla., and built a million-dollar causeway to it and put a million-dollar hotel on it, Santa Claus arrived in Sorolla and opened a distributing office there. The syndicate was ostensibly headed by Julius K. Boadman, Jr., but the elder Boadman's money was behind it, and it survived the collapse of the boom. "We're here to stay," young Boadman says. "I believe in Sorolla's future." What is more important, he believes in his own, which is also backed by the elder Boadman; and he lives in his father's New York house, when he is at home, and occupies himself with other Boadman enterprises when he is not busy with Sorolla.

About the same time that Santa Claus came to Sorolla, the Comic Opera Guild of America got under way in New York. Its sublime object was to foster and promote the production of native American comic operas and to aid in the development of Gilberts and Sullivans in the United States. Its public offices are in the Times Building on Broadway, but its private throne is located in a little yellow house on Fifty-third Street, near the corner of Lexington Avenue where Mrs. Boadman and her youngest son anonymously helped the authors to write the first of the Guild's productions, "Pocahontas."

The night that contracts were signed for "Pocahontas," a detective named Duff called at the house in pursuit of a runaway boy, named Mickey McQueen, alias Jimmy Crawford, of Syracuse. Mickey slipped out the basement door while Duff was interviewing Mrs. Boadman in her studio, and Duff had to cut short his interview so as to take up the trail again hotfoot. It was a shock to Mrs. Boadman to find that she had been deceived by Jimmy Crawford but she was too absorbed in her sons, by this time, to grieve much over her disappointment.

"All right, Duff," Boadman said, as he paid him off. "Things have turned out so well that I suppose I'll have to forgive you— but if I ever employ a detective again on my family affairs, I'll carry a heart stimulant as an antidote. You all but killed me."

THE

PARSON

CASE

THE PARSON CASE

I

AS THE DAILY EDITORIALS SAID, it was as if the crowded sidewalk of Fifth Avenue, on a Saturday noon, had opened under the feet of Isabel Parson and swallowed her whole. She had walked out of Foyer's shop, near Thirty-fourth Street, with her purchases, and vanished. She had ceased to exist as suddenly as if she had been struck on Foyer's threshold by some mysterious thunderbolt that had silently annihilated her, blown her into invisible atoms, destroyed her without leaving a trace. At one moment she was a handsome young girl, in smart spring clothes, on her way from her parents' apartment in Park Avenue to a week-end visit on Long Island, with a little fitted "week-end case" in her hand. A moment later, she had dropped out of sight into some undiscoverable abyss; and neither her frantic relatives, nor the police, nor a thousand eager newspaper reporters, could find even a reasonable explanation of what had become of her.

The family chauffeur had driven her, in her father's limousine, from the door of the apartment house on Park Avenue to the Harriman National Bank in Forty-fourth Street. At the bank, she drew out several hundred dollars from her pin-money account. The chauffeur motored her, then, down Fifth Avenue to Foyer's, and there she told him that he need not wait. "I'll take a taxi to the station," she explained. He saw her go into Foyer's. Apparently, she intended to buy herself a silk sweater in Foyer's, but she did not find any that she liked. She bought, instead, a pair of silk pajamas, a negligee, and some underclothes that proved irresistible. With these in her week-end case, she walked out blithely—into whatever bottomless gulf had swallowed her.

Her friends on Long Island waited till Sunday morning before they telephoned to ask why she had not arrived. By Sunday noon her worried father was calling up the hospitals and the police. The newspapers got the story Sunday night, and they were short of news, so they spread it on the front page Monday morning. They described her as "an heiress," a "Fifth Avenue girl," a "prominent debutante," a young personage of wealth and fashion. According to them, she had everything in the world that a happy girl could wish. They could discover no shadow of a reason why she should have run away. Consequently, they decided that she had been kidnaped and carried off into some criminal den of white slaves. Her photograph showed her appealingly pretty and spirited—an alert and breezy girl with a boyish bob—and she looked at you from the printed page with an air of confident youth and privileged security that made it horrible to think of her as attacked, betrayed, tortured, suffering.

It happened that one ingenious editor had been crusading for a better police control of taxi-drivers, and he scented something fruitful in her statement to her chauffeur that she would finish her trip to the railroad station in a taxicab. So, on the following night, while one of his reporters was standing at the corner of Fifth Avenue and Thirty-fourth Street, a fainting woman flung herself from the door of a passing taxi, and gasped out a terrible story of how she had felt herself losing consciousness in the cab and discovered a rubber tube beside her from which a flow of faintly sweet-smelling poisonous gas was slowly stupefying her. She had called to the chauffeur to stop. He had put on speed. She had fallen against the door, too weak to open it, struggling feebly with the handle. And then the brakes were clamped on with a jerk as the cab was caught in a jam of traffic at Thirty-fourth Street and Fifth Avenue, and the sudden jolt threw her weight on the handle, and the door flew open, and she fell out.

The reporter caught her. He might have caught the taxi-driver, but before he could understand from her what had happened, the cab had darted forward again and disappeared.

As his paper said next morning, she had been almost "Isabel Parsoned" within sight of Foyer's. And by the time the evening editions issued, a new terror had been added to the imaginary dangers of life in New York. The "lethal taxicab" had been invented—the lethal taxicab that prowled about the streets at night, a chamber of horrors on wheels, diabolically prepared to catch unprotected girls in all their happy innocence and carry them, drugged and helpless, to the infernal regions of the underworld.

It was a more plausible myth than the "kissing bug" of 1899 that stung beautiful actresses on the lips and left them to faint away in the streets. It was more terrifying than the "poison needle" of a decade later, that was jabbed into poor girls in the subway rush, with the result that the unsuspecting victim, having felt only a pin prick in her arm, began to grow faint and dizzy, accepted aid from a stranger who caught her as she staggered, and slowly lapsed into a walking trance from which she woke Heaven knows where. Compared to these earlier sensationalisms, the lethal taxicab was an invention of genius. It not only tapped the romantic emotions of all the suppressed Puritans for whom tales of white slavery had a horrid fascination: it appealed to the animosity of every timid soul who had ever been cheated by a taximeter; and it revived the resentment of every pedestrian who had been almost run down (and completely bawled out) by a careless taxi-driver. The papers became daily melodramas, full of Isabel Parson and the lethal taxicab, with diagrams to show how the deadly gas could be piped from a tank under the driver's seat to the nostrils of his victim. They all but provoked a race riot, with mobs of lynchers pursuing fleeing taxis up and down the howling streets.

Among the New Yorkers who read these stories skeptically, one of the most skeptical was Detective Duff. He knew something about New York's underworld. He knew that it was governed by the same commercial laws that ruled the rest of the town. He knew that the supply of girls in it was greater than the demand, that the girls had to practice the same arts of salesmanship as a book agent, that Isabel Parson as a white slave was as impossible as an insurance solicitor in chains.

"People," he complained, "are so darned romantic about vice. They don't seem to realize that it's a business. These girls have as much trouble making a living as the rest of us. It's only the cleverest of them that ever earn more than day's wages. You might as well talk of kidnaping girls and selling them as clerks to department stores. Pickles! This Parson girl ran away, or I'm a sap."

He came out with these judgments flat-footedly to anyone who mentioned the Parson case. He had no hesitation in voicing them. He never expected to be involved in the Parson case himself. And he was contemptuously frank in expressing his opinions to a stranger named Ewing who called on him in his office with a letter of introduction, one morning at the height of the Parson furor, when Ewing naturally got to gossiping about the Parson case after his own small trouble had been laid on Duff's desk.

Duff was not impressed by Ewing. Ewing had an exterior that was prosperous and fat and self-important—the exterior of a successful self-made man of money—but out of his eyes there looked another sort of person altogether. He had a way of staring at you too fixedly.

His gray hair was brushed back too defiantly from his forehead. He seemed too aggressively clean-shaven. He held his mouth in a stern expression and frowned all the time, but behind his forbidding mask Duff seemed to see a frightened small boy confronting

the big bully, life, with a show of facing him down. In spite of
everything, Ewing's features were weak and white and soft; and
his eyes were as if steeled against his own timidity.

At Duff's declaration that the Parson girl must have run away,
Ewing asked, glowering, "What makes you think she ran away?"

"She drew money enough to run away with, didn't she?" Duff
replied. "She had a suitcase, and nobody knows what was in it.
She knew she wouldn't be missed for four or five hours, didn't
she? And she bought the sort of things a girl takes with her when
she elopes. Her father must be a darn fool, or he'd know where she
went and who went *with* her."

And at that, Ewing turned red in a stare of mortified rage.
"Look here," he said hoarsely, "my name's not Ewing. It's *Parson*. I'm her father."

Duff's first impulse was to laugh. He did not yield to it. He
glared at Parson almost as malevolently as Parson glared at him.
"Where is she?" he asked.

"I don't know."

"Who's with her?"

"I don't know that either."

They bristled like a pair of unfriendly dogs, eyeing each other
angrily—only Duff was a large and shaggy mastiff of a man
whose growl was a sort of good-natured warning not to provoke a
fight, and Parson had the peevish manner of a fat house pet snarling to keep up its courage.

"Well," Duff said, "you're not suffering from the general delusion that she's been kidnaped, are you?"

He smiled dryly as he said it, and something in Parson weakened when he tried to outface that smile. He dropped his eyes.
"No," he admitted. "I don't believe she was kidnaped."

"You think she ran away."

"Yes," he said sulkily, "I do."

"Why do you suppose she did it?"

"I don't know."

And he didn't know. Under Duff's continued questions, it became clearer and clearer that he didn't know. He had left the girl
and her affairs to his wife, and there had been no more trouble between mother and daughter than there usually is in these days of
rebellious youth. Neither he nor his wife knew of any lover to
whom she might have fled. She had one recognized suitor, a
Horace Chilton, well-to-do and eminently eligible, whom they had
hoped that she might marry, but they had not tried to influence her.

They had felt that she was still too young to consider marriage seriously. She was just out of school. They had wanted her to go to college, but they did not insist on her going when she announced that she was sick of books and teachers. They let her stay home and take singing lessons. She was musical. She played the piano—chiefly jazz. And she was mad about dancing. During the past winter, she had been out to dances with Chilton on an average of three times a week. Chilton was a solid, sensible fellow, older than she, and when she refused to be chaperoned—because no girls were chaperoned any more, you might as well send her out with a governess—her mother had compromised by letting her go alone wherever Chilton took her.

"We gave her her own way," Parson complained bitterly. "In everything we possibly could, we gave her her own way. We didn't even force her to go to church with us when she said she didn't want to any more. We didn't interfere with her reading, and she was free to go to matinees by herself. We didn't want her out at night alone, especially at these so-called 'clubs' where young people dance and drink till all hours, but we even let her go *there* if Horace took her, and we didn't ask any questions about it."

Duff watched him while he talked. Here the man sat, at the heart of all the tragedy and mystery and emotion of the famous Parson case, a wholly commonplace and inadequate parent with a grievance. It was funny. It had all the burlesque quality of reality at its most real. The one emotion in Parson's shallow soul seemed to be resentment. He was angry at the girl, at her mother, at the police, at the newspapers, at the situation in which he found himself, and at the world that saw him in that situation.

"Well," Duff asked, "what do you want me to do? Find her?"

"Yes. Of course I want you to find her."

Duff slumped down in his swivel chair, hunching up his shoulders, his chin on his chest. "It isn't going to be easy, or some one would've picked up her trail before this. She must've had her cover all ready before she started. If the police and the newspapers can't locate her, I haven't a chance—unless I can find some indication of where she was going, in her mind, before she went."

"In her mind?"

"Yes."

"Huh!" Parson grunted. "How are you going to do that?"

"I haven't the faintest idea," Duff admitted.

There was something about Parson that was "off normal," as Duff would have said, and Duff was puzzled to know what was the matter. Being puzzled, he avoided all appearance of being puzzled. He avoided any show of interest in Parson. He frowned gloomily at his desk calendar.

"Your wife," he said, "must be pretty well knocked out by this whole business. If she had a nervous breakdown, now, it'd be perfectly natural. And it'd be perfectly natural for you to hire a trained nurse to look after her. I want to put an operative in among your servants, and a trained nurse is the only sort of servant that wouldn't be suspected. I have a girl, a Miss Browning, who acts as a trained nurse. I use her in cases of this kind where the ordinary detective would stick out like a patrolman at a ball. If I can put her in your household, she'll work her way into the confidence of the servants—particularly the chauffeur—and find out whether they know anything they're holding back from you. I'll have to have somebody rope Chilton, too, and see whether *he* has anything. Your daughter may have dropped a hint to him that he hasn't noticed; she must've been planning this move for some time. But we'll have to keep under cover. I don't want the reporters to know I'm on the case, and I don't think we ought to tell the police."

"Damn the police," Parson broke out. "I shouldn't've told them in the first place. All my wife's cursed nonsense . . ."

"Ah!" Duff said, suddenly illuminated, "you heard from the girl after you called in the police!"

"Now, look here," Parson blustered, "this is confidential. I'm not going to be made to look like a fool. You're not going to give it to the newspapers, and you're not going to tell the police. Let them find it out if they're so smart. They started all this talk about white-slave taxicabs, and they can finish it their own way."

"Certainly," Duff soothed him. "Quite so. What've you heard from her?"

He drew a note from his pocket and threw it angrily on Duff's desk. It was written in lead pencil, on a cheap ruled letter paper. And it read: "I'm all right. Don't worry. And don't try to find me."

"When did you get this?"

"I didn't get it till Monday morning. It was posted to reach me Saturday, and it was either delayed in the mail or mislaid in the house. I didn't see it till Monday morning, and by that time"—He made an impatient gesture of disgust at the ridiculous hullabaloo that had been raised around him—"I couldn't admit that she'd run away. It'd make me look like a fool. Besides, I thought that with all this publicity, some one would be sure to trace her, and I wanted her brought back."

Duff had been turning the note over in his fingers. "It came in an envelope, of course," he said.

Yes, of course, it had come in an envelope, but Parson had not dared to carry it around in its envelope for fear he might lose it from his pocket and betray himself. The note, without the envelope, did not give any name. No one could guess that it was from *her.* He had destroyed the envelope.

"Where was it postmarked?" Duff asked.

"New York."

"What post office?"

He did not remember.

"Well, it doesn't matter," Duff said. "If you'll get your wife to go to bed with a nervous breakdown, I'll prepare Miss Browning to take the case."

He rose to end the interview.

And as soon as he got rid of Parson—which he only succeeded in doing after fifteen minutes of last doubts and final reassurances—he called Miss Browning in at once.

"Martha," he said, "this crazy Parson case has come to us, very confidentially, and I'm turning it over to you. Between ourselves, the girl's parents are a couple of poor boobs apparently. They don't know anything about anything. There's something phoney about their reactions to the girl's disappearance. I don't understand them. You'll have to trail back over their relations with the girl and give me a full report on it. And I want to know what's been going on in the girl's mind. See if you can't find a definite love-image for me. Trace back her action-patterns and see if we can't figure out, from *them,* what has become of her. It's our only chance. It's a psychological case, and we'll have to handle it psychologically, see?"

Martha Browning was a large and placid young woman who looked as little like a detective as the huge Duff himself. She listened to his instructions with the professional detachment of a newspaper "sob sister" taking an assignment from a city editor. "When do I go on it?" she asked.

"Some time to-night or to-morrow morning. Parson's to phone me. I'll let you know later."

"All right," she said. "I'll have to make arrangements. I can't leave my mother alone."

"How is she?"

She smiled, quite humanly. "Oh, she's better, thanks."

She went off, to make her arrangements, and Duff turned to his office phone and asked for an operative named Bundy.

"Is that you, Charlie?" he said. "Well, listen. That crazy Parson case has come in, confidentially, and I want you to report, under cover, to Parson in his office, and let him put you next to a man named Chilton—Horace Chilton—the guy that the girl was supposed to be engaged to. I've a hunch that Chilton may know where she is." This was a lie, of course. "At any rate, I want you to find out what their relations have really been and what kind of a girl Chilton really thinks she is. You'll have to rope him. I don't know how you'll do it. Parson may be able to help you. All right. See you later."

II

So Duff undertook the Parson case. And the longer he worked on it, the less it looked like the Parson case that was agitating the public mind. Though George E. Parson lived in a Park Avenue palace—in a fifteen-room apartment that cost a prince's ransom every year in rent—he was not truly "class" in the popular sense. He was the son of a Long Island dairy farmer. He had come to New York as a boy to work in a lunch room. It was an older brother, Ned Parson, who got the idea of opening a restaurant in Nassau Street, and the two brothers went into it together. That was the first of their string of "Homestead" Dairy Restaurants, on which the Parson fortune was based. After the brother's death, George Parson made a merger of the Homestead restaurants with a rival firm that operated lunch rooms under the so-called Food Trust, and he was now merely vice-president of this consolidation—of which Horace Chilton was the executive manager. Parson occupied himself with real estate. His father's farm on Long Island, cut up into building lots, had been as profitable as an oil field. He had bought and built in all directions and in no direction had he gone astray. All his development schemes had succeeded marvelously. He was now a very rich man, convinced of his ability and his importance, living in a continual happy downpour of rents and dividends, and really as simple-minded still as when he first arrived in Manhattan to work as a waiter in Dennett's.

And Martha Browning's reports made it evident that Mrs. Parson was only a feminine version of her husband. She had been a Miranda Baker, daughter of the Rev. Enoch Baker of Flushing, when Parson married her, a choir soprano with fair hair and a nasal voice. For the first ten years of their married life they had lived in boarding houses, both working in the original Homestead Dairy Restaurant. Then when Parson was nearly forty and she was thirty-five, they added their only child to the family and went to live in a flat. "I don't think the mother wanted a child," Martha Browning wrote. "She speaks always of having done her duty by the girl, but she seems to have done it without affection. She says that Isabel was always wild. She acts as if she were in some way obscurely gratified because her daughter has fulfilled her constant predictions that the girl would come to a bad end."

The conflict between mother and daughter had been a quarrel between two opposing ideals of conduct. To Mrs. Parson, life was made up of duties mostly—her duty to God, to her husband, to her daughter, to her neighbors, and to her position in the world. She sat down to the good things of life convinced that her appetite for them was sinful, and determined to restrain herself and her family from self-indulgence in them, and solemnly prepared to make her self-denial a good example to her neighbors. The girl sat down beside her with an eager young appetite and a long reach. As an infant, the mother could control her, but at six years old she ran away with some rowdy children from across the street; at eight, she tried to elope with the elevator boy of the house in which they lived; at twelve, she was sent to the discipline of a strict boarding school for girls because her parents could do nothing with her; at sixteen, she was in sturdy revolt, openly independent, contemptuous of her parents as "a couple of back numbers," and doing pretty much as she pleased.

She had been clever enough to wheedle her father secretly over to her side of the war with her mother, but she had never tried to force him to stand frankly with her; she must have understood the intimidated sternness of his frown. And she had been masterly in her handling of Horace Chilton. She had convinced him that his only hope of winning her lay in giving way to her in everything. She used him to deceive her parents, making him take her to all the forbidden places that she wished to go to, and forcing him to lie about them loyally. She had a lot of wild young friends for whom she deserted him at dances, leaving him to wait for her in a corner like a faithful watch-dog, and rewarding him, when she returned, with humorous endearments. She called him "Chilly." She had persuaded him that he was her ideal of a husband—that he need only be patient till she was ready to marry him and settle down.

"Well," Duff said, "what we get out of all this is simply an action-pattern that shows the girl was set to run away some time or other." And he phoned to Martha Browning, "Find out whether the elevator boy wore a livery—the boy she tried to elope with when she was eight."

They learned little of any value from Horace Chilton. Parson had told Chilton, in confidence, of the letter from the girl, and Chilton had undertaken to find some trace of her among the wild young friends with whom she used to drink and dance. He put the detectives on every boy who had ever jazzed with her. They discovered nothing. "No," Duff said, "if she'd wanted to elope with any of those cake-eaters, she could've gone openly. She must've picked up some rowdy boy, like the children she ran away to play with when she was six." And when Martha Browning reported that the girl's first love had worn a livery, Duff called in two of his operatives and ordered them to cover the Parson chauffeur.

Nothing came of that, either. The chauffeur was a young Irishman named Larry Farrell who lived respectably with his mother and a younger brother in a flat on Third Avenue not far from the Parson apartment. He had been a newsboy and a garage mechanic before he took service with the Parsons. Out of his earnings he had set up his brother in a tire-repair shop, and they were planning to open a garage of their own as soon as they had saved capital enough. When he was not on duty for the Parsons, he was home asleep. It would have been difficult to "rope" him in any circumstances, but now he and his brother and his mother, too, had been so pestered by reporters and police and plainclothes men that it was impossible for any stranger to approach them unsuspected. One of Duff's detectives tried to get work with the brother in the tire shop, and the brother said: "Chase yerself out o' here, bo. We're not hirin' any private dicks." An operative who attempted to shadow Larry, the chauffeur, reported: "This guy's been tailed so much that he walks backward when he goes to bed." Another operative tried to make his way into the Farrell flat as an inspector of gas meters, so as to see how the family lived, and the mother stopped him at the threshold. "That meter's been inspected three times this month," she said, closing the door in his face. And Martha Browning reported from the servants' gossip: "The chauffeur has been so cross-examined and interviewed and third-degreed that he is planning to go out West, as soon as the excitement blows over, and open a garage with his brother—probably in Los Angeles."

She had little else to report from the servants. There were only two of them—an old housekeeper who had come to the Parsons, years before, as a nursemaid for the daughter, and a personal maid who waited on both mother and daughter. The rest of the service was supplied by the apartment house—as in a hotel. The housekeeper acted as a butler and answered the door; the personal maid served as a sort of second man and kept the place in order. In the details of the daughter's daily life which these two unconsciously supplied to Martha Browning, there was one curious incident which had no recognizable significance. On the morning that the girl disappeared, she had slept late. At ten o'clock, a woman called with a gown that had been ordered from a Madame Stojowska. This woman—an elderly gray-haired woman, rather shabbily dressed—had insisted on seeing "Miss Parson," to try on the gown. The mother was out. After some carrying of messages between the sleepy girl and the implacable dressmaker, Madame Stojowska's representative was admitted to the bedroom, and Isabel Parson said sulkily: "Well, what the devil do you want?" The woman closed the bedroom door before she answered. And nothing more was heard of her. She left the apartment without being seen by the servants; and, after she had gone, when the maid brought in the girl's breakfast tray, the box containing Madame Stojowska's gown lay, still unopened, on the foot of the bed.

The servants supposed that Isabel had quarreled with the dressmaker and sent her off without allowing her to try on the gown. But the gown was an evening frock which the girl had bought to wear on her weekend visit. She had taken it with her in her suitcase. If there had been any doubt of its fitting her, it seemed strange that she should not have tried it on.

"Better see this dressmaker," Duff directed Martha Browning, "and find out what happened. She appears to've been one of the last persons, outside of the family, to talk with the girl before she beat it."

At once, a difficulty developed. To Martha Browning as Mrs. Parson's private secretary, Madame Stojowska explained that there had been no question of the gown's fitting. Isabel Parson had tried it on, in the shop, two days before its delivery, after all the necessary alterations had been made. Moreover, Madame declared, the dress had been delivered to the Parson apartment by a young girl and not by an elderly gray-haired woman.

Martha Browning said: "Let me see the girl."

The girl was produced. And she admitted, immediately, that she had not delivered the dress. On her way downstairs, from the workrooms on an upper floor of Madame Stojowska's establishment, she had been overtaken by a Mrs. Moore who said that Madame had ordered *her* to deliver the dress to Miss Parson and see that it fitted.

"But I told her notdings of such a kind," Madame put in.

Mrs. Moore was a sewing woman, intermittently hired when business was brisk. She had taken the dress for Miss Parson from the girl, and the girl had gone on with some other packages which she had to deliver.

"But no!" Madame protested. "I did not told her."

"Let me see this Mrs. Moore," Martha Browning said.

And Mrs. Moore was not forthcoming. She had not worked for Madame Stojowska "since some weeks"—not, in fact, since that Saturday on which she undertook to deliver the gown.

Martha Browning wrote down Mrs. Moore's address. "Please say nothing of this to any one," she warned Madame Stojowska, aside, "or you may be involved in publicity that will hurt your business."

"I say not at all," Madame promised fervently. "I do not like the trial of murders. No, not with *my* shop."

Martha Browning went at once to the nearest telephone, not daring to make another move till she had consulted Duff. And Duff said: "Good! I don't know where we're going, but I think we're on our way at last. Don't do anything about this. Leave it to me. I'll look up Mrs. Moore as soon as I've thought the thing over. Go back to your invalid and don't say a word."

She returned to her role of trained nurse, and Duff settled down to "think the thing over" in a manner that was peculiar. He sent an operative to "cover" Mrs. Moore at her address. He called for the complete file on the Parson case. He gave orders that no one was to disturb him in his office till he said the word. Then he planted himself at his shabby old desk, in his creaking swivel chair, and began to read his operatives' daily reports in a dreamy idle-minded mood, with one eyebrow raised and his lips pouted. It was an absurdly childish expression on the face of such a man. It was almost the expression of a blinking baby with a bottle to suck and its eyes on a daydream.

In the midst of Martha Browning's reports on the domestic relations of the Parsons and their daughter, he smiled lazily and reached for his phone. "Get me Parson," he ordered, in a sleepy voice, and went on reading with the receiver to his ear.

"Mr. Ewing," he said to Parson, in the same tone of abstraction, reading as he spoke, "I'm phoning from the office where you consulted me, last week, about that legal tangle of yours. Yes. Could you drop in to see me, this afternoon? Yes, as soon as you can. Right away, if that's possible. Yes. I've something important to report. Yes. Yes." He let his voice trail off languidly as he hung up. "Quite so," he added, after the receiver was on its hook. He put aside the reports and lay back in his chair. "Well," he said, "I must've been deaf and blind." He shook his head sadly. "I must be losing my mind."

III

He was still sweetly downcast and self-depreciative when Parson arrived. "I'm afraid I've been pretty dumb about this case," he said as they shook hands. "Pretty damn dumb!" And Parson, dressed in black, as formally solemn as an undertaker, received the confession with an air of meek self-conscious satisfaction. He took it, evidently, as a proof that Isabel Parson's father was not such an obvious "darn fool" even if he didn't know where his daughter was hidden.

"The fact that you didn't tell me who you were, at first," Duff continued, "and failed to tell me about the letter you'd received, and all the rest of it—I should have known that the impulse to concealment—" He left the sentence unfinished with a vague gesture that motioned Parson to a chair. "I suppose I took it for granted that if a man called in a doctor, he wouldn't lie about his symptoms, or deceive his lawyer about the facts in a case that had to be defended." He sat down. "Well, well," he said. "Live and learn. Live and learn."

He sat down and left Parson standing. And Parson stood, reddening like a guilty schoolboy, his hat in his hand. "Look here," he said, in a weak bluster. "What're you talking about?"

Duff gave him a dark look. "Whose child is this girl, anyway?"

" 'Whose child'?"

"Yes. She's not your wife's. And I don't believe she's yours. Whose is she?"

It was possible to watch, in Parson's features, a certain hardening that indicated a sulky determination not to answer Duff. He was no longer merely guilty; he was guilty and on his defense.

Duff shot at him, quickly, "Who is Mrs. Moore?"

And the question acted like a shell exploding inside his defenses. His face seemed to break up, at once, in a painful dissolution of his stubbornness. He stared at Duff, pale and shocked, but apparently no longer clearly aware either of Duff or of himself. It was as if the name of Mrs. Moore had raised her, in the flesh, between him and Duff, with the whole story open before both of them; and it was as if acknowledging her, necessarily, in her presence, that he replied, in a breathy huskiness, "She's her mother."

"Who was her father?"

"My brother Ned."

He sat down. That is to say, his body sat down, as though the impact of Duff's questions had overcome and weakened him, but he was evidently unconscious of his own movement, and he gazed at the floor, with a look of empty-eyed tragedy.

"I'll have to know the whole story," Duff said. "You'd better tell it to me."

Parson remained a long time silent, but it was an unconscious silence, not a stubborn one. His habitual frown and all his timid aggressiveness had vanished from his face. He looked as if he were going to cry.

"My brother Ned was a fine fellow," he said, pathetically, "but he wasn't happy with his wife."

He paused on this for so long that Duff, at last, said, "No?"

He shook his head. "No. That's why he fell in love with *her*—with Katie Moore. She was a waitress in one of our restaurants."

After another interminable silence, Duff prodded him again. "I see."

"I didn't know anything about it," he went on, "till some doctor told him that he had heart disease—that he was likely to drop dead any minute. Then he told me that Katie was going to have a baby, and he asked me to look after her if anything happened to him. And then he dropped dead, one day on the street, before the baby was born, and I got her away to a place over in Jersey City, and I told my wife about it, and we agreed to adopt the baby, because Katie hadn't any way to take care of it—or anything—and my wife went away for the summer, and when she came back she brought the baby with her and pretended it was hers."

"The girl—Isabel—did she ever know?"

"No. Nobody knew—except *her*—the mother. We didn't even tell Ned's wife. She died without knowing it."

"Has Katie Moore made any attempt to—"

"No, no. Never. Never. She was a good girl—a pious girl. She knew she'd committed a sin and she wanted to suffer for it. That's why she wouldn't take any money from us, or anything like that. She earned her own living, as a waitress, and then sewing. She was—She was afraid her sin'd be visited on the child, so she wouldn't come near, for fear some one might suspect. She wouldn't take any money from us—not even Ned's money after his wife died. She wanted it all to go to the baby. She wanted her to grow up a good girl and never know she'd had a bad woman for a mother. She wouldn't let us know where she was or anything. She was afraid something might happen. She was queer. The last time I ran across her I thought she was—I thought she'd been drinking."

He did not ask how Duff had learned of Katie Moore. He took it for granted, apparently, that his wife had inadvertently betrayed their secret to the nurse. And when Duff said, "Well, you'll have to come along with me and see this woman," he rose, without asking any questions, very much as if he were in the hands of the police.

It was not till they were outside, in a taxicab, that he remonstrated, "Why do we have to bother *her?*" And when Duff replied, "Because I think she knows where the girl is," he protested, feebly, "How is *that* possible?"

"You'd better let her tell you, herself," Duff answered.

He fell silent again. He rode, indeed, with Duff, like a mourner in a funeral who had his eyes and his thoughts fixed on the melancholy past that was being carried to the grave, in the hearse, ahead of them. He did not move when the cab stopped at an old brownstone residence in a row on Lexington Avenue that had been converted into rooming houses. "Here we are," Duff said.

There was a cleaner and dyer in the basement. Up the flight of battered brownstone steps, a hairdresser advertised in the parlor windows. Duff's operative, loitering on the sidewalk, came up to report with a brisk casualness: "She's on the third floor back, Chief. There's no one lives with her. She sounds like she was alone in there, sayin' her prayers."

Duff nodded, and the man, walking away quickly, disappeared again. "Come along," Duff said to Parson.

Parson got out as if they had reached the cemetery.

He followed the detective upstairs, blindly, to a door in the rear of the dark hallway on the third floor. Duff knocked without an answer. He knocked again. The third time, a muffled voice called through the door, "Who is it?"

"Tell her," Duff whispered.

And Parson answered: "It's me, Kate. It's George. George Parson."

They heard a bolt withdrawn, and then the door opened on a strange sight.

Katie Moore stood back, in a man's overcoat and bare feet, with her gray hair wild and hanging in her eyes. Behind her, the room, all its blinds drawn, was bright with lighted candles, like a chapel, and with altar lights that burned on the mantelpiece before small statues of the Virgin Mary and Saint Joseph and images of the Sacred Heart. She had the strong face of an old witch, her eyes bloodshot and exalted, her head trembling. She held the overcoat closed at her throat with one hand, and with the other she kept putting back her hair from her face distractedly. "It was the devil in her," she said in a hollow voice. "Even unto the third and fourth generation. It was the devil in her, the same as it was in me."

Duff edged Parson into the room and closed the door behind them. "Where is she?" Duff asked.

And she replied to Parson, as if she did not see Duff at all: "She's gone her own ways. She laughed at me. There, in her bed, with them nightclothes on her like a bad girl, she laughed at me when I told her. 'It's the devil in you,' I said, 'like it was the devil in me at *your* age,' I said, 'an' yuh needs must fight against it before it's too late. I seen yuh in his arms,' I said. 'Yuh clung to him an' yuh kissed him, the same as I did, an' I yer mother.' "

"Who? Where?" Duff interrupted her. "Who was she kissing?"

She blinked at Parson. She dropped her voice to answer, in a saner tone, "The chauffeur."

"Where?"

"At the head o' them stairs," she whispered, "on the way up to the fittin' rooms, where he'd gone to call her, because he couldn't wait no longer with the car. An' when they seen me watchin' them, they came downstairs past me, gigglin'. An' I knew her the minute I set eyes on her." Her voice was rising again to a crazy chant. "An' I prayed an' prayed, an' God sent me the girl with the dress in a box, an' I took it, an' I went to her, an' I told her she was on the brink o' Hell because o' what she was, an' I her mother. An' she jumped up an' says, 'D'yuh tell me, then I'm not their daughter?' An' I said, 'No. Not *you*. Yuh're the daughter o' sin,' I said, 'an' me a bad woman.' An' the devil in her laughed.

An' she leapt out o' bed with villainy, an' she said, 'Tell me, then, who *am* I?' An' I told her. An' she flung up her hands an' laughed an' laughed. An' I seen the devil in her face, an' I knew she was lost, an' I run away to pray—fer nothin' can save her now but prayin'. Nothin' but prayin'." She waved her hand to the tapers and the images on the mantelshelf. "Yuh'll pray with me, now," she said; and throwing off the overcoat, she knelt down in a long white garment that looked like a priest's alb; and blessing herself, she began to repeat a muttered litany, very rapidly, bent double, and beating her breast.

The room was stifling with exhausted air and the smell of guttering candles. Parson wiped his forehead with a trembling hand. Duff took him by the elbow. "Come along," he said under his voice. "We'll get nothing more here."

Parson shook his head, without turning around, fascinated by the pathetic huddle of devotion crouched on the floor before them. "We can't leave her like this," he whispered. "She's—she's gone crazy."

"She'll be all right," Duff argued. "My man'll look after her till we get back. You can have her taken care of—in a sanitarium or something. There'll be lots of time for that. But now we've got to move fast, if we're going to find your daughter. We're only a couple of jumps ahead of the newspaper men, if anyone down at that dressmaker's begins to babble. Come along, quick."

He had opened the door while he talked. He drew Parson out and shut it gently after him. "I was right about that chauffeur in the first place," he muttered, "if I'd only had sense enough to go after him myself."

Parson, behind him, blundered along the dark hallway and stumbled down the stairs, blinded with tears. He was still carrying his hat in his hand when they came to the street door. "Pull yourself together," Duff said harshly. "Put your hat on. Draw it down more over your eyes. All right. Come along. We can get in the cab before anyone sees you."

He hurried Parson to the waiting taxi and gave the driver the Farrell address on Third Avenue. He sat back, frowning busily, without so much as a glance at the silent man beside him. And when Parson said at last, "Poor Ned! I hope he's nowhere that he can see her like *that!*" Duff turned on him.

"Now, look here," he threatened, "if we're going to get anywhere with this job, we'll have to have some sense about it. You're not to blame this girl for running away, you understand.

Your wife's a good woman, but you know as well as I do that she wasn't as crazy about the child as she would've been about one of her own. She's been trying to do her duty, but duty's no good with a child, and this girl's been running away from it ever since she was old enough to walk. You'll have to make up your mind to let her go. The best you can do is to help her get away without a whole lot of newspaper holler that'll raise a yell around her wherever she gets to. Between her crazy mother and the rest of you, you've just about ruined her life. The best you can do is to try to help her to find a little happiness with her chauffeur-boy, if that's possible."

Parson asked dully, "Where is she?"

"There's only one place she *can* be, but if I let you see her, you've got to promise to do nothing but help her. You've helped to make Katie Moore what she is, with your darned nonsense. Now you've got to help me get this girl a chance for her life."

"What've *I* done?" Parson protested, brokenly.

"You should've let that woman keep her baby," Duff scolded. "You could've covered the whole thing up, so nobody would've been any wiser. Then you wouldn't have a crazy mother on your hands and a daughter that's trying to destroy herself. You'll let this girl have her lover, now. You'll cover that up for her, and you'll cover it up right."

Parson did not try to defend himself. He was obviously broken. "What do you want me to do?"

"I want you to help her and the boy get away where the newspapers can't find them. I want you to give her her money—every last cent of it—and set the boy up in business somewhere, and let him have a chance to make good. I don't care a damn about your piety or your morality or anything else. You're going to do what I tell you, or I'll drop the whole case, and the newspapers'll find her and make you look like a fool."

"I haven't said I *wouldn't,* have I?"

"All right, then. I'm your lawyer, understand. I'm your lawyer, and I'll do the talking, and you'll agree to everything I say. Your chauffeur lives here with his mother and his brother." The cab was pulling up at the Farrell number. "They'll let *you* in when they mightn't let me, so you'd better ring the bell, and ask to see the mother, and I'll do the rest."

IV

But when Parson rang at the door of the Farrell flat, it was Mrs. Farrell herself who answered, and to Duff's surprise she was not Irish. She was a small, motherly-looking Englishwoman in gold-rimmed spectacles, dressed in black and a kitchen apron, with a basting spoon in her hand. "Well, sir," she asked, "what is it?" And before Parson could reply, Duff explained: "This is Mr. Parson. I'm his lawyer. We'd like to have a few minutes' talk with you in private."

She hesitated only a second or two while she looked them over, unembarrassed. "My boys're not back from their work yet," she said, "but come in. Larry'll be here any minute." She held the door open for them to enter, and she closed and locked it behind them when they were in. "Sit down if you will."

There was no inner hall to the flat, and they had come directly into a living-room that made no pretentions of being a formal parlor. The furniture was old and worn; there were newspapers scattered about on the rag carpet; a disorder of pipes, tobacco, playing cards and automobile catalogues covered the center table; a sewing machine stood by the window; a kitten was asleep in a sewing basket on the seat of an old rocker. As her only gesture of hospitality, Mrs. Farrell put the basket and the kitten on the sewing machine, silently, and laid down her spoon.

Duff liked her, and he liked the room. If he had put his feeling into words, he would have said: "This is a shrewd and capable woman. She understands that the essential thing in a home is the happiness of the human relationships in it. She lets that govern her housekeeping, and she doesn't worry about appearances. I'll bet she makes those boys comfortable."

He said to her, "We didn't come to see your son. We came to see you. We think you can help us."

She clasped her hands over the waistband of her apron, patiently. "How can I do that?"

"Sit down and I'll tell you." He motioned Parson to a chair beside the table. He drew up a chair for himself, to face her rocker. She sat down before him with the appearance of being only politely and impersonally interested. But behind him, and in front of her, were the portieres of a doorway leading into the next room. They were cheap chenille curtains, with a ball fringe, hanging on a curtain pole and closely drawn. She never glanced at them, but he could see that she was as acutely aware of them as he was himself.

"On the day that Mr. Parson's daughter disappeared," he said, "she wrote her father a note to tell him that she was all right, that he wasn't to worry about her. That was a Saturday, as you may remember, and the note was either delayed in the mails, or mislaid in some way, so that he didn't receive it till Monday morning. In the meantime, he'd been so worried that he'd notified the police. And all this uproar started. He let it go on in the hope that so much publicity would make it certain she'd be found. And he wanted her back at any cost, you understand, but now he realizes that she was unhappy at home, that he'll have to let her go if she wants to go; and all he asks is to help her to get away without being caught by the police or exposed by the newspapers or anything like that."

Duff was speaking over-loudly, for the benefit of the portieres. Evidently Mrs. Farrell could not decide whether he thought that she was somewhat deaf or whether Parson was. She kept looking from Duff to Parson and back again to Duff. "I see," she said, when Duff paused for some word from her.

"She can't get away by train, or by boat," he continued. "She's sure to be recognized. Her only chance is to go by automobile, and even so it won't be possible for her to stop at any hotels, or to go through any cities where newspapermen might spot her. She'll have to travel in a machine with some sort of camping outfit. As soon as she's ready to start we'll notify the police and the newspapers that she's been found—that she's been suffering from a loss of memory, or some bunk of the sort, and she's written her father and he's put her in a sanitarium. That'll stop them from looking for her around here, and in a few weeks the excitement'll die down and they'll stop looking for her anywhere. In the meantime, she'll be well on her way across the continent—say to Los Angeles."

"I see," she said. "And how can I—? "

"In this way. Your son Larry has been planning to open a garage, with your other boy, as soon as they've saved up enough money. He's even mentioned the possibility of doing it in Los Angeles. You'd want to go with your boys, of course, and there's no reason why—if you went with them—they couldn't drive the girl across the continent in the way you suggest. In order to pay them for this, Mr. Parson'll put up all the capital they need to start in business for themselves in Los Angeles. Also he'll supply the machine, with the camping outfit, and pay all the traveling expenses, and give you a salary, if you want it, for as long as the girl needs you. She has money of her own coming to her through an uncle who died some years ago, and that'll be placed at her disposal right away. All Mr. Parson wants is to let her be happy in her own way. She can marry anyone she pleases or do anything she likes. We know she'll not do anything too wild as long as *you're* looking after her."

Mrs. Farrell studied him a long time, doubtfully. "I'll have to talk to Larry," she said.

"Naturally," Duff agreed. "And of course we needn't warn you not to talk to anyone else." He gave Mrs. Farrell one of the cards that he used when he was posing as a lawyer. "Tell him to phone me first thing in the morning. We'll turn all the necessary money over to him as soon as he says the word. And tell the girl, when you see her, that she's free to marry anyone she wishes, even the boy she kissed on the stairs at the dressmaker's, if she wants to."

She took this without so much as blinking. "I'll tell her," she said, and she went to open the door.

Parson had been listening vaguely. He rose when he saw Duff saying good-by. He looked around him, blankly disappointed, as if he had expected something dramatic to happen. "Come along," Duff said, "I want you to write some checks for me."

"Yes," he said, "but where is she? Isabel? I want to see her."

"No," Duff urged him on. "Not till she wants to see you."

And, at that, the portieres were flung back with a cry of "Dad!" and the girl rushed to throw herself in his arms. They clung together in silence for a moment, and in that silence Duff whispered to Mrs. Farrell, "Tell him I'll wait for him downstairs, in the taxi."

He slipped out quietly. "Oh, Dad!" the girl was laughing and weeping as he closed the door. "I've been so miserable and so happy. I'm sorry I did it, and I'm not sorry, I'm glad . . ."

~ ~ ~

A few days later, the Parson case, as far as the newspapers were concerned, suddenly blew up. Parson notified the police that his daughter had been found, that she had suffered "a loss of identity" and wandered away from home, but she had written her mother as soon as she recovered her memory, and she was now resting in a sanitarium. He refused to name the sanitarium because he wished to protect the girl from any further publicity. On the day that this announcement was made, the Parson chauffeur resigned his job. His brother had sold his tire shop, and the whole family were going to Los Angeles, where the two brothers intended to open a garage. They were sending their trunks ahead of them by express and

most of their household furnishings by freight, and they were following in a touring car that was ingeniously fitted up for camping
out.

Their neighbors were much excited. They planned to give the
Farrells an enthusiastic send-off on the Saturday morning on
which they were to start. But when Saturday morning came, it was
discovered that the Farrells had slipped away in the middle of the
night. "Larry had a bride with 'm," the policeman on the beat explained, with a grin. "He said to tell youse all he didn't want to
start with a bunch of ol' shoes tied to his axle."

JAMES

ILLINOIS

BELL

JAMES ILLINOIS BELL

I

DUFF SUSPECTED, AT ONCE, that the man was lying to him, though there was no obvious reason why he *should* be. He had come to Duff's office, to consult the detective, voluntarily, and Duff knew nothing whatever about him or his case. His story was entirely plausible. He answered Duff's questions with none of the ingratiating nervousness of deceit. There was nothing to be gained by misleading Duff—as far as Duff could see—quite the opposite, in fact. Yet Duff remained suspicious of him and in doubt.

His name, he said, was James Illinois Bell. He was a Westerner, an oil man from Oklahoma, and he wished to engage Duff to find his daughter. He had lived in Denver, he explained, from 1903 to 1914, and during the autumn of one of those years—about 1905 or 1906—he had met a show girl named Mabel Dodgett and had an affair with her that lasted "for the week that she played Denver." He was, at the time, a reporter on the Denver *Republican,* and he met her through a theatrical publicity man in the Denver Press Club. After the show moved on to the Pacific coast, she sent letters to him at the Press Club, but he did not reply to her; and when she wrote to him from New York, next summer, telling him that she was in the Maternity Hospital and asking him to send money for his child, he did not answer that letter either.

"I was cleaned out," he said. "I hadn't a nickel. And, of course, I couldn't be sure that the baby was mine, anyway. So I let it ride."

There was a boom in farm land around Denver, especially in apple orchards, and he began to speculate in fruit ranches. He made enough money, in that way, to promote some fake mining schemes; and when "the gold-mine graft petered out" he moved on into oil. Here, at last, he "struck it rich." He made several millions, but in the meantime he lost track of Mabel Dodgett and her daughter.

"When she wrote me from the hospital, she said she was calling the girl 'Bell' after me. And last year, I saw in the papers that she'd been killed in a joy ride over on Long Island somewhere—the mother, I mean—and I wanted to come on and find the girl, but I wasn't able to get away then, and now I don't know where to look for her. She must be about eighteen or nineteen, and she's on the stage by this time, probably."

Duff kept murmuring, "I see. I see. Yes, of course. Of course," in his best confessional manner—the manner of a tolerant giant with a sympathy as broad as his shoulders. He sat back in his desk chair, genial, experienced, and thoughtfully receptive; and his eyes seemed to look at Bell's story rather than at Bell himself; but, all the time, he was noticing that Bell told his story as impassively as a gambler playing his hand, and this professional impassivity had the air of being somehow guarded and defensive.

He spoke the Western vernacular in a slow drawl but with a broad "a" that was either English or Bostonian. He wore his hair in a bang across his forehead; and under that bang his eyes were a colorless gray and stony while he spoke. His clean-shaven face was as hard as bronze and heavy with jaw-muscles. It was a face that reminded Duff of some antique bust of a vicious Roman emperor—a face that showed a sort of debased culture—the face of a man who knew the worst of himself and of the world, and dominated others more easily than he controlled himself.

" 'Bell Dodgett,' " Duff said. "Would she use that name on the stage?"

"Probably not," he admitted. "Her mother used the name of Cornish—Constance Cornish."

"The daughter would probably be Cornish, too?"

"Maybe."

"You have no description of her at all? Blonde or brunette?"

He shook his head.

"Do you suppose she knows that you're her father?"

"I don't know it myself."

"Would her mother tell her you were?"

"I don't see why."

"Do *you* intend to tell her?"

"I'll face that after you find her."

"I see."

Duff was enjoying himself. Here was a formidable and astute man who had come to him, all carefully buttoned up, with an innocent-looking project that might very easily be wearing a mask. It delighted Duff to have anyone try to deceive him. It awoke a hunting instinct in him. And Bell was wary big game, having made his living for years as a superior sort of confidence man exploiting the public. He was curt to the point of tacit contempt in the indifference of his manner, and there was something coolly arrogant in the way he replied, "I'll face *that* after you find her," when Duff tried to probe him about what he intended to do with Constance Cornish's daughter.

"Well," Duff said, "let's see what I've got to work with. Back about 1905, a girl named Mabel Dodgett—Was she married?"

"I don't know. She didn't have any husband with her."

"Probably not married, eh?"

"Probably not."

"A girl named Mabel Dodgett—What was the name of the play she was in?"

"I don't remember."

"Remember any of the scenes, or the plot or anything?"

"Not a thing. It hadn't any plot. It was a musical show. She just sang in it."

"Remember any of her songs?"

"No. What's all this got to do with it?"

"If we could find out the name of the play, we might look up the cast and get hold of some friend who remembered her—and her daughter."

"Oh!" He thought it over. "I never really saw the show. I just went in to watch her once in the last act while I was waiting to pick her up at the stage door."

"Would your friend remember her?"

"What friend?"

"The press-agent that you met her through."

"I lost track of him years ago."

"Remember his name?"

"He was just one of the newspaper boys that did the publicity work for the Tabor Grand. He left Denver before I did. Went to 'Frisco, I think."

"What was his name?"

"Hall. Tommy Hall. But there's no chance that he'd remember her or the show or anything else about it. He wasn't interested, and he didn't know *I* was."

"I see. I might wire our correspondent in Denver to look up the newspapers around that time, and see if he could find Constance Cornish in any of the casts."

"I should think it'd be a damn sight easier to look her up in some of the casts she played in here."

"That's a good idea."

Bell eyed suspiciously the simplicity with which Duff accepted the suggestion; and Duff, realizing that he had overplayed the role of innocent stupidity, smiled broadly at Bell. "Who sent you to *me?*" he asked.

Bell regarded the smile and the question until he had evidently made up his mind what was behind them. Then he drew from his waistcoat pocket a roll of yellow-backed bills, counted off five hundred dollars, and dropped them on the desk. "You can reach me at the Marbridge any time you want me," he said as he rose.

He put on his hat and walked out.

Duff frowned over it a moment before he took up his office phone. "Find Bilkey," he ordered, "and tell him I want to see him."

Bilkey was the operative who made a specialty of confidence men, but it was not for this reason only that Duff wished to put him on the case. Bilkey, out of office hours, was a devotee of the theater. He was as devout a first-nighter as Diamond Bill Brady.

As a boy he had collected cigarette pictures of stage favorites; now, with the same enthusiasm, he accumulated acquaintanceships with the actors and actresses themselves, with show girls and chorus ladies, specialty dancers, pony ballets, producers, stage directors, house managers, box-office boys, doorkeepers, ushers, and even chorus men. It was his private boast that there was no theater in New York to which he could not go, during the last act, call the doorman by his first name and walk in unchallenged to find a seat in the last row, with a nod to the usher. They knew him as a Central Office man, who had long since left the force, having saved a lot of easy money. They did not know that he was on Duff's staff.

He looked like an actor. He looked, indeed, as if it were his ambition to look like John Drew at forty. He dressed in the most quiet good taste, and he preserved always the simplest sort of interested and observant silence. When he came to Duff's room, now, in answer to Duff's summons, Duff was busy with a file of reports that concerned a case on which he was engaged, but he put it aside eagerly. He enjoyed Bilkey. The man was an artist in spite of his affectations. "Sit down," Duff said. "I think I've got a job that'll interest you."

Bilkey seated himself silently in a chair near Duff's desk. It was a comfortably padded leather armchair, and he sank back in it and crossed his legs without freeing his trousers at the knees. He understood that a gentleman of leisure, with an unlimited wardrobe, did not worry about bagging his trouser legs.

"I've just had a bunk artist in here," Duff explained, "named James Illinois Bell. He says he's made a fortune in Oklahoma oil.

He's stopping at the Marbridge. He wants us to locate the daughter of an actress named Constance Cornish. Ever hear of her?"

"Constance Cornish." Bilkey put his elbows on the arms of his chair and rested his finger-tips on either side of his nose. It was a prominent and bony nose, and he was accustomed to fondle it in thought, as another man might stroke the chin. "Constance Cornish."

"She was in a musical show, on the road, in Denver, about 1905 or 1906. So he says. She was killed in an automobile accident somewhere on Long Island, a year or so ago. Her real name, he says, was Mabel Dodgett."

Bilkey rubbed his nose. "Constance Cornish. Mabel Dodgett."

"There's something phoney about him, but I don't know what it is."

"I never heard of her," Bilkey said, as if he were surprised that such a thing could be.

"He says she had a daughter by him, the year after she was in Denver—a girl named 'Bell'—named after him. He wants us to find this 'Bell'—'Bell Cornish' or 'Bell Dodgett.' He thinks she's probably on the stage."

Bilkey shook his head. "Never heard of her."

"Well, it shouldn't be hard to find her. The mother's probably been off the stage for years. He didn't seem to know anything about that. But there must be some one around that trouped with her in the old days, and they ought to be able to put you on her trail."

"Sure."

"And I want you to get a line on Bell himself, if you can. You'll have to go slow on it, of course. He's foxy. I think he's trying to use us. If we locate the girl, we'll have to find out what he wants with her. See?"

Bilkey nodded. "All right, Major. See you later."

II

His first move was simple enough. He went to the Hotel Marbridge and consulted the house detective, McGraw, who was, of course, an old professional friend of his; and, in half an hour, McGraw had gathered everything concerning James Illinois Bell that was known to the clerks at the desk, the bell boys, the elevator men, the telephone and telegraph girls, the chamber maids and the dining-room staff. It amounted to nothing. No one had called on

Bell by telephone or otherwise. He had received no telegrams and
no mail. He usually rose late, ate his breakfast alone in his room,
went out to attend to whatever business had brought him to New
York, and did not return until about six o'clock in the evening. He
dined alone in a quiet corner of the basement grill, took a taxi to
the theater, and returned to his room by midnight. He had a wardrobe trunk full of "case goods," and he ordered nothing from the
bellhops but ice water for highballs. He asked no questions. He did
not talk even to the waiters. A girl on the newsstand who sold him
theater tickets was the only person who had especially noticed
him, and she had been struck by the fact that he bought only one
theater seat and bought it always for the same play, an unpopular
comedy of manners called "Modern Marriage." He had been to see
that three times.

"Thanks, Mac," Bilkey said. "I guess I'll have to take him from
the other end."

"Nothing serious against him, is there?" McGraw asked.

"Oh, no," Bilkey assured him. "He's trying to put over a deal
here, and the people concerned just asked us to look him up. See
you later."

He went from the Marbridge to the Columbus Theater, where
"Modern Marriage" was billed to play a matinee that afternoon;
and he found, on the program, the name of "Isabel Cornish" in a
minor part.

He reported, at once, to Duff by telephone, and Duff said: "This
guy's good, eh? Well, let's see. The poor simp! We'll have to run
a few rings around him. Get in with the man who's producing the
play. Pretend you want to buy a piece of it. Or no! Tell him you
have a sucker with money and you think you can sell an interest to
him. When you get the producer hooked, let me know, and we'll
work out the rest of it. Go slow, now, and don't stub your toe."

Bilkey went slow. He knew the Columbus Theater as a
"morgue." It was a huge house, on the outer fringe of the theater
district, so that it "caught no drip" from the Broadway successes,
and it was not controlled by either of the trusts, so that it got no
help from the ticket agencies. It had to draw its audiences all the
way from the dinner table to the box office, and it only succeeded
when it had the assistance of a popular star in what Broadway calls
a "wow."

Its latest owner had gone into bankruptcy, and the receiver had
leased the house to an independent producer—who was a friend of
his—at a rental ridiculously low. The producer had put forward

"Modern Marriage," an intimate sort of little highbrow comedy, on this vast stage that had been built for musical shows, before an immense and echoing auditorium decorated morosely in enough dark green and rusty gilding to depress a roaring farce. The result, both artistically and financially, was summed up by the dramatic critic who wrote: "The play sets out to ask 'Is modern marriage a failure?' Its answer is 'Yes.' And the box office makes it unanimous."

Bilkey sat through two acts of the afternoon performance in the stolid aloofness of expert contempt. The play was losing money, so the producer was trying to save on his necessary expenses. He had cut down the lights in the auditorium and the coal in the boiler room; consequently the theater was as chill and gloomy as a Mammoth Cave. He had reduced his orchestral music to a pitiful thin trickle of piano and violin. The box-office man, in an attempt to "dress" the house, had scattered the audience over the whole orchestra floor, and every little group of possible enthusiasts was entirely surrounded by the cold insulation that comes of unoccupied seats. There was the hushed, meek hopefulness of failure in the air. The curtain rose as sadly as Melancholy opening its eyes.

It disclosed a party of young people, laboriously gay, in one of those scenes of smart life for which Clyde Fitch set the pattern. Everybody on the stage was pretending to laugh and chatter, but it was a hollow pretense in that atmosphere of doom. Bilkey looked for Isabel Cornish. There she was—a tall, dark girl of nineteen or twenty, overgrown and drooping, with a wistful and sensitive face. Naturally, she had been cast to play the role of a lively flapper, in a kittenish voice, with an excess of bounce in her movements; and she flapped through her scenes in a sort of giggling panic that threatened to become hysterical. Bilkey frowned and watched her. What did James Illinois Bell want with this poor ham?

His eyes remained on the play for two acts, but his thoughts were elsewhere. They were occupied with Bell, and the producer, whose name was Livingstone. He knew Livingstone. Livingstone was a newspaper man who had come into the theater as a press-agent for a play in which he took a five per cent interest in lieu of salary. That play had run a year and paid him like a hundred-to-one shot. He had then bought a quarter interest in a second play that made him a little money, and he had now staked all his winnings on this third play which he owned outright. Bilkey judged that he was probably on the high road to bankruptcy.

At the end of the second act, he went to see Livingstone in his private office, upstairs, on the front of the theater building, and bankruptcy was evidently staring Livingstone in the face. It was a pale, fat face, and clean-shaven—the face of a man who always got what he wanted from the world by appearing ill and worried and pathetic. He had a touchingly mild manner, a gentle voice, and a way of looking at you that was distressed and winning. He gave Bilkey a limp hand without rising from his desk chair. The box-office statement and the afternoon's ticket stubs were on his blotter. He put them aside as if he were afraid to look at them lest he burst into tears.

Bilkey sat down, uninvited. "I've got a chance," he said, "to make some money for myself—and you—if you'll help me with it."

Livingstone did not change the hopeless stare of his pale eyes.

"There's a sucker on here from the West with a roll bigger than his head, and I think I can sell him a piece of this play if you'll give me a good commission."

It was in an exhausted, death-bed voice that Livingstone murmured, "Five per cent do?"

"No," Bilkey answered harshly, "nothing less than ten."

Livingstone closed his eyes, put his hat back from his moist forehead, drew a long breath, and sighed deeply. "All right," he said. "Bring him around."

"Not till I know how much you can sell us," Bilkey retorted, "and how much you want for it."

That led to a long negotiation in which Livingstone finally showed his books and allowed Bilkey to make elaborate notes from them. Bilkey wanted to find out how much the play had lost on the road before it reached New York and how much it was losing now. He insisted on having the salary list of the actors and an exact account of the expenses of the theater itself. He made a copy of Livingstone's lease from the receiver, and separated the weekly cost of the theater from the weekly cost of the play. "You're about twenty-three thousand dollars in the hole to date," he summed it up, "and you're going down at the rate of twelve hundred dollars a week. You could afford to turn over the play and the theater to us for nothing at all and save money. The play's a flivver, and the theater's always been a morgue. Anything you can get from us is pure velvet. You can't hang on much longer, can you?"

Livingstone looked, despairingly dumb, at the figures he had added on his scratch-pad.

"All right," Bilkey said. "I'll see what I can do. The play's no good for the movies, and a few hundred dollars would cover all we'd ever get out of stock rights. Good-by." He held out his hand.

Livingstone rose unexpectedly to dismiss him. "I haven't said I'd sell," he murmured.

"No. And I haven't said we'd buy," Bilkey replied. "I'll have to do some tall lying if I'm to put the deal over. I'd never try if it weren't that this poor nut has gone sweetie on a girl in your cast."

He hurried back to report to Duff, and Duff summoned into conference another operative named Col-burn—a distinguished-looking moron with an impressive forehead who could pass either as a butler or a bishop. He was to act, for the evening, as a business man to whom Bilkey wished to sell an interest in "Modern Marriage," and they coached him in his part for a patient half hour. When they sent him home, at last, to put on his dinner clothes, it was with instructions to be at the Hotel Marbridge by seven o'clock.

"He'll be all right," Bilkey complained as he gathered up his notes, "if he doesn't forget himself and call me 'Sir.' "

"Well, don't worry," Duff encouraged him. "If this doesn't work, we'll try something else. We can bring Bell out into the open, any time, by notifying him that we've located his daughter."

"What do you suppose his game is?"

"You run along and find out," Duff advised him.

III

When the head waiter in the Marbridge's basement grill ushered James Illinois Bell to his accustomed corner for dinner that evening, Colburn and Bilkey were already seated at the adjoining table, busy with their soup and a discussion of "Modern Marriage." Bilkey was talking to Colburn, who had his back to Bell's table; and, at first, Bilkey lowered his voice at Bell's arrival, in a natural desire to keep their conversation private, but as he got deeper into his account of what business the play had done on the road, he became more unguardedly enthusiastic. "If they'd taken this show into a small house," he argued, "it'd probably have made money from the start, but it's lost in the Columbus. It'll never get over while it's *there*. The Columbus has never made money with anything but a musical show, and it never will. Never. Look at what they did with 'Modern Marriage' in Albany. Here's the box-office statement. And here's Schenectady, before that. Look at this." He was plying the silent Colburn with papers. "The newspaper notices were so good that they thought the play could carry anything, and they loaded this white elephant on its back, and it hasn't been able to do more than crawl since. I tell you, Mr. Hemingway, if you'll put up the money to take this play to a small up-to-date theater, you can make a clean-up on it."

Colburn looked at the papers and grunted, unconvinced.

"What's more," Bilkey continued persuasively, "you could put a musical show into the Columbus and make five thousand a week easily. Livingstone's got a lease for a year at next to nothing a week. He could clean up, himself, if he hadn't run so low that he hasn't enough left to turn round on. If some one doesn't buy him out pretty soon, he'll have to close the play. There's no use lending him money. He's a poor showman. What you ought to do is to buy him out. Then you'd be in a position to put Miss A. in any part you pleased, without asking any one to do it for you. As it is, you're paying out money for her and getting nothing but a little gratitude. If you owned the play, so as to be able to star her or fire her as you chose, it'd make a big difference in the way she felt."

Colburn grumbled some inaudible protest.

"Well," Bilkey said, "there's no use deceiving ourselves about these girls. They're on the make, and nobody looks quite as good to them as a manager. Your name needn't come out at all. You could be a sleeping partner."

Colburn said, "Let me see those figures again."

Bilkey began all over from the beginning, with the original cost of building the sets, hiring the stage director, rehearsing the play, and trying it out on the road. He never let his eyes wander for a moment from Colburn to the man behind Colburn, but he could see that Bell, while he pretended to read his evening paper, was getting what detectives call "an earful."

"A play like this," Bilkey explained, "usually costs the management ten thousand dollars, at least, before they get it opened in New York. It can't make any real money on the road until it's had a New York run, you understand. Livingstone did so well on the road that he was only five thousand dollars behind when he reached the Columbus. If the theater'd been right, he could have made that up in a week. As it is, of course, he's been losing ever since, but, at *that,* he's got the theater so cheap that if he had any real money behind him he could shift his play to a smaller house, put a musical show into the Columbus, and make a clean-up. Look at this. Here's his lease on the theater, and here's his salary list for everything in front of the stage. It's a cinch, Mr. Hemingway, for anyone who has the money to swing it."

Colburn ate, and listened, and studied Bilkey's figures, and ate some more. Bilkey snatched his mouthfuls of food—in the pauses when Colburn was reading his memoranda—and talked and talked and talked. It was one of those interminable business conferences between a voluble salesman and a "prospect" who cannot make up his mind. It lasted through the soup and the meat and the salad, and came to the coffee tired but doggedly dragging along. Colburn ended it by glancing at his watch, on a signal from Bilkey. "I've got to go," he muttered.

"Well, I'll leave it with you," Bilkey continued undiscouraged. "You can reach me at the Bryant any time, but you'll have to give me a decision in a day or two if you want to take it up. Good-by. Don't wait if you're in a hurry. I'll take care of the check."

Colburn grumbled an apology and moved ponderously out. Bilkey sat down again, to light a cigarette and finish his coffee, staring down into his cup. James Illinois Bell cleared his throat. Bilkey did not look up.

"Are you in the theatrical business?" Bell asked.

Bilkey blinked at him as if he had been wakened from a day-dream. "I beg your pardon?"

Bell was settled back in his chair, smoking a thick cigar. He eyed Bilkey a moment in a sort of sulky challenge. Then he leaned forward across the table, and said, through the cigar smoke: "Do you want to make that proposition to me?"

Bilkey was naturally surprised. "What proposition?"

"The one you made to *him.*" He indicated the departed Colburn with a sideways jerk of the head toward the door.

Bilkey looked down at his papers, embarrassed. "That was confidential," he said.

"All right." Bell settled back in his chair again. He drank his coffee and looked around him for a waiter, taking out a pencil to sign his check.

There was no waiter in sight and the pencil, consequently, was an obvious bluff. Bilkey studied his cigarette a moment, dropped it in his coffee cup, gathered up his memoranda deliberately, rose without a glance at Bell—and joined him at his table. "Are you stopping here? At this hotel?"

"Yes. My name's Bell. James Illinois Bell."

Bilkey put out his hand. "Chester Bilkey. I didn't know I was talking loud enough for you to hear me." They shook hands on it indifferently, regarding each other with no pretense of anything but wariness. "Are you in the theater?" Bilkey asked.

"No. And I haven't been for years. I'm in oil. Out West. I've cleaned up there and quit it. I came to this damn town, thinking I could find something to get interested in, and I haven't found anything yet that wasn't a con game." He mumbled it, scowling, as if he were disgusted with New York and aggrievedly suspicious of it—and of Bilkey.

Bilkey smiled a metropolitan smile. His varnished black hair was brushed back from his forehead in the style. His dinner jacket was smooth and snug on his shoulders. He looked sleek and expert and self-confident before the careless informality of Bell's mode and manner. "Well, if you're afraid of con games," he said, "I don't want to sell you into the New York theater."

"Pretty crooked, are they?"

"They'd sooner cheat you than play straight any day."

Bell nodded. "I guess I can take care of myself. What've you got?"

"The trouble is I can't very well sell it to a stranger."

"What do you want to know about me?"

Bilkey thought it over, fingering his notes. "Well," he decided, at last, "I'll show you what it is—and take you over to the theater and let you look into it for yourself—and then, if you want to go ahead, we can discuss the personal end when we come to it."

Bell nodded again. "Shoot!" he said.

Bilkey shot, but not with the continuous rapid-fire that he had used on Colburn. He took his time, in the manner of a man entrenched who intended to await the attack, not make it. Bell was reluctantly compelled to offer the advances, ask the questions, and leave the shelter of his silence to feel out Bilkey's position. It gave Bilkey an advantage, and he kept it. He was polite and smiling, but he maintained the unconvinced attitude of having something to sell which Bell wished to buy, and he affected to be silently skeptical of Bell's credit and good faith. He forced Bell to propose that they should go to the Columbus Theater together that evening, to look at the play. "I'll not introduce you to Livingstone," Bilkey said, "until we get a little further along."

He did not introduce him to Livingstone or to anyone else. He left Bell in the theater lobby while he got seats from Livingstone, and between the acts he sat in Livingstone's office and allowed Bell to wait alone in his orchestra chair. He made no attempt to "sell" the play to Bell; he showed no interest in Bell's opinion of it, or in Bell's emotional reactions to it, although he was acutely aware that whenever Isabel Cornish appeared on the stage Bell at once became secretly tense in an unblinking attention that was as still and staring as an animal's. When the final curtain fell, it was Bell who suggested that they should go back to his room in the Marbridge to talk matters over. And when they were sitting in Bell's bedroom, with highballs in one hand and cigars in the other, it was Bell who began: "Well, what do you want to know about me?"

IV

At four o'clock next morning, they separated. Or rather, at four o'clock, Bilkey rose slowly from his seat, glanced at the empty bottles on the bedroom table, and, with the same air of final and indifferent appraisement, looked at Bell sunken in his low arm-chair, with his chin on his chest and his hands hanging down to the floor on either side of him. Bell had been rather maudlin toward the end. He had wept at his story of his early life, his struggles, his hardships, and the malevolence of the world. He slept now, as exhausted as the empty bottles.

"Well," Bilkey said to himself, "I guess I've got everything." He poured himself a glass of ice water unsteadily. "I'll have to go to a Turkish bath," he thought, "and get this booze boiled out of me. If Duff wants anything else, I'll pick it up later."

His one difficulty had been in deceiving Bell about drinking the whisky, and that deceit had been progressively easy after the third highball. He was only fuddled in his feet as he made his way to the elevator; his head seemed clear enough; and he was solemnly absorbed in trying to rearrange, in some logical sequence, the long, rambling and muddled story that Bell had told him. By the time he reached the baths on Forty-second Street, his report to Duff was beginning to take a coherent shape. "That'll be all right," he assured himself. "Once you get sobered up, that'll come straight from there on—if you don't forget some of it."

He clung to his memory through the long ritual of the bath, fighting to clear his mind. And lying under his sheet, with his predatory beak pointed to the ceiling, he struggled against sleep for fear that some of his recollections might be blotted out before he could fix them. Sleep came, in spite of him, but it was only a cat-nap; he awoke in a moment, as alert as a wild animal and as refreshed. He remembered everything; he continued to sort it out

and pick it over while he took his cold shower, dressed absent-
mindedly, and drifted out, for his morning coffee, to a hotel restaurant where he began to make cryptic little notes in his microscopic
handwriting, on the pages of a loose-leaf diary, with a gold pencil
that was dainty enough for a social secretary.

At eight-thirty, when Duff arrived in his office, Bilkey was
ready and waiting for him, as fresh as the new day, his whole report arranged and accurate in his mind. Duff listened with the
twinkle of amused congratulation that was his usual expression
when he was working with Bilkey. The affectations of the man
were combined with a sober precision of thought and a con-
scienceless accuracy of method to make a contrast that was as
amusing to Duff as the profanity of a dowager duchess.

"Well, Bilk," he said, "you've certainly turned this poor long-
horn inside out. We ought to have some fun with him now. Do you
want to go on with his theater scheme?"

"I'd like to make the ten per cent out of Livingstone."

"That'll be all right with me," Duff assured him. "I can frame
Bell without tipping off your hand. Drop in at his hotel and phone
me as soon as you find he's up and doing. I'll call him over here
and give him a surprise. We can't let any Oklahoma con man put
up a game like this on us and get away with it, eh?"

Certainly not. But Bilkey considered that this part of the affair
was "off his beat," as he would have said; and having waited in the
lobby of the Marbridge till McGraw reported that Bell had ordered
his breakfast brought to his room, Bilkey phoned the news to Duff
and went home to get another nap. He had the happy faculty of
being able to sleep whenever he wished to sleep, and to sleep for
as long as circumstances permitted.

James Illinois Bell was evidently not so adaptable. He answered Duff's phone call as if he had had a bad night. "You can
drop the case," he said irritably, when Duff reported that he had
located Isabel Cornish. "I don't need you. I've found her myself."

"Yes," Duff replied, "but something else has turned up that
may make trouble for you. I'd like to have a talk with you."

"What about?"

"I can't tell you over the phone. It's too serious. We ran into it,
last night, after we found the girl. I'll expect you here right away."

"You can expect what you damn please," Bell replied, at his
surliest. "I can't get over there for an hour anyway."

"Good," Duff said. "I'll expect you in an hour, then." And he
hung up.

Bell showed his independence by taking not one hour but two, and he came at last with an air of sulky indifference that evidently covered a suppressed and angry apprehension. He would not sit down. "I'm in a hurry," he said. "What've you got?"

Duff sat and smiled at him in a pose of gigantic placidity. "There's something wrong about this case of yours," he said. "Our correspondent in Denver phones us that the only time Mabel Dodgett played Denver she had her daughter Isabel there with her—an infant four months old."

"Who the hell—He's crazy!"

"No. He says you never had an affair with Mabel Dodgett at all. She turned you down flat and you were furious about it. You kept hanging around—"

Bell clapped his hat on. "You can go to the devil," he said. "I don't need you—"

"No," Duff cut in, "but Isabel Cornish may."

"What do you mean by that?"

"That you can't tell Isabel Cornish you're her father. I'll not let you get back at her mother by any such dirty trick."

Bell stuck out a venomous forefinger and shook it at him, enraged. "You rotten welsher! If you try to double-cross me—"

"You poor boob!" Duff said. "Did you think you could come in here and play me for a sucker? I knew you were lying before you'd talked to me two minutes. Sit down there. I'm going to tell you something about yourself."

"Sit down nothing," Bell blustered. "I'm through with you. You're like the rest of these private detectives—you're a blackmailer."

"Shut up and listen to me. When you ran away from your home in Boston, as a boy, you took your little sister with you, and you went crooked for the sake of that girl. You lied and begged and cheated and stole for *her,* because you had to have money and you didn't know how to get it honestly. It wasn't until after she'd died, in Denver, that you quit gambling and the race-track, and became a sports reporter. Isn't that true?"

"What the hell!" It was so true, and it was so unexpected— coming from Duff—that Bell stared at the detective as if Duff had suddenly summoned up the ghost of this sister out of a past of which no one in the world knew anything.

Duff pointed to the chair. "Sit down!" he ordered. And Bell sat down.

"Didn't Constance Cornish remind you of your sister when you saw her in Denver? Didn't she *look* like her?"

If the ghost had asked him, he could not have been more unable to reply.

"And doesn't this girl, this daughter here, Isabel—doesn't she look exactly like her mother?"

He answered only with the blink of his bloodshot eyes, evidently so confused by the thousand questions in his mind that he could not get past a bewildered amazement.

"Well," Duff said, "this Mabel Dodgett, or Constance Cornish, or whatever you called her—the moment you saw her in Denver, it gave you a terrific kick. You got hold of the publicity man and went after her, but you started to treat her like a chorus girl, and she turned you down flat. You spent the rest of the week mooning around the theater, and trying to waylay her, so as to put yourself right with her, and she wouldn't look at you. You were so sore you wanted to shoot her—or yourself—and you ended up by getting drunk and making a fool of yourself all over the place—at the stage door and in the Press Club."

Duff was using Bilkey's story, of course; but he was feeling his way through it in the manner of a fortuneteller, ready to hedge at once if he saw, by any change of expression in his client's fascinated gaze, that he—as a detective—was failing to guess the inner truth of the incidents which Bilkey had reported to him.

"Then you decided that if you'd been a millionaire, she wouldn't've been able to resist you, and you started out to make a fortune—a crooked fortune—in farmland swindles and fake gold mines and wildcat oil stock. You made the fortune, and I don't know how many women you tried to buy with it, but I can guess that it didn't get you what you wanted, because you threw it all up, at last, and came to New York to get away from it. Well! Here you run across Constance Cornish's daughter, and she's enough like her mother to start you off again where her mother left you, and you think you're going to get your revenge on the mother by blackening her memory to this girl. You think you're going to get even with the mother by pretending to her girl that she was your mistress. And you try to plant the story with *me,* as part of some crazy scheme to use me on the girl. You try to get *me* to find her and tell her that you're her father. You big dumbbell! You don't seem to know what you're trying to do—nor why you're trying to do it. If you don't get wise to yourself, you'll end in a worse smash than you made of yourself in Denver!"

Bell asked, hoarsely, "Where did you get this stuff?"

"What stuff?"

"This stuff about me."

"That's *my* business," Duff replied, contemptuously. "And I'll tell you something else about yourself. Last night, you happened to hear a theatrical man, named Bilkey, trying to sell a piece of a play to a crooked old Wall Street angel. And when you found out that the play was the one that Isabel Cornish is in, you took Bilkey into camp and started to use him the way you wanted to use *me*— as an approach to this Cornish girl. And I warn you that I'll tip Bilkey off to your whole dirty game if you try to go an inch further with it."

Bell swallowed, like a guilty small boy about to make a repentant confession. "I'm not."

"You're not going ahead with it?"

"No."

"You're not going to tell her you're her father."

"No."

"No! And I'll tell you why you're not," Duff said, with a sneer. "You act on a pattern that you don't understand. You act according to that pattern without knowing why you do it. And then you invent reasons and motives to explain your actions to yourself— fool reasons that would be disgusting if they weren't so ridiculous. Shut up! When you saw Mabel Dodgett, out in Denver, you wanted to act toward her as you'd acted toward your sister. You wanted to help her and protect her, but you're such a damn fool about yourself that you didn't know it. You tried to play the regular stage-door Johnny with her, and you couldn't get away with it. She gave you the air. And you started out, with her in your mind, to go crooked again—the way you went crooked for your sister. And every woman that you fell for—instead of realizing that you wanted to help her and protect her—you tried to get your revenge on her. And you couldn't do it. And when you saw Mabel Dodgett's daughter, you began the same boob program with *her,* instead of understanding that what you really wanted was to behave to this girl as if you were her elder brother. You come in here to me, full of bad whisky, and plant a story that would ditch you both if I'd fallen for it, and then when you've got that off your chest and you're feeling ashamed of yourself, you run into a chance to buy in on this play and get next to Isabel Cornish in the way you *really* want to get next to her, and naturally you jump at the chance. You poor fish, you don't even know that you're not naturally a crook. You don't even know that you're still a kid on the streets, lying and cheating and swindling because you've never learned how to make a good living honestly. And if you try to cheat, now, for this Cornish girl, the way you cheated for your little sister, these hard-shell crooks like Bilkey will skin you alive. You're the cheapest imitation of a con man that I ever ran across—and I've known a lot of them—and unless you're going into this theatrical game to do the square thing by the girl and Bilkey and all the rest of them, you'd better go back to Denver and drown yourself in Cherry Creek."

Bell had listened to this tirade exactly as if he were the bad little boy whom Duff described. He looked silly. He looked sheepish, with his boyish bang, and his shamed eyes, and his faltering attempts to interrupt and defend himself. And when he pulled himself together, at last, it was with a boyish bravado that he spluttered: "Is *that* so! You think you're a hell of a fellow, don't you? You can go and chase yourself. I'm not asking for any advice from you, and I—"

"Run along and sell your papers," Duff cut in. "I'm busy." He took up his telephone. "All right," he said, to his outer office. "Who's next out there?" And when Bell had risen and started out, he added: "I'll keep an eye on you, and if I find you're not doing the square thing by Isabel Cornish, I'll trip you up so quick—"

"Aw, you go to hell," Bell muttered, without turning, as he went out.

~ ~ ~

"Well, Bilk," Duff asked, some weeks later, "how's your friend Bell getting on?"

"All right," Bilkey said. " 'Modern Marriage' is paying expenses over at the Forty-fourth Street Theater, and his musical comedy's cleaning two thousand a week at the Columbus."

"Good. How's he getting on with the girl?"

"All right. I don't know whether he intends to marry her or adopt her. He wants to give her the lead in 'Modern Marriage,' and I'm using that as an excuse for selling out my interest to him."

"Don't intend to stick and make a fortune in the theater, eh?"

"No. You'd have to have a flock of oil wells behind you to play the game the way Bell plays it. I'm getting out."

"Good. I want you to go to Chicago on a case, as soon as you're free."

THE

LOVE

CHARM

THE LOVE CHARM

I

AS SOON AS DUFF called in his secretary, that morning, to dictate his letters, he saw that there was something wrong with her. But he did not speak of it. As a detective, whenever he happened on anything that he did not understand, he pretended not to notice it—so as to be able to observe it better. He went on with his dictation, as usual, and considered her in a private corner of his mind.

He knew all about her. The work she did for him was often dangerously confidential, and he had investigated her for months before he promoted her to her position. Her name was Helen Manson, and she was the daughter of a J. Franklin Manson, an insurance agent and real-estate man in Redhouse, Long Island. Manson was a respectable failure whose one sufficient weakness was his appetite for alcohol. His oldest daughter ran his insurance agency and his real-estate business. His wife kept up his home. His younger daughter, Helen, had left Redhouse and come to live with a girl friend on East Fifty-seventh Street, when she began to work for Duff, and though she sent part of her earnings regularly to her mother, she did not often visit her parents. They were not a demonstrative family. Life had not been easy for Manson's wife and daughters. They had stiffened to keep up appearances and hardened to resist adversities that would otherwise have worn them out.

This stiffness, this reserve, had helped to make Helen Manson perfect for Duff's purpose. She had been an ideal office slave, as regular, silent, and impersonal as a timeclock. He had warned her not to tell her family or her friends that she was employed by a private detective; that would arouse their curiosity; they would be always asking her questions. "Tell them," he said, "that I'm a lawyer. It's the only disguise I ever use." And she had told them that. He investigated, after she had been with him for three months, and he found that not even the girl she roomed with knew the truth. He promoted her, then, to be his confidential secretary; he dictated to her his summaries of his operatives' reports when he was closing up a case; and she was the only person in his office, besides himself, who really knew what most of his cases were about. Since his summaries were usually followed by an arrest, it was necessary that she should be completely trustworthy.

And she had seemed to be merely a stenographic machine, as indifferent as her typewriter to any report of guilt or misery. She had never made a comment on one of his cases, even to him. A patient, sturdy, rather simple-looking young woman, she had bent above her notebook in a placid absorption in her task. He had never seen her show an emotion of any kind. Consequently, he was at once puzzled and concerned to see her now, pale, obviously worried and showing what he took to be traces of overnight tears in her swollen eyelids.

He decided that if there had been illness in her home, he would have heard of it before it came to the weeping point. She would not have arrived for work if anyone were dead. She was not sufficiently fond of her family to grieve over any of their worries. No, it must be a personal trouble. It might be something to do with her relations with her roommate.

He came to the end of his correspondence. He took up a letter that he had already answered, and he went on dictating, as if in reply to it:

"Dear Madame: I was aware, when you were last in my office, that you were very much disturbed about some personal matter, outside of the business that brought you in here. I could see that you had been, perhaps, crying. I do not want to force your confidence, but I should like to be of some assistance to you, if I can. If you have worries outside of the work in which we are engaged, they may tend to impair your efficiency in that work. During my life as a detective, I have learned a great deal about human nature, outside of its merely criminal aspects, and I might easily be able to assist you in your private problems, if you would give me the opportunity. Trusting that you will not hesitate to confide in me, I remain, et cetera. That's all."

He threw aside the letter which he had been pretending to answer. Helen looked at it vaguely, where it had fallen. She looked at it with a somewhat bewildered frown, as if she were just waking from a daydream in which she had been lost. Then she read again the last stenographic notes that she had made at his dictation, and she read them as if they contained the dream from which she had been roused.

At last, she said: "You didn't give me any address for that letter, Mr. Duff."

Duff affected a preoccupation. "What letter?"

"The last letter you dictated."

"I don't recall which that was. Read it to me."

She read it to him, tonelessly, word by word; and it was evident that the words meant nothing to her.

"Oh, that one?" he said. "Address that to Miss Helen Manson, care of Mr. John Duff, et cetera."

That woke her. She was startled. She gave him a frightened look and dropped her eyes to her notebook and read what she had written, the color flooding to her face in an embarrassed blush. She did not raise her eyes again, when she had finished. She said to her notebook: "It's nothing. Nothing that anyone can help me with. It's just myself."

"What is it about yourself?"

After all, she seemed merely a bashful child. She was at least twenty-five years old, yet she sat there reddening over her notes like a confused schoolgirl interrogated by her teacher. She said: "I can't talk to people."

"What kind of people?"

"Oh—*you* know—artists, musicians—"

"Men or women?"

She looked up, at that, and smiled. "Men," she said, and her smile was charming.

He had never seen her smile before. It changed the whole flat timidity of her face to something shyly alluring and sweet. There was a warmth in it that warned Duff she was not thinking of talking to men in general but to one desired man in particular. Nevertheless, Duff assured her: "You don't have to talk to men. You only have to listen to them. They hate brilliant women. If you look into it, you'll find that all the fascinating, witty women that men rave about, just listen to them and applaud them. They're considered witty because they laugh well."

Her smile faltered and showed doubt.

"It's true," said Duff. "Think of it. What *is* conversation? Ordinary social conversation? With most men, it's a sort of exhibitionism. They're showing off. Well, what's the use of trying to show off to a woman who won't look at you?—won't look at you because she's busy showing off herself? It's all stuff. Why am *I* talking now? To help you? Pickles! I'm only trying to show you how clever I am." He settled his huge bulk back in his chair and beamed at her, his black eyebrows tilted humorously, his heavy cheeks crinkled in an infectious grin.

"Yes," she said, "but I can't get *them* to talk to *me*, either."

"That's easy." He put up a broad hand and patted the air towards her. "I can tell you how to do *that*. There's one thing a man always wants to talk about, and that's himself. And there's one thing about himself that's always lovely and romantic to him, and that's his boyhood. Ask him about his boyhood. Do it this way. Say: 'I met a man, the other day, and he told me he could remember something that happened to him when he was only four years old. Do you think that's possible? How far back can *you* remember?' See? He'll start to tell you, and then you'll just lead him on a little, and in ten minutes you'll have him completely enthralled—perfectly delighted. He'll be laughing and touched, and all wet around the eyelids, and fairly stumbling over his teeth to get it all out."

"Is that really true?" She did not ask it unconvinced. She was at the feet of her private oracle, now, looking up at him with admiration.

"Of course, it's true. Don't you realize that for most men—and most women—their childhood is a sort of Golden Age. They had love and protection and irresponsibility. They didn't have to work for money. They lived a natural, animal life, eating and sleeping and playing around like pups. Hell! They've never had anything like it since, and they love to recall it."

She shook her head. "My childhood wasn't like that."

"No," he said, "but then your father didn't protect you and your mother was worried. You probably had to grow up too soon."

"It wasn't only that. My sister was so much cleverer than I was, and she was Mother's favorite, and I was naturally kind of stupid—I was daydreaming all the time—and I sympathized with Father more than they did. I was like him, I was so impractical. And they hadn't any patience with me, any more than they had with him. Even when I grew up, I couldn't sew or do anything with my hands, the way Bell could. I wanted to moon around and play with dolls, and then, later, I was all the time reading—what they called 'trashy novels.' "

She was chattering eagerly, smiling, her eyes a little wet. Something in his expression stopped her suddenly.

He reached out and patted her hand. "There you are!" he said. "See how it gets you going? Try it on anyone. I never knew it to fail."

She rose. "I'm sorry. I didn't mean to bore you."

"Nonsense," he said. "I like you. I think you're a great girl— only you don't appreciate yourself. And you don't realize how simple most people are. You let them frighten you. Just try this thing on them and see how childish they are. And if there's any one of the men you want to get eating out of your hand, tell me what he remembers about his boyhood and I'll show you how to work him to a fare-thee-well."

His slang made her smile again. "All right," she promised, as she gathered up her notes. "I'll tell you."

And Duff said to himself: "That's the answer. She's in love with some one. He isn't interested. And she's so sorry for herself, she's been crying about it."

II

The house in which she lived on East Fifty-seventh Street had seen better days and many of them. For all its brownstone stoop and its marble-tiled vestibule, it was little better than a shabby tenement. Some one on the ground floor advertised "Pinking and Pleating" in a parlor window. A Greek peddled coal and ice from the basement. The upper floors were let to poverty and labor in various forms. Only an experienced New Yorker, accustomed to such discrepancies, would have guessed that behind that rusty and weather-worn front, Helen Manson and her friend could be living in rooms that were "adorable" to everyone who saw them— including Helen Manson.

To Helen, they were miraculous. Her roommate, Evelyn Stickle, was an artist, an amateur decorator, a sensitive esthete, and Evelyn Stickle had contrived to make their three dingy rooms into three masterpieces of delicate taste. She had treated their living-room from a line of Keats: "Daffodils and the green world they live in." She had done the walls in a true daffodil yellow, a vibrating yellow, full of life. She had painted all the furniture a tender April green that was almost as sunny as the yellow. By one of those fortunate accidents that happen only to genius, she had found a chemical calcimine that would "take" on leather—and not rub off—and she had transformed two stuffed leather chairs into priceless pieces of green Cordovan. With white woodwork and yellow curtains, cushions of green and yellow and rose-red and the blue of larkspurs—and yellow lamp shades and a grass rug as green as a lawn—she had made the room sing like a flower garden, at once cool in its atmosphere and warm in its feeling, restful, cheery, refreshing. She had made the kitchen into a Dutch gem of Delft blue. The bedroom was a smiling boudoir in Dubarry pink. She had painted and sewed and dyed and stenciled in the inspired frenzy of Michelangelo decorating the ceiling of the Sistine Chapel, and with the triumph of her artistry she had transformed Helen Manson's life.

All day, in Duff's office, those rooms glowed for her, behind stenography, like the secret felicity of a double life. She hurried home to them, after work hours, as if she were on her way to romance and a love-nest. In that dingy old house, they were a miser's jewels hidden in squalor, and when she opened the door on them she was the gloating miser unlocking his strongbox. She swept and scrubbed and washed and polished them devotedly, and she shopped and cooked and made the beds with the happy willingness of a neophyte dressing the altar and serving in the sanctuary. Evelyn was the high priestess of the temple. She did nothing but preside over it.

She was a tall and beautiful ashen blonde—long-legged, flat-chested, as bloodless as a white flower—with more warmth for Helen than for any young man who flushed and looked silly when she smiled at him. She smiled at him alluringly. She played the piano to him with such a delicate, slow touch that even ragtime sounded like the melancholy yearning of some secret dissatisfaction calling to him to console it. She danced with him in a lonely dream. She gave him her hand to hold, appealingly, and then forgot it. She talked about herself till she tired, and then, with her head on his shoulder, she yawned and sent him home. When he was gone, she took off her evening frock with the relief of a workman getting out of his overalls; she washed off her make-up—her dark eyebrows, her scarlet lips—and bathed and creamed herself refreshingly; and, turning in front of the pier glass, as if to admire herself as she really was and as only Helen and she knew her, she discussed him with complete cynicism, his weaknesses, his vanities, his absurd egotism. "What fools men are!"

Those final moments were the most delightful of Helen's day. Evelyn was such a slim and satin beauty in her glorified blonde boyishness, and her contempt for men was so consoling, and her conquests among them were, in some way, vicariously, such victories for Helen, too! None of the men ever noticed *her.* It was she who cooked for them when they came to dinner, and mixed the cocktails, and carved and served at the table, and saw that they had cigarettes. They accepted everything from her as if she were an upper servant, a combination of housekeeper and paid companion for Evelyn. They did not even notice her absence, after dinner, when she shut herself in the kitchen to wash the dishes. If they danced they let her preside over the phonograph. She made them hot chocolate when they stayed late, or cool drinks if it was hot weather, and they accepted her attentions from invisible hands. She did not force herself on them; she was shy and she did not seem to resent their neglect. But when they had gone, and she was washing the chocolate cups or the glasses in the kitchen, and Evelyn was before the mirror in the adjoining bathroom, with the door open, then she had her satisfactions and her revenge. "What fools men are!"

That remained true of all men until a chorus boy named Tod Powell arrived on the scene. He arrived inconspicuously, in the background of a call from a decorative artist named "Hank" Overton, an old friend of Evelyn's who had long admired her with the un-possessive ardor of a connoisseur before a museum piece. He brought Powell to look at his special bit of beauty with an air of showing him a Botticelli in a neglected gallery, saying nothing—words would be useless—but letting esthetic charm overwhelm the happy soul in silence. And Powell was not overwhelmed. He was a peculiar looking youth, rather frog-faced, with prominent eyes and a flat profile, and a childishly round and bulgy forehead, and an innocent, dumb air. He watched and listened to Evelyn respectfully, but one could imagine him saying to Overton: "Yah. I'll take your word for it. I guess it's off my beat. I'm not up to this sort of thing, maybe." And he turned to Helen Manson, as some one on his own level.

To Evelyn, his level was low. He had no self-respect, she said, no human dignity. He was a clown. He had been a juggler's assistant in a vaudeville act, and when he was helping Helen to wait on the table he did comic stunts with the dishes, pretending to drop them and only catching them again, in an agonized convulsion of fear, at the last moment before they crashed. Or he pretended to trip at the kitchen door, with a platter in his hands, and he stumbled headlong, falling at every step, across the entire width of the room to the dinner table, and reached it miraculously—and then put the food down as if nothing had happened. These antics enraged Evelyn. She was polite, sarcastically polite, but she was cutting. He looked meek when she scolded him, and he wiped his forehead, with a face of embarrassed stupidity that was the funniest part of his clowning, while Helen laughed till the tears came, and Overton screamed a high falsetto cackle.

After two or three scenes of the sort, Evelyn decided that the only dignified thing was to ignore him, and she left him to Helen to entertain and appreciate. And Helen did not know how. They were all right in the kitchen; he was an experienced cook, and he taught her all sorts of strange tricks of seasoning—like salt in coffee, to bring out its flavor, and a Roquefort cheese dressing melted into broiled steak—and as long as they were too busy to talk, they got along swimmingly; but when she was washing the dishes and he was drying them, she searched the world in vain for something to talk to him about, and she felt that he must despise her silences. She knew nothing about acting or the theater. She felt that she knew even less about painting or music or any other of the arts that Evelyn and her friends discussed so emotionally. "Do you like acting?" she asked Powell. And he replied, "Well, it's *one* way of making a living." And that was as far as it went.

He told her, one night, that he was out of the chorus and rehearsing a small part in a regular play; but he said it so casually that she failed to appreciate what it meant to him. The play was a hit. He was praised by the critics. He had a minor role, but it was a comedy role in a series of tense situations where everybody else was terribly serious, and his matter-of-fact lines, delivered with a slangy naturalness, exploded roars of laughter in the audience. He played it straight, a little sourly, as if he were both stupid and hard-boiled. Broadway began to talk about him. One of his lines, about prohibition—"It's better than no liquor at all"—became the most famous line in the English language, for the amusement district, overnight.

All this was received with mixed emotions in Evelyn Stickle's circle. None of them, from Evelyn down, were commercially successful. They regarded themselves as devotees of pure, not applied, art. They were above the business of debasing their minds to the level of the practical and the popular. They spoke as contemptuously of commercially successful art as a research scientist of a patent medicine. And yet they were not quite superior about it. A cynical observer might have thought them envious. They were too bitter. And, at the same time, when they came into personal contact with the successful, they stared. They were flattered; they were not quite themselves. "Well," Evelyn said of Powell, after he had made his hit, "I imagine that's the last we'll see of him."

She pretended to say it with relief, but it had the undertone of a grievance.

She knew that many of the esthetic youths who came to what she called her studio were drawn by the food and the drinks. She had a monthly allowance from her parents in St. Paul, and Helen earned a comfortable salary, but most of Evelyn's admirers were uncertain where their next check would come from, and as soon as their checks began to arrive regularly they were not such regular arrivals themselves.

She did not realize how grateful Powell was. She did not know that while he had been rehearsing, without salary, the food he got at her table was all the food he had to eat. He borrowed an advance on his first week's pay and phoned at once to ask her and Helen to come out to dinner with Hank Overton. She declined the invitation. She did not propose to be patronized. "Why can't you both come up here?" she asked.

They came, although Powell had to be in his dressing room by eight. And she did not greatly change her manner to him; for, after all, he was still only a clown. But two days later she read, in one of the accredited organs of the intelligentsia, an article that applauded his rhythm and his timing and the expert-ness of his pauses and the cosmic significance of his pragmatic mood. And she saw a great light. The same critic had opened her eyes to jazz, and to Charlie Chaplin, by the same magical use of words. He merely described a lowbrow art in the sacred phrases of classical estheticism, and the curse was lifted.

She began to laugh at Powell's antics, now, as if he were a Shakespearean clown whose gags were unintelligible without footnotes. She discovered a most engaging quality in him—that he never made fun of anybody but himself—and this no longer appeared as a lack of dignity to her, but as an excess of kindliness. He professed to know nothing about rhythm or cosmic significance or pragmatic mood, but she replied, "Of course not. Like every real artist, you know these things unconsciously, without knowing that you know them." She even delighted in his slang. "Real slang, after all, is the poetry—isn't it?—of popular speech." And she began to monopolize him so successfully that Helen was in despair. She could not compete. He was so busy listening to Evelyn that he could not even help Helen to wait on the table. He had to hurry away to his theater while the coffee was being served, and Evelyn rode down with him in a taxi so as to finish their discussion; and Helen, left alone to clean up, wept into the dishwater.

She blamed nobody but herself. Ugly, stupid, speechless, boring—who else was there to blame?

It was next morning that Duff noticed her swollen eyelids. And it was the following Sunday that she got her first opportunity to follow Duff's advice on how to be fascinating to men.

Powell and Overton were coming to Sunday evening dinner, and Evelyn had invited a select group of her most intelligent friends to drop in after dinner and meet her young comic genius—"the actor who's made such a furor, you know, in 'The Stuffed Shirt.' Have you seen him? Oh, you must go before Sunday. You must see him. He's superb."

She saw that she was going to have a lion in her studio, and she was prepared to make the most of him. She had decided, as she told Helen, that he was one of those unconscious artists who obtain their effects blindly, and she was sure that his range and scope could be greatly increased if his eyes were opened to the whole field of art and beauty. Especially beauty. That was what he lacked, a sense of beauty, of poetry, of eloquence and mystical emotion. He needed to see that beauty was the rift in the veil of appearances, through which one caught glimpses of the true reality.

All during dinner, she talked to him in those terms, or across him, to Overton. After dinner, she went to the piano to play for them while they smoked. She believed, with Beethoven, that music was the "wine of inspiration" for the other arts, and she poured out Debussy as an intoxicant that should affect Powell to ends of poetry and uplift, unawares. Helen, being tone deaf, took advantage of the interval to wash up. She slipped into the kitchen and closed the door on her complete defeat. She had not had an opportunity to say a word to him, and when the after-dinner guests arrived, the opportunity would be still less. "And what's the use?" she thought. "I don't know anything. I'm no good. Evelyn can help him, but I can't. I couldn't do anything but wash dishes for him. What's the use?" At that, Powell tiptoed in, guiltily, and closed the door behind him, and leaned against it in a burlesque attitude of exhaustion. "Gee," he said, "all this is miles over my head. I don't know what they're talking about, half the time. It's like the music. I hear it, but I don't know what it's all about."

"Neither do I." She turned to him with a breathless laugh. "Listen," she plunged. "I want to ask you something. I got into an argument with a man the other day. I was telling him about something that happened to me when I was only four or five years old, and he said it wasn't possible—that I couldn't remember so far back—and I said it was. And I was wondering. Can you remember things like that—at four or five?"

"Gee," he said, "I should think I could." He took the dish towel from her. "I can remember—Why my mother died when I was only seven and I can remember years before that! I can remember when my little sister was born, and she was only three years younger than me."

"Really?"

"Posilutely. I remember them showing her to me, on a pillow. It was in a hotel room somewhere. We were on tour."

"On tour?"

"Yes, my father was an actor. James T. Powell. Old school, you know. Shakespeare and melodrama. Out in the sticks. And Mother was his leading woman." He was off. He could remember the first time he saw his father play "Othello," with his mother as Desdemona, and he was so small that when he stood in the stage-box he could just peep over the rail. "The funny thing was, you know," he said, "I seemed to be wise, from the beginning, to what a rotten actor Pop was. He was about as good an actor as William Jennings Bryan—and about as popular, out there. They were nuts about him. And Mom was the real stuff—the pure McCoy—and I don't think she ever got a hand in her life. She never spoke a line that it didn't sound as if it was something that just struck her. She *thought* her stuff over the foots. And *he* couldn't say 'What do you know?' without making it sound like an oration. They never knew that she was acting at all, but they never made any mistake about him. He acted all over the place."

She died of tuberculosis when he was about seven, and then his father married "a big, blonde tragedy queen," and he hated her. "She could act about as much as the Woolworth Building. She hadn't a thing but a chest-heave and a voice like an empty church—*you* know—hollow and solemn. When she and Pop got together on the stage, they made so much emotion you couldn't understand a word they said."

He was full of memories of those days, the last great days of the road, before the moving pictures killed cheap melodrama and the barnstormers. He had seen the famous James T. Powell go down to defeat, unable to pay his salaries, his scenery seized for a hotel bill, his company disbanded, stranded in Kansas City and consoling himself with alcohol until he weakened to the point where he caught pneumonia and died. "She's keeping a boarding house out there, now. I think she's married again. It's a funny thing, isn't it? Both of them thought they were great artists, and they'd neither of them do a thing to cheapen what they called their art, and they went down with their flags flying and their chins up—and neither of them was an actor for a minute, really. All they knew of acting was how to pose about it. If they saw what I'm doing now, they'd be ashamed of me. Comedy? Fooey! Nothing but clowning!"

"Where did you learn to act?" she asked, busy with the dishes and as happy in his flow of reminiscences as if she were a prospector who had struck oil.

"I never learned," he said, "unless from watching Mom. And then there was a boy at Notre Dame—They sent me there to get rid of me when they were trooping—and he was so funny I was plumb hipped by him. I learned from him to look dumb and keep my face straight when I asked fool questions in class. He was a wow!"

He began to tell her a long story of a practical joke which this boy and he had played on a bully during their schooldays; and though the story was no funnier than most stories of the kind, he told it with choked laughter and smiling tears, as if it were a masterpiece of pathetic humor. He was no longer the sophisticated clown, hard-boiled and sad-faced. Something boyish had come to the surface and transformed him. And the change in him changed *her*. She found herself delightfully emotionalized and released in her feeling for him. She laughed with him, hysterically, struggling against a sort of flattered desire to weep.

When Evelyn came in on them, they were both talking at once, flushed and happy. "Well, Helen," she said coldly, "I think you might leave the dishes till the others have gone." And Powell and she felt as if they were a pair of children reproved by an elder. They looked guilty.

"We're—I'm almost done," Helen stammered. "I can finish them. You go on in," she said to Powell. "I'll be done in a minute."

Evelyn saw him hesitate. She took the dish towel from him. "Come along," she said. "I want to show you the decor I've been doing for the witches' scene in 'Macbeth.' And don't you dare to say it reminds you of Gordon Craig."

She led him out and shut the door on Helen. And Helen, left alone, began to giggle like a naughty little girl, caught in mischief and reproved but not punished. She was elated. She knew that she and Powell had arrived at terms which Evelyn would never reach by talking art to him.

She finished her dishes and went back to the daffodil sitting-room, to find Evelyn monopolizing Powell while Hank Overton rested in a corner of a cushioned divan, gorged and silent, smoking cigarettes. She sat down beside him. She said, seriously: "We've been having an argument in the kitchen. He says he can remember things that happened to him when he was only three years old. Do you think that's possible? How far back can you remember?"

"Well, now," he reflected, eyeing his smoke, "let us see. Yes. Oh, yes. Quite possible. I can recall—I was an orphan. I don't remember my mother, but my father died when I was only four, and I recall his funeral perfectly. I went to live with my two aunts, his sisters—"

And *he* was off. He had none of Powell's enthusiasm; he was detachedly artistic in his recollections; but he proceeded to describe, in pallid detail, the lives of his two maiden aunts in a suburb of Boston; and he described them almost poetically, through the eyes of the pale and wistful little boy whom they had protected from contact with any rough reality, even if it were only the summer heat and the danger of sunstroke.

Helen listened, delighted. She loved the gestures he made with his long hands, and his long fingers, and his long cigarette holder with its long cigarette. She loved his description of the two little spinsters, living in rooms where it seemed to be always twilight, surrounded by a peace as sweetly severe as the atmosphere of Whistler's picture of his mother. He smiled a thin-lipped, ascetic smile. He spoke in a low and affectionate voice, looking at her with eyes that were deep and soft with the emotions of his childhood. And Evelyn, laboring in her attempts to interest Powell in the new stage of the expressionists, kept glancing jealously at this tender tête-à-tête that went on so confidentially, in such a fluent murmur, at the other end of the room.

It was broken up when the visitors arrived, but, throughout the evening, both Powell and Overton, whenever they could escape from their social responsibilities, drifted to Helen's side, and confided to her something new that they had just remembered. A little fat man, who had come there with an artistic wife, fell a victim also to her new technique; and, at one time, all three men together were with her on the divan, trying to prove to her how accurate were their memories for events that had happened while they were still babes in arms. The fat man insisted that he could remember crawling on a bearskin rug, before a lighted fireplace, in a house which he had left when he was only nine months old.

"What in the world were you talking to those men about?" Evelyn asked, when she was drying herself from the bath, after they had all gone.

"Oh, we were just gossiping," Helen replied, "about things that happened to them in their childhood."

"I should think," said Evelyn, "that you would've been bored to death."

And Helen answered, evasively, "Yes."

III

She came to Duff's summons, next morning, her eyes downcast, suppressing her smiles, and she sat down demurely, to take his dictation, in the character of the willing female slave who has no life outside of her servitude; but that was because she supposed that he had probably forgotten all about his advice to her; and when he saw her air of hidden excitement and asked, "Well, how did it work?" her laughter and her blushes were the sounded trumpets and the flags of triumph suddenly unfurled. "Oh," she cried, "it worked—it worked marvelously!"

"Talked, did they?"

"Oh, yes. All the time. All evening. No matter what was going on. They kept coming back to me until even Evelyn was jealous."

"Evelyn's the girl you room with?"

"Yes, and after they were gone she said, 'What were all those men talking to you about?'—because she'd been trying to get one of them to talk to her, and she couldn't."

"Did you tell her how you'd done it?"

She shook her head, mischievously. "No."

For a person who was ordinarily so set and colorless, she had an amusing air of innocent deviltry, and her excitement was out of all proportion to the ostensible cause of it. She could not have worked up all this delighted emotion out of the fact that a number of men had talked to her about their boyhoods. No. It must be that she had succeeded particularly with the one desired man. Duff undertook to find out who he was. "What did they tell you about themselves?" he asked.

"Oh, everything! Everything as far back as they could remember. There was one man insisted he remembered things that had happened before he was a year old."

"Who was he?"

She described him, and it was obvious that he had only amused her. She repeated her conversation with Overton, and for Overton, plainly enough, she had felt no more than friendship. But when she began to speak of Powell, her whole secret showed in her face, and Duff led her on until he had got from her every incident that Powell had told her of his youth. "Well," he said heartily, "he sounds like a nice boy. And clever, eh? I must go around, some night, and see his play. He oughtn't to have any more trouble about money, after making a hit like that. You like him, don't you?"

She nodded, trying to be bold. "Yes."

"You're an old-fashioned girl, aren't you?" He leaned his elbows on his desk and smiled at her.

That confused her with self-consciousness. "Am I?"

He was studying her with a deeply reflective eye, in spite of his twinkles. "Do you want him?"

He asked it in a low voice, confidentially, and at once her whole face began to change and tremble with pathos and wistfulness. She struggled with her eyebrows and bit her lips, looking down at her notebook as if she were afraid that she might cry.

"All right," he said. "I'll get him for you."

That alarmed her. "How?"

"Never mind. I'll bet I can do it. Don't you worry. I have a little plan."

"Oh, please don't," she begged. "Please don't interfere."

"I'll not," he promised. "You'll never know about it—and neither will he—or anybody else. All you'll know is—if nothing happens—that I've failed. It's just as simple, when it works, as getting him to talk to you. You go ahead in your own way, now, and don't ask me any questions."

"You'll not do anything that I'd—I'd be ashamed of—if he found out!"

He drew himself up in a travesty of haughtiness. "Young woman! Am I an old blunderer? Have you worked for me all these months and arrived at this kind of opinion of me?"

"Oh, no! No!"

"Good. Then take these letters and forget your private affairs for a minute. We have some work to do. Take a reply to this Henry Johnson. 'Dear Sir—' "

He pressed her so hard with his dictation that she had no time to think of anything else, and her "chest heave" subsided and her face cleared as she followed his long sentences. He dictated a rather pompous letter always, dignified and legalistic. He even spoke in that way when he was not speaking frankly. He found it effective, because the person to whom he was speaking, involved in sentences that were difficult to follow, had less attention free to suspect what the sentences might conceal.

"All right," he finished. "That'll do for the present. Get those out for me, and by that time I'll have some more." She hesitated after she had gathered up the papers, and he added: "I'll not do anything about that affair of yours till I've talked it over with you again. Run along now and don't worry."

With that, she went, relieved; and as soon as she had closed the door, he took his office phone. "Send Jenks in here to me."

Jenks was a newspaper man, temporarily unemployed, who had come into Duff's office to do the simpler sorts of leg-work until he could get back to his profession. He was a dark, good-looking, easy-going Southerner in a blue serge suit and a derby—inconspicuous, self-assured—one of those phlegmatic, fat young men whom nothing can put out of countenance. He strolled into Duff's office, now, his hat in his hand, and stood beside Duff's desk in silence, and watched him with an inquiring, quiet brown eye.

"Look here, Bob," Duff said, "there's a comedian in town—he's just made a hit in a play called 'The Stuffed Shirt'—and I want you to interview him, see? His name's Powell, son of an actor named James T. Powell and an actress whose name I don't know. It's the mother I particularly want to get a line on, understand? Could you do a ballyhoo about him for one of the Sunday sheets?"

Jenks ran his hand over his sleek black hair, fingered his necktie thoughtfully, and said: "Sure. Barney'll let me do it for his Sunday page."

"Good. The information that I want is kind of peculiar. It's psychological. Sit down a minute."

He put his hat on Duff's desk. He drew up a chair. He sat down comfortably and reached into his pocket for a cigarette.

Duff asked: "Do you know the low-down on true love?"

He studied his cigarette a moment and then shook his head. "No. I don't believe I do."

"Well," Duff said, "you know if you take a hungry dog and show him a mutton chop, his mouth'll water. Then if you ring a bell every time you show him the chop—and keep on doing it till you set up a connection between the sound of the bell and the sight of the chop—you'll get him to the point finally where his mouth'll water when you ring the bell without showing him the chop. See? You can educate him to respond, as they say, to a stimulus that he'd naturally be indifferent to. Get me?"

"I think so."

"Well, you can do the same thing with a child—not only with his appetite for food but with any other of his so-called instincts. For example, he has an instinct of affection. It's aroused, first, by his mother. She's the mutton chop in the case, see? And whenever he sees her he has this warm glow of affection, the same as the dog's mouth waters. But, of course, there are all sorts of things about her that are like the ringing of the bell. There's the sound of her voice, or the color of her eyes, or the shape of her nose, and he gets educated to respond to those things about her, automatically, without knowing it, just as the dog gets educated to the bell, until finally the boy will respond to the bell even when the chop isn't there. See? He'll just naturally like anyone that has a voice like his mother's or eyes or a nose like hers. And that continues after he grows up, unless his mother does something to put him off, see? Any girl who comes along and rings the bell, he'll have that warm glow of affection for her. He'll be attracted to her. It'll feel like a case of love at first sight, see? And he won't know why. He won't know what's done it to him. Any more than the dog. Get me?"

"It listens well," Jenks conceded. "I can believe it."

"Good. I want you to locate, with this boy Powell, every conceivable thing about his mother that could possibly ring the bell on him. Get any photographs you can. He was pretty young when she died, but it's just possible he kept a kid's scrapbook about her. Bring it to me, even if you have to steal it. You won't have any trouble making him talk about her. Pretend you want to do him as the son of James T. Powell, and then let him switch you over to her. He gives her all the credit for everything about him. Write the article any way you like, but bring me this information, and keep the whole business confidential. Understand?"

Jenks nodded and put on his hat. He asked no questions. He had been doing odd jobs for Duff, for years, even while he was at work in Newspaper Row, and he knew with what ingenuity Duff usually concealed the real goal of an investigation from his operatives, so as to prevent a leak. Consequently, he believed that Duff's talk about true love was nothing but a blind. He did not waste any time

asking questions about it. He went off to cover his assignment like
a good reporter under orders from his editor.

IV

That was Monday morning. Late Tuesday afternoon, Jenks delivered to Duff's desk an old scrapbook that had lost half its cover,
and a collection of theatrical photographs; and one of the photographs so interested Duff that he studied it a long time, through a
reading glass. On Wednesday, an operative brought him a handful
of shell-cameos, and Duff chose a small one, about the size of a
quarter dollar, carved with a head of Athene. In the course of the
afternoon, he sent for a woman operative, and said, "Get me a
black velvet band, will you?—the kind that a girl might wear tight
around her neck. I want one broad enough to carry this cameo.
How do they fasten the band? Does it buckle at the back? Well, fix
it up for me, will you? And leave it here to-morrow morning. I
want to use it in a case."

And, on Thursday morning, with everything prepared, he called
in Helen Manson. He dictated his letters to her, as usual. He
waited until she had gathered up her papers to leave him. And then
he said, as if it had just occurred to him: "Listen. I want you to do
a good turn for me, if you will. One of our boys is working on a
crooked gang down at the Hotel Antwerp, and they're sticking so
close to him that we can't reach him. There's a dance down there,
Sunday night. The moving picture people are giving a supper and
a show and a dance, and I want you to go there—I've got four
tickets for you, so you can take your roommate and a couple of
escorts. I want you to go there and get an envelope that he'll give
you, and pike right back here with it as fast as you can. Will you
do it?"

"Why, ye-es," she said, surprised. "I guess so."

"There's no danger at all," he assured her, "except to him. I
daren't send anyone that might be recognized as one of our operatives. That's why I'm asking you. Have you a black evening
gown?"

She nodded, a little frightened.

"You're to be in black, and you're to wear this." He took the
black velvet band and the cameo from an upper drawer of his
desk. "Around your neck. *You* know. Up about here. He'll recognize you by it, and he'll find a way to slip the envelope to you
without letting anyone see it. You may find it under your plate at

the table—see?—when you come back from dancing. Or some one may say, 'I think you dropped your handkerchief,' and when you take it, you'll find the envelope pinned in it. Anything like that. And then you just call a taxi and run down here. One of the boys will be on the lookout, at the door, to get the message from you."

She knew that Duff's operatives were constantly engaged in escapades of the sort. As his secretary, she had been living behind the scenes of many such little adventures, seeing them in the case reports which he dictated. But now, like a dresser in the theater who had always stood hidden in the wings, she was suddenly invited to put on a costume and walk out on the stage in a part; and though it was only a super's part, with no lines to speak, it gave her stage fright. "Oh, dear," she said, trembling, "suppose I don't do it right?"

He made a contemptuous gesture. "Nonsense. You can't go wrong. You've nothing to do. You go to a supper and a dance—that's all. Take your roommate and those two boys, Powell and his friend. If nothing happens by ten o'clock, you'll know that Charlie can't reach you, and you can leave, then, any time you like."

"Ten o'clock."

"Yes. As a matter of fact, I'm not sure that anything *will* happen. I'm just sending you there, with this identification mark, in case he can use you. You don't have to worry. Nothing can happen as far as you're concerned. He'll not come within a mile of you, unless it's perfectly safe." He put the velvet band in an envelope and gave it to her. "You'd better not tell the others what you're doing. It might make them nervous."

She stood with the papers in one hand and the envelope in the other, looking at them, as if she were unable to move.

"All right," he said. "Run along now and do your letters. I'll talk it over with you again, in case there's any change of plans."

She went out, with a divided mind. She sat down to her typewriter, distracted. She began to transcribe her shorthand notes, on the machine, but she hardly knew what she was typing. She kept seeing herself, in a black evening gown with a ribbon around her throat, standing helpless in the midst of a situation which she could not understand, while strange men besought her with silent but meaningful glances to do she did not know what.

Since she was not at all of a nervous temperament, she carried this inward apprehension stolidly. It no more than made her seem absent-minded at her work and deeply thoughtful outside of the office. "I've been given four tickets for a supper and a dance on

Sunday night, if you'd care to come," she told Evelyn. "We could get Mr. Overton and Mr. Powell." And she was so vague in reply to Evelyn's questions, that Evelyn merely thought her more dull than usual. She got out an old black evening gown and shortened the skirt to make it half-way fashionable, but she could not explain why she had decided to wear "that old rag," and Evelyn shrugged her shoulders cynically. There were times when Helen Manson seemed as stupid as a servant. And naturally, like a servant, she was at her best in the kitchen—if she would only stop dragging the men in there!

In there, alone with Powell over the gas stove, she seemed to him to be "pepped up a lot." She released, with him, enough of her secret agitation to light up the surface of her mood, and he was touched to find her so girlishly excited by the prospect of going to a dance. It made him feel superior and protective. He patted her on the back as she leaned over the dishpan. "You're all right," he said, affectionately.

She looked around at him, appealingly. "You'll help me," she whispered, "won't you? No matter what happens?"

"I sure will," he promised. His arm slipped down to her waist. He gave her a little reassuring hug. She smiled over her shoulder at him and went on with her work, so absorbed in her anxiety that she did not really notice his caress.

And, on Sunday evening, that hidden anxiety was so obsessive that she noticed nothing at all. When Powell and Overton rang the bell, she went to open the door of the apartment to them, in her black gown and her neckband—withdrawn in her concealed excitement to the point of appearing just tensely calm. "Do I?" she replied politely, when Powell, blinking in a sort of pleased confusion at the sight of her, said, "Gee, you look swell!" She smiled formally, as unself-conscious as if she were quite used to hearing men say things like that. "Gee, you're a knockout in that gown!" His voice even shook, but she was not aware of it. And when Evelyn and Overton had gone ahead into the outer hall and she and Powell were locking the apartment door behind them, he said, "Gee, I like you in black. You look swell!" and she caught his hand and squeezed it in a mixed impulse of gratitude and relief to have him with her, though she did not actually appreciate the emotion with which he spoke.

The others very quickly appreciated it—not in the taxicab, for there Evelyn did all the talking and only Overton replied—and not while they were making their way through the crowded lobby of the Antwerp—but certainly as soon as they had left their wraps in the cloakroom and met again outside the vast ballroom in which the supper was to be served. Evelyn intended to have Powell take her in; she spoke to him and touched his arm. He neither heard her nor saw her. He was staring quite stupidly, she thought, at Helen. And Helen had the most peculiar air. She stood as if she were all alone in the midst of the hubbub, placidly silent and self-contained, gazing straight ahead of her at nothing, bright-eyed, erect and somehow expectant, but as though she were expecting to see an apparition or to hear a voice out of the air, rather than searching for anyone in the unregarded throng that chattered and crowded around her. Powell gave her his arm. She took it mechanically without looking at him. They led the way into the ballroom, and Evelyn followed with Overton, frowning.

She was piqued. She was unpleasant throughout the supper and the vaudeville show that accompanied it on a stage at the far end of the room. And she was unpleasant in vain. Powell seemed to be clearly aware of no one but Helen, and Helen was not clearly aware even of him. She smiled excitedly and tried to listen when he spoke to her, but it was evident that his words only reached her outer ear. And Powell smiled when Evelyn spoke to *him,* but his eyes went back to Helen absent-mindedly, even while he listened, and his replies were brief and perfunctory. "What's the matter with them both?" Evelyn complained to Overton, and Overton rubbed his puzzled forehead and answered, "I'll be blessed if I know."

He knew well enough. They both knew, but they could not believe their eyes. Helen sat, pale, with her chin up, her shoulders squared, looking suddenly mature in black—and dominating. When she replied to Powell, she was poised, possessive, almost condescending. He bent to her, fascinated. They were both completely wrapped up in each other and apparently thrilled with a mutual emotion to the exclusion of everybody else. They did not seem to know what they ate, to hear the music, or to see the vaudeville show that went on with applause and laughter throughout the supper.

"What has happened?" Evelyn said to Overton, under her voice, as he lit a cigarette for her. "Are they married?"

"Well, if they're not," he answered, "it's a nice scandal."

The supper had begun at half-past eight. It lasted until after ten. Then some one announced from the platform that the tables would be removed and the floor cleared for dancing if the guests would go into the reception room and the halls for a moment. Everybody rose. "What time is it?" Helen asked. Powell glanced at his watch. "It's twenty minutes after ten."

"After ten?" She clutched his arm. "Are you sure?"

"Yes. What's the matter?"

She stood frightened, bewildered, transfixed, in the stream of people that pressed around her and bumped into her impatiently.

"What is it?" he said. "What's the matter?"

She gasped. "I don't know. I'll have to phone. To Mr. Duff. To the office."

He drew her arm through his. "Come along then. The phones are outside here."

She was afraid that Duff's scheme had failed through some fault of hers—that she had forgotten something he had told her to do—and she kept going over his directions in her mind and trying to recall everything that he had said to her. Suddenly, with a horrible distinctness, she remembered his words: "There's no danger at all, except to *him.*" And she turned cold with the thought that while she had been eating and chatting at the table, something horrible had happened to a man whom she might have—

"What number is it?" Powell asked.

She told him. He gave it to the phone girl at the switchboard. In a moment, the girl said, "Number five," and when she failed to understand, Powell repeated, "Booth number five," and led her to it, and stepped back to wait for her.

Duff's voice came to her at once. "Yes. What is it?"

She had expected to hear the telephone girl in the outer office. "Oh, Mr. Duff," she wailed, "it's after ten. It's after ten and nothing has happened. No one—"

"That's all right. I didn't really expect it to. Don't worry. Are you still there? At the dance?"

"Yes. Yes. I'm still here."

"Then go ahead and enjoy yourself."

"What?"

"Don't worry. It's all right. Go ahead and have a good time. I'll see you in the morning."

She heard the click as he hung up, but she stood, with the receiver at her ear, as if waiting for something more, her lips puckered in a noiseless "What?"

It was too sudden. The relief was too sudden and too violent. She drew a slow, tremulous breath, and put up the receiver weakly, and wavered out of the booth. Her knees had begun to shake under her. The long nervous tension, abruptly relieved, left her feeling as unstrung as if something taut and pulling on her had been cut. She tried to smile at Powell, but she could not control her lips.

"What is it? What's the matter?"

"Nothing. Nothing," she said hoarsely. "It's all right. We can go back."

"Do you want to?"

She looked around her blankly and shook her head.

"Neither do I. Come on. Let's beat it. I don't want to dance. I want to talk to you. Come on. Let's get our things and hop off."

He hurried her to the cloakroom. By the time she got her wrap, she had collected her wits. "Evelyn!" she said, reluctantly, when he rejoined her. "She'll wonder—"

"Let her." He started her off down the hall, his hat in his hand, his coat on his arm. "I've been wanting to talk to you, all evening. It seems to me—you and I—we're always either cooking or eating or washing up." He had a funny breathless air, as if they were running away to something secret and clandestine.

She began to redden. "Where are we going?"

"Anywhere that we can be alone a minute." His voice cracked on "alone," and something caught her, sympathetically, in the throat. She found difficulty breathing. Her heart was pounding. She could not speak.

Neither could he.

He managed to say "Taxi" to the doorman, and when he had handed her into the cab, he cleared his throat to say "Central Park" to the chauffeur, who grinned. He still had his hat in his hand, and he tripped over his coat as he climbed in after her. The starter, missing a tip, slammed the door on him before he was seated. The cab started with a sudden jerk that threw him into her arms. He dropped his hat and coat, and clutched her in an involuntary embrace, which he did not relinquish as he fell into the seat. "Darling!" he said in a sort of jolted sob. He kissed her. He turned her face to him and kissed her on the lips. "Tod!" she mumbled, into his mouth. He drew his hand down her cheek to her neckband and followed that to find the cameo, and at the touch of it she felt him shudder with a violent emotion. "I'm *crazy* about you," he whispered.

~ ~ ~

"It's all right," Duff assured her, next morning. "We got a message from him about midnight. He didn't dare to try to reach you. It wasn't your fault at all."

"I'm afraid I'd never make a detective," she said, smiling, with no regret.

He turned over in his fingers the neckband which she had given back to him. "Do you want to?"

"No! I don't think so." She put a bold face on it. "I'm going to be married."

"Congratulations. Who is it? Powell? When did it happen? Last night?"

She nodded and nodded, brightly mischievous and blushing. "Yes. Just after I phoned you."

"Good! Then you ought to keep this as a souvenir." He gave her back the ribbon and the cameo. "As a love charm," he added.

"Oh, thanks," she said. "I'd love to." And she had no suspicion of what he really meant.

She did not suspect, even months later, when she saw among Powell's photographs the picture of his mother which Duff had studied so carefully through his reading glass. It showed her in a black evening gown with a cameo on a velvet band at her throat. She was looking down, Madonna-like, at her infant son in her arms, and he was reaching up a tiny hand to the cameo.

"Don't ask me," Duff says. "I'm nothing but a dumb detective. I can't explain human nature. I only know how it works."

ABE ENGER

AND THE

PRINCESS

ABE ENGER AND THE PRINCESS

I

IT WAS LIKE meeting Jesse James. At least, it was like that to Duff. It was like meeting a rich and triumphant Jesse James who had come back from the outlawry of his youth and held up the community for so many millions, now, that he was as respectable as a bank. Duff had never seen him before, but he had heard of him often enough, for thirty years past. And what years! The years of an old wolf who had never been trapped by the law, never so much as scratched in his long life of preying and fighting and fleeing to cover.

He had sent for Duff. "Mr. Enger wishes to see you," the message read. Duff's secretary had it when Duff returned from lunch. "Is it Abe Enger?" Duff asked, in the tone in which one asks the incredible. And it was Abe Enger.

"Well," Duff said, "that's what it is to be a detective. You can never tell what sort of criminal you're going to meet next. See if you can make an appointment for four o'clock."

He was really flattered. After all, there was only one Abe Enger in the world. Enger was unique—not in kind, perhaps, but in degree. Like a true genius, he was the product of the social conditions of his day, the fruit of the contemporary tree; and the tree was now loaded with lesser Abe Engers, but he was on the topmost bough, fat and juicy in the unobstructed sunlight, the first and finest of the crop.

"He must be growing old," Duff thought. "I'd like to see him before he drops."

The secretary reported that Enger would see him at four o'clock.

"That's funny," Duff said to himself. "He must have made room for me. I wonder what he wants."

What *could* Abe Enger want? What could he want of a man like Duff who made a point of being an honest private detective with a reputation for refusing any case that might put him on the wrong side of the law? It was on the wrong side of the law that Enger had lived and thrived so long and so gorgeously. "He must be planning to use me as a camouflage," Duff decided.

Abe Enger, born in the Ghetto, had first gone to work as an office boy in a bucket-shop, during the day, while he studied law at night. The world did not hear of him till he appeared in the police courts as a young attorney for the lesser criminals of his district, for the cadets and petty thieves and gangsters who had been his boyhood friends. These he defended with conspicuous success. Then, with their aid as ambulance chasers and perjured witnesses, he began to prey on all the traction companies and insurance companies that could be sued for damages; and, in this way, he made his first reputation as a dangerous man; and he made money, but he also made powerful enemies. They stirred up against him the District Attorney of that day, an eloquent reformer who was on the way to becoming Governor and perhaps President. He summoned Enger before a Grand Jury and indicted him on a charge of forging evidence for a crooked client, and Enger took a holiday in Europe, a fugitive from justice. The District Attorney's detectives pursued him, and he went into hiding abroad, no one knew where, his career apparently ended.

But not so. He still had his criminal friends. They attacked the District Attorney's political ambitions. They helped to prevent him from getting a nomination for the governorship. They helped to defeat him for reelection to the office of District Attorney; and the new District Attorney was properly grateful; and Abe Enger returned to his old haunts, unmolested.

And now a queer thing happened—a queer thing but the usual thing in Enger's practical world. All his powerful enemies, all the shrewd business men on whom he had preyed—seeing him return to the practice of the law and seeing themselves threatened with a renewal of his old activities—hastened to retain him as their lawyer, to subsidize him and his friends, the little criminals, in defense of just such damage suits as Enger and they had once prosecuted. From that foothold, he climbed quickly until he was the eminent and learned counsel for most of the richest corporations in most of the conspicuous cases in the courts of New York. He made millions. He was a new kind of lawyer, the lawyer who studies a statute as a doctor studies a disease, in order to outwit it. He was called in on every sort of doubtful financial scheme and questionable incorporation, to devise ways by which to make a large dishonesty safely legal, and his fees were as big as blackmail. He organized New York's famous "bankruptcy ring" of lawyers who forced ailing enterprises into insolvency and then bled them to death. It was said that he had never lost a jury case, because he always had the jury fixed in advance, but that was never proved, and the reputation did him nothing but good because all the honest lawyers, when they were confronted with a jury case against him, advised their clients to accept a settlement rather than to go to trial. He was hated and feared and flattered and imitated.

Duff knew all this. Everybody knew it who knew anything about lawyers in New York, and Duff had been especially aware of it, of late, because he had been engaged to investigate a bankruptcy that looked as if it had been manipulated by some of Enger's bankruptcy ring. He had not found Enger in the case, perhaps because Enger had been growing inactive, of recent years, declining in virulence, reposing on his wealth. And what Duff was wondering was this: had the old crook decided to become respectable? And was it because he had decided to become respectable that he was sending for Duff on a case, instead of using the private blackmailers whom he generally employed as his sleuths?

"Well," Duff thought, "maybe I'll find that out when I see him."

Duff had no moral judgment to pass on the old scoundrel. He had been working among human beings long enough to know that the unsocialized man has little moral sense outside the circle of his family and his friends. It was not to be expected that a boy of Enger's birth and training would grow up with any feeling of responsibility to the community. That was the community's fault. It was the community's business to see that he was taught to be an honest and loyal member of the community.

"There they are," Duff reflected as he sat among them, in a crowded subway car, on the way downtown to Enger's office. "They pay for the schools, the hospitals, the churches, the courts, the police, the firemen, the armies and the navies that protect and educate and defend a man like Enger from every sort of moral and physical enemy, while he picks their pockets. You'd think they'd take the trouble to see that when he was young and teachable he was taught to go straight. Not they. It's a great little civilization, this. I wonder whether Enger has a sense of humor. I wonder whether he ever looks out his office window at the people and laughs."

His office was in an aspiring skyscraper on lower Broadway. "A noble and majestic building," Duff said to himself, as he approached it through the crowds. "Lift up your eyes to its sublime heights, all ye people, and see Abe Enger enshrined above you in the skies."

Abe Enger was on the twentieth floor, and he rented most of the floor for himself and his score of assistants and their clerks and stenographers; but there were no partners' names on the glass of his double entrance doors; there was no name but "A. Enger," in letters large enough to occupy the entire transom. "There's an ego," Duff thought.

He opened the door on a crowded reception room. A railing cut him off from the waiting list, and a girl at a desk guarded the gate in the railing. She was a rosy blonde in pink who looked as if she should have been in the ticket kiosk of a movie palace. "Some of Abe's protective coloration," Duff decided.

He gave her his name. She murmured it to a desk phone. The phone answered nothing audible, but she beckoned to an office boy across the room and then nodded to Duff. The gate was opened to him silently, and the boy muttered, " 'S way."

The crowded room watched Duff pass in ahead of them—dozens of them—waiting patiently to be let in to Enger, or his assistant leeches, to be bled. "It's a great business," Duff thought. "He doesn't have to go out on the street and hold people up. They come to him and ask for it." He passed into a law library, lined to the ceiling with shelves of law books in the conventional leather. The books did not look as if they had ever been used, and neither did the library table nor the padded chairs. At the far side of the room, another girl was sitting, at a typewriter desk beside a solid door—an older woman, dark and Oriental-looking. She stared at Duff officially, taking him in with a swift scrutiny that ran from his heavy black eyebrows to his big feet—and then returned to her typewriter like a watchdog to its kennel. (She was really wondering what it must be like to be married to such a giant.) "Mr. Enger is expecting you," she said.

Duff reflected: "Women are better, for him, than men. They're more loyal and less honest. He doesn't need a bodyguard. He isn't afraid of being strong-armed, because he's in right with all the stick-ups, and the people he loots are law-abiding." He opened Enger's door.

And he opened it, to his surprise, on flowers and sunlight and fresh air.

The outer offices, the reception room and the library, were stuffy and windowless. They were lighted with electricity but they were unventilated inside rooms. Enger's private office had rows of windows on two sides, looking toward the Hudson River and the Bay, and a bright sea breeze had filled it with a soft stir of autumn freshness. It was also filled with flowers, September flowers—chrysanthemums, asters, zinnias, and dahlias, as well as hothouse roses and some golden-rod, in vases on side tables, on Enger's desk, on low bookshelves around the walls. Among the flowers were photographs, in silver frames, of Enger's wife and children; and, among the flowers and the photographs, Enger was sitting, at his mahogany desk, in his swivel chair, reading some foolscap pages that were fastened together at the corner with a paper-clip.

"Here's a swell set-up," Duff thought. "Or is it real? Maybe he likes flowers. Maybe he's a good family man. Why not? After all, he's human."

Enger did not greet him. He did not look at Duff. He went on reading, patiently absorbed, his face expressionless, his mind entirely occupied.

Duff closed the door, looked around the room at his leisure, studied Enger at a distance, and then approached to sit in a convenient chair across the desk from him. Enger moved his head, as if in a nod that acknowledged Duff's presence, but he continued to read.

He was old. He was bald. He was gray. He had the serenity of aged indifference. There was nothing crafty about his face; it was neither keen nor wrinkled. He looked merely like a tired business man, in business clothes, rather bored. His flat features were not markedly Jewish. If anything, they were markedly commonplace. "Well, there you are," Duff thought. "That's how he does it. He just looks like nothing at all."

And yet decidedly he was the authoritative center of the room. The flowers were smiling for him to enjoy them; the photographs watched him; the telephones on his desk were turned expectantly toward him; Duff and the general silence and all the business of the outer offices waited for him to be done with his reading and take them up.

He continued to read, very slowly, without glasses, as though he were not used to reading and had to take it word by word. His hands, Duff noticed, held the foolscap pages in stiff fingers that were shiny and claw-like. The skin on them seemed to be too tight. "Gosh," Duff thought, "if any of his victims see those horrible hands!"—and then he remembered. There had been a fire, a domestic accident of some sort, wasn't it? A servant girl? Her clothes had caught fire in the kitchen, and Enger had burned his hands beating out the flames.

Duff put his hat down, and settled back in his chair. It wasn't going to be possible to judge Enger from appearances. It was going to take time.

And then Enger spoke. He laid down his typewritten pages, and with his eyes still on them, he said: "There's a Russian woman in town—a Princess Sipiagin. Have you ever run across her?"

It was a deadly voice. There was no other word for it. It was toneless, indifferent, inhuman, very low, dry, chalky. Coming from a man of Enger's sinister power, it was the sort of voice you might expect to hear from the small mouth of a shark.

Duff was startled. His reply boomed from his big chest, "Sipiagin? No. Never heard of her."

Enger aligned the papers with the edge of the blotter on his desk. He continued, indifferently, "She has some letters from a client of mine. We want to get them back."

"Have you tried to get them?"

"Yes. We sent a man after them."

"What happened?"

He answered, coldly precise: "He was killed."

"I see," Duff said. "Who is she?"

Enger swung around in his swivel chair to give Duff his profile. "She's a Russian refugee. She met my client on the boat from England, and he fell in love with her. He must have had softening of the brain. She's using his letters to blackmail him. We put a detective on her and he tried to steal them. She's surrounded by a lot of Cossacks, Turks, Georgians, and people like that. They knifed him in the hallway of a tenement house."

"How do you expect *me* to get them?"

Enger shook his head. "That's up to you. We don't care how much it costs. We're paying her a thousand dollars a month now. She hasn't the letters in her possession. She's turned them over to one of her outlaws. If anything happened to her, it wouldn't help us. The letters would still make my client look like a damn fool. He can't afford to have them used. His public wouldn't stand for it. He'll pay anything to get them."

Duff had been watching him curiously. He had not so much as glanced at Duff. His face had remained expressionless. His lips alone had moved, in a precise utterance that must have been carefully acquired by a man of Enger's antecedents, but that precision of speech was the only concession that he made to his listener.

Otherwise, he might have been talking to himself. It was as if he were entirely self-centered in a world of enemies whom he did not fear, whom he had no desire to placate, who did business with him at their own risk—and be damned to them!

"Well," Duff said, "I'll look her up and let you know."

Enger swung back to his desk and reached out for his foolscap pages again. "You'll find her in the phone book—Madame Marya Sipiagin. She has what she calls a studio where she sells Russian things made by her friends."

Duff stood up. "All right. Good-by."

Enger did not answer. He had begun to read. And when Duff glanced back at the door, he was still reading, absorbed, his face expressionless, his mind entirely occupied, just as he had been when Duff first entered. Throughout the whole interview, he had not once looked at Duff, so far as Duff knew. "Well," Duff promised himself, "he'll look at me before I'm done with him. I'll make his eyes pop, if *I* know myself. Gosh, what a voice!"

He decided that Enger had sent for him, not out of any impulse toward decency, but because he had vainly tried every crooked means of getting the letters and now he was willing to try something honest. "He probably intends to see me as far as I'll go, and then ditch me for some one who'll finish the dirty work. It must have been his damn fool client who told him to put me on the job. Gosh, what a voice!"

II

It proved easy enough to get a line on the Princess Sipiagin. He called in little Dottie Parkins, a newspaper woman who had worked for him when he was Major Duff of Military Intelligence, and he said to her, "Look here, little Bright-eyes, there's a Russian refugee in town with a whale of a story. Here's a note on her. You ought to be able to sell her to one of the women's magazines. Give me a good report on her. I don't care what it costs. Go as far as you like. Only don't be seen around *here* while you're doing it. She travels with a lot of Russian refugees who're nervous about their pasts. If they get an idea you're spying on them, they'll stick a knife in your fair young gizzard. Send your reports to me by mail."

Dottie Parkins dimpled with smiles. She seemed perhaps twenty-five years old, in her short skirts and her leopard skin coat and her little cloche hat that looked as if it should have been lined around her face with rosebuds. But then she had been looking twenty-five for the last ten years at least. She put the note about Madame Sipiagin in her handbag and asked: "What's the case against the lady?"

"No case," Duff assured her. "Just a commercial inquiry. She's trying to get capital for some sort of business she runs—selling handicrafts for her refugee friends."

"Yes?" Dottie said. "What a liar you are, Major." She wrapped her leopard skin around her like a bath robe. "All right. I'll send you the dope. You want everything, do you?—past, present and future?"

"Everything you can get."

"Don't fret," she fluted. "I'll get plenty. I'll tell myself I'm working on space rates. Ten cents a word, say? Toot-toot."

And she certainly got plenty. And she certainly delivered it like an oil gusher. She became an unlimited flow of words impelled by an inexhaustible enthusiasm. "The most wonderful woman I have ever met" gave her "the most interesting story I have ever heard," and she poured it out on Duff in pen, pencil, or typewriting, at the top of her literary voice, breathlessly.

To believe her, the Princess Marya Sipiagin was a true aristocrat. She was beautiful, charming, distinguished, petite, spirited, brave, gentle, ferocious, chaste, affectionate, witty, musical, artistic, truthful, educated, imaginative, and everything else that was dazzling, contradictory and delightful. And her story was beyond words. For instance, her father, the old Prince Sipiagin—he was one of the Czar's advisers and he had been in America at the Russo-Japanese Peace Conference which met, under President Roosevelt, at Portsmouth, to end the Russian-Japanese War—and this Prince Sipiagin, a widower at the age of forty-two, being piqued at his family, had married a beautiful gypsy girl, and the Princess Marya was her daughter. That was why she was so temperamental, and that was why, once in Petrograd, when she saw an officer beating a soldier, she went up to the officer and slapped his face. There was a terrible row about it, and she was sent away from Court and kept in a sort of exile on her father's country place near Moscow. And years later, after the Bolshevist revolution, when she was a refugee on the streets of Constantinople, she met this Cossack whom she had defended from his officer, and he—"But that comes later," Dottie wrote. "I mustn't get ahead of my story."

Or take her marriage. After the Bolshevist revolution, her father fled from Petrograd to his country estates and lived there, in retirement, with her and her mother and her two maiden aunts. Her two brothers, who were Czarist officers, were killed by the Bolshevists, and their home in Petrograd was looted, but most of the peasants on their country place were loyal, and though the horses and cows and farm stock were all seized and the agricultural machinery stolen at night and taken away, their house was not attacked and they were allowed to live in it with some of their old servants. Then a Bolshevist Commissar, named Yakov, came to the village to organize it, and he confiscated all their furniture and rugs and pictures and sent them off to Moscow to be sold, and when he saw the Princess Marya he fell in love with her, and he told her that he had orders to execute her father and mother, but he'd spare them if she married him. And she said "Never!" So he called in some soldiers, and they took out the two old aunts and shot them both, in front of the house; and when Yakov came back for her father and mother, she said, "No. I'll marry you!" So they were married, that afternoon, in the church down at the village, and he slept with her that night, and the next morning he took her father and mother out in the garden, under her bedroom window, and shot them both.

"At that," wrote Dottie, "she went kind of crazy. Something happened to her eyes. Everything looked small, as if it were a long way off, and everything sounded distant. She could see and she could hear well enough, but people didn't seem to be near her any more, and their voices were tiny little voices, and she had to strain to catch what they said. Nothing mattered either. It was all small and far away."

She seemed not to be angry at Yakov. She said, "They were old. Their world is dead. What had they to live for? They are better off." But there was a deaf mute who did chores around the kitchen and fed the pigs, and he was a huge half-witted giant whom they called "Baba" because that was the only sound he made. She had always been kind to him and he was devoted to her. She got him to steal her some boy's clothes, peasant's clothes that would fit her, and a pair of heavy boots; and she got from him the sharp knife that he used to kill pigs with when it came time to butcher them in the autumn. She hid the clothes and the knife in her bedroom. And one night when Yakov came to her, drunk, she coaxed him to go to sleep, and then she slit his windpipe with the pig-knife so he couldn't cry out, and she threw herself on him and held him down till he bled to death. "Pig, cut with a pig-knife," she kept whispering to him, "die slowly. Die slowly." He was too drunk to struggle much. When she was sure that he was dead, she cut off her hair, like a boy's, dressed herself in the peasant's clothes, and ran into the woods with Baba.

They were not caught. They got away. Of course, they hid during the daytime and only traveled at night until they were miles south, below Moscow; but there, the roads were so full of refugees, tramps, pilgrims, demobilized soldiers, beggars, thieves, and all the human wreckage of war, famine, and revolution, that they were in no danger of pursuit. They were nearly a year on the road. The Princess could recall very little about it, and that only dimly. After the murder of Yakov, she seemed to see everything through a red mist. "I walk in my sleep," she said. "It is a nightmare. I think it is not all true. I dream it. I don't know which is dream and which is true."

They had started out in the late winter, about March. They arrived in the Crimea in the autumn. There Baba was shot while he was stealing food for her, in some seaport town whose name she never knew, and she was pursued to the waterfront where she succeeded in stowing away, unseen, on board a French destroyer, bound for Constantinople.

When the sailors found her, she told them who she was and they took her to the captain. He shrugged his shoulders. "Very well," he said, "if you so prefer to starve to death in Constantinople instead of here, why not?" There were thousands of Russian noblewomen on the streets of Constantinople. "It had one good," she told Dottie. "There were so many women to give themselves for a plate of food that no one attacks me."

Her adventures in Constantinople were a new Arabian Nights. She met her Cossack while she was disguised as a gypsy playing a guitar and singing on the streets, and he got her work as an entertainer in a restaurant where he washed dishes. He lived in the native quarter with a lot of brigands from the hill tribes above Armenia—thieves, counterfeiters, outlaws and murderers who adopted her with delight. "They were the most kind," she said, "of all the peoples I ever met, and the most loyal." She lived with them very comfortably all winter, learned to cook, to speak Turkish and to play the *tar*, and she made a manuscript collection of their folk songs and dance music. In the spring, her Cossack got himself killed in a street brawl, and the gang decided that she had better leave Constantinople. One desperado brought her a passport which he had altered to suit her needs, being a professional forger, and the original owner of the passport having died suddenly. Another of the gang contributed a pillowcase full of Turkish paper money, "warm from the oven," as he expressed it. He was a counterfeiter. Thus equipped, she got passage on an English boat for Liverpool—where the people all looked to her "as if they were coming out of a fit, their faces were so dumb."

At this point in the story, Dottie Parkins decided that she would help the Princess write her autobiography. She interested a magazine editor in the idea and got an order to go ahead. Naturally, she had to begin at the beginning; so in her reports to Duff, she returned to the childhood memories of the Princess, in Moscow, in Petrograd, and on her father's country estate. Duff groaned: "Gosh! She's going to write me a novel." He got her on the telephone. "Look here, Dottie," he said. "Come down to date, can't you? How's she living now? Where does she get her money? Give me some dope on the friends she has around her." Dottie plunged eagerly into that assignment. The Princess had a studio-flat, on East Twenty-third Street, near the edge of the Turkish quarter, and she employed a group of exiles and refugees whose stories were only one degree less picturesque and melodramatic than her own. They dyed and painted silks for her to make into dresses, negligees, shawls, handkerchiefs, and pajamas, with the assistance of some Circassian sewing women and a little Russian adventuress who was a genius as a costumer. Those of her friends who could sing or dance or play the guitar, she helped to get vaudeville engagements, to find work in cabarets, or to appear as after-dinner entertainers at fashionable homes. When they became involved with the law, she went to court with them. She took them to the hospital, when they fell ill. She sent word throughout the Russian colony that the key of her studio was under her doormat for anyone who found himself on the street at night without a bed; and sometimes as many as a dozen homeless tramps would file down her front steps at dawn and disappear for the day. One of her American friends remonstrated: "But, Marya, how *can* you sleep? With all those strange men in the next room to you?" And she replied: "I should care if they were in my bedroom! Imagine that I once kick the soldier in the ditch with my foot and say, 'Move over, comrade, and let me sleep where you have warm the grounds.' "

She had a small income from the rental of property in Paris that had belonged to her father—or so she told Dottie Parkins, anyway—and she used this money to support her business and her friends and herself. She used very little of it on herself. She asked of life only two things: "Each day a good dinner, and each night a soft bed." She once had possessed everything—youth, beauty, wealth, rank, envy, adulation, and every enjoyment of culture and the most refined esthetic sense. She had lost everything except, as she said, "the breath in the lungs." And she had found that nothing really mattered to her except food and sleep. "You people are such great fools," she philosophized. "You have not a bed in America." She had hers piled high with feather ticks and down coverlets and fat pillows. And every day she shopped herself, in all the foreign food markets, for the native specialties that only cosmopolitan New York can supply. She was her own cook. She had assistants, but she allowed them to do only the apprentice work of carrying out her instructions. "I would as rather let one court for me as cook for me," she said. "Eating and loving! It is only with animals that they are to satisfy the appetite—just." And Duff said to himself: "This is the first sensible woman *I* ever heard of."

After a month of such enthusiastic reports from Dottie Parkins, it began to dawn on Duff that the Russian lady was not only sensible but shrewd. She was too shrewd for Dottie. In all the varied transports of their intimacy, not a word had been said about Abe Enger's client, about his letters, or about the monthly blackmail which he paid—unless this was referred to as the income from property in Paris. "She's a damn smart woman," Duff assured himself. "Dottie'll never make her. I'll have to try another approach."

After much pacing up and down his dingy little office, he sent for Chester Bilkey, the operative who worked chiefly in the theatrical district. Duff gave him a list of the Princess' musical protegees. "These people," he said, "are all being helped to get work by this Sipiagin woman, see? I want you to rope some of them and get next to her. You can make friends with them and try to land them theatrical engagements. That ought to bring you into touch with her. Be careful. They're dangerous. They knifed one of Abe Enger's detectives."

He sent for another operative whose business it was to know the underworld. "Here," he said, "are the names and addresses of some people from Constantinople who had criminal records on the other side of the pond. Go slow with them. They bumped off one of Abe Enger's dicks not so long ago. Don't touch them yourself.

Get a line on them from some of the gang that travels in the Turk-ish quarter. I want to lead into that Sipiagin woman if I can."

And he telephoned to Dottie Parkins, "If your young Russian friend gets into any legal difficulty, recommend me as a lawyer. You don't know anything about me except that I'm said to be hon-est. You met me in Washington during the war. Give her my office number and tell her to look me up. If she finds out that I simply use the law business as cover for a detective agency, you're sur-prised, understand? You didn't know anything about that."

It was true that before the war, Duff had been a lawyer, and to all outward seeming he was a lawyer still—an unsuccessful law-yer, sitting all day at his old walnut desk, in his shabby old office, on the second floor of a shabbier old building just off Union Square. And at his desk, or pacing up and down his dingy little office, he prepared the maneuvers—the plots and "plants" and in-tricate conspiracies—by which his operatives discovered for him whatever it was that he wanted to know. They reported to him, in his chair, by telephone, and he directed them, from his chair, at his leisure, like an expert playing a half-dozen games of chess at once. Every morning their typewritten accounts of their previous day were waiting on his desk blotter to be studied. He went over them in the intervals between dictating letters, summarizing cases that were closed, receiving his clients, and instructing his men. And, sitting at his desk, he saw an endless monotony of small crime and dull tragedy pass across the typewritten pages of his blotter, in the peaceful silence of his law office, between the shelves of legal volumes that were his camouflage, under the rusty engravings of Washington crossing the Delaware or Lincoln freeing the slaves.

In that atmosphere, the reports that arrived about the Princess Sipiagin and her entourage were glimpses of an impossible world. She was promoting the success in vaudeville of a violinist, a hand-some blond young Russian who looked as if he had just left Eton. His whole family had been tortured and killed during the revolu-tion. He had become a spy among the Bolshevists, and it was his proudest boast of revenge that he had once got into a hospital of the Bolshevist army and cut the throats of a whole ward of wounded men. That did not prevent him from being a sweet and charming person who played the violin with an angelic fury. His boon companion was a Petrograd professor of bacteriology who had come through the revolution so disillusioned about humanity that it was his one ambition, now, to get work as a keeper in the Zoo and associate for the rest of his life with animals only. In the circle that surrounded them—and the Princess—were hereditary chieftains from the mountain tribes of the Caucasus, men who traced their ancestry back to Genghis Khan, men who had held the power of life and death over their people—and they were working in radio factories in New York, or wrapping up toilet articles in the shipping room of cold cream manufacturers, or opening taxicab doors in front of Russian restaurants, or singing tribal songs and doing dagger dances in night clubs and cabarets. "Well," Duff thought, "if Abe Enger wants to get his throat cut, here are the folk to do it for him."

They were completely peaceable and law-abiding. Whatever monstrous way of life had been imposed on them by the atrocities in Russia, they were no more bloodthirsty now than any demobilized soldier who has seen too much of war. Duff's underworld sleuth reported that none of them were known to the professional criminals of the quarter. "So much the worse for Enger," Duff concluded. "None of his little jackals will be able to warn him if these lads go after him."

And then his underworld operative reported something else. He found a "tip" among the local gangsters, that Duff was on the trail of these Russians. "Don't know where it came from," he phoned Duff. "Ducked as soon as I heard it. Didn't want to spoil my cover." And Duff replied: "Back out of it. For the time being. Wait till you hear from me."

He was puzzled. If there was a leak in his office, how could it have reached these people of the underworld? Not through Dottie Parkins. And not through Bilkey, his operative in the theatrical district. No. And no one else in his office knew. The leak must have come from the outside. It must be that some one in Enger's office—

Among the cases on which Duff had been working, there was that bankruptcy proceeding which he had been employed by a suspicious creditor to investigate. The reports of his operatives involved an obscure lawyer who had guided the bankrupt through a series of devious evasions of the law. Duff had been trying to find out how that young attorney had come into so important a case, and who had put him in charge of it, and where he had learned to cooperate so smoothly with the shyster lawyers of the "bankruptcy ring." All this was in the background of his mind along with a mass of similar matters no more relevant to the Sipiagin case— while he mulled over his operative's tip that the underworld knew he was on the trail of the Russians. And suddenly, out of nowhere, with a certainty that came upon him in a cold chill, he saw Enger concealed behind the young lawyer in the bankruptcy case; and he saw that Enger, when he found himself endangered by the bankruptcy investigation, had conspired to rid himself of the investigator by putting him on the trail of a dangerous gang of "outlaws" (as Enger believed them to be) and then sending them a warning that he was on their trail.

Duff did not see it in such logical terms, however. That was not how Duff arrived at his so-called "hunches." He did not perceive it as a deduction, intellectually. No. What he saw was Enger, as Enger had received him, that day, among the flowers and the family photographs. He saw him sitting there, reading his foolscap pages, absorbed and expressionless. He saw him, in profile, talking indifferently, with his peculiarly deadly voice. He saw that Enger's coldly precise admission of the death of the previous detective was probably an admission which he made to assure himself that he was concealing nothing; that Enger's indifference in the whole interview was unconsciously assumed so that he might not later accuse himself of having pretended any friendship for the man whose murder he had plotted; that Enger had been saying to himself: "You and I are enemies. I don't pretend any friendship. If you want to work for me, do it and be damned to you. Here's a dangerous case. Take it if you want to. Take it at your own risk. You can't blame me, if you get tripped up in it. That's your own affair. You're trying to trip me up in this bankruptcy investigation. Go ahead. We'll see who'll do the tripping."

That was what had made his voice so deadly. "Gosh," Duff thought. "I might have known it. That's Abe Enger, all right. Not a doubt of it."

He remained seated at his desk, hunched forward, resting on his elbows, staring ahead of him at nothing, thoughtful and impassive. He said "Huh!" He closed one eye as if he were looking through a telescope. When he opened it again, he puckered his lips in a soundless whistle. He nodded. "Why not?"

He took his office phone. "Is Denny up there? Yes. Put him on." He blew his noiseless whistle while he waited. "Denny? Drop that Russian business. Yes, quit it cold. Find out for me about Abe Enger's family, who lives with him, how many children he has, if there're any grandchildren, how many servants, whether any of them are foreigners, what's his home life, whether he's a good family man, and so forth, see? Be careful, but give it to me as quick as you can."

He telephoned his Broadway operative: "Hello, Bilkey. Lay off that Russian outfit. Absolutely. They've been tipped off. It's too dangerous. I'll handle them myself."

He called up a friendly official who was connected with the Department of Labor in Washington. "Clem," he said, "I want you to make a little passport trouble for a young Russian violinist who's in this country as a student. Yes. Just as a plant to bring him in to see me. I'll drop down this afternoon and tell you about it. Three o'clock do? Good. How's everything?"

And finally he called Dottie Parkins. "You know that young violinist your Princess is ballyhooing? Well, there's going to be some trouble about his passport. As a lawyer, I'm an expert on passport troubles and I work quite a pull in Washington, see? Recommend me to your little playmate. I'd like to have dinner with you both. Yes. I'll tell you the whole story and relieve your mind. No. Relieve it of the suspicion that I'm trying to do your young friend any dirt."

III

These maneuvers worked out so well that, three days later Dottie Parkins brought to Duff's office the Princess Sipiagin and her protege, young Vladim Khalkoff, the violinist. She brought them to consult Duff, as a lawyer, about Khalkoff's passport. Khalkoff had been admitted to the country, temporarily, as a musical student, and the Department of Labor wished to be assured that he was really studying music; and since he had not been really studying music, he was in danger of deportation. When Dottie Parkins had heard them discussing that danger, she said: "I know the man that can help you. He's a passport lawyer and he has a lot of influence in Washington. I'll take you to see him." And technically she brought them. But, from the moment that they opened the door of Duff's inner office, it was in no way evident that the Princess Sipiagin had been brought. She entered the office as if she owned it, with Dottie Parkins in the role of an ornamental escort. At the sight of Duff, her little dark face lit up with an expression of delighted recognition. "But it is Baba!" she cried. "Truly, it is my Baba!" She threw back from her arms the long black street cloak that she was wearing, and coming to Duff, with both her gloved hands outstretched, she took charge of him and of the situation and of the interview; and Dottie Parkins dropped into the colorless background and chorus of the scene, to support it only as an echo and a smile.

"And who was Baba?" Duff asked as he took her hands—although he remembered well enough that Baba was the deaf mute who had saved her life.

"No, no," she said. "Some day. Not now." She was as small as a boy, and like a boy she took off her little turban hat and threw it on Duff's desk. She shook out her black hair, bobbed like a gypsy musician's, brushed back from a childish forehead that did not show the faintest line of worry. "Not now," she said. "Now you must help me again—as Baba did." Her mouth was infantile. Her nose was as delicately waxen as a doll's. She gazed up at the giant Duff, smiling in a child's solemn confidence, with eyes that were anything but childish under eyebrows that might have been drawn, in the single sweep of a camel's hair brush, by some Chinese artist with a passion for the perfect line of beauty. "You must help me, and you must help this baby."—She indicated the blond Khalkoff who smiled and bowed, bashfully silent, because he knew very little English although he looked as if he had just come from an English public school. "They say they send him back to Russia. If he arrive, he is shot."

"Sit down," Duff said, "and tell me about it."

They seated themselves around his desk, and she began a long and rapid recital of Khalkoff's troubles with the guardians of Ellis Island. It was a pretty garbled English that she spoke, with French inflections, and d's and z's impartially substituted for th's, and much confusion of syntax. And this, Duff kept thinking, this was the woman who had suffered every physical and moral horror that the atrocities of war and revolution could inflict. He could imagine no explanation for her. "It must be," he thought, "that the worst calamities can come like a blow on the head with a club. You go through them dazed. You don't realize them, and you come out of them blank."

Not that she looked exactly blank. She looked animated, but unworried, as if her animation were only the surface sparkle on a deep serenity. Even when she recalled a revolting agony of her past and Khalkoff's, there was something that the old tragedians called "the sublime" in her expression—in the beautiful reflection of remembered horror in her face. Duff could imagine her accepting any unspeakable thing as an inevitable aspect of life, regarding it calmly, and going on with a firm, light step, her head up, carrying herself like a young poet.

He listened to her account of Khalkoff's difficulties interest-edly, although he knew all about them already. He studied the papers that she had brought, and frowned and nodded like a judge. "I understand, "he said. "When Miss Parkins phoned that you wished to consult me, I got in touch with a friend of mine in the bureau here, and asked him a few questions." He tapped the papers with a portentous forefinger. "There's more in this than meets the eye."

"But, yes," the Princess agreed. "Surely yes. But what is it we don't know."

"It's something," said Duff, "that I would like to discuss with you in private."

She spoke a few words of Russian, pleasantly, to Khalkoff. Dottie Parkins had already risen. Khalkoff made a smiling, awk-ward bow. They went out unnoticed as the Princess leaned forward, innocently expectant, toward Duff, and Duff, resting his elbows on his desk, regarded her with a large inscrutable intentness.

"You have some letters?" he asked.

"Letters?" She did not seem to recall them.

"And a lawyer named Abe Enger has been trying to get them from you."

"But, of course," she said eagerly. "I am stupid. It is those letters, you think?"

"One of his men, a detective, was killed trying to find out who had them."

She opened her eyes very wide. "It is true, then? They did not know who he was. They feared he was a spy from Russia who follow them. It is not safe for anyone to follow men who are so nervous."

"Enger doesn't know who killed him but he knows it was one of your friends. He doesn't know who has those letters, but he knows it's some one in your circle. This man Enger is very power-ful, very determined, very unscrupulous. Starting with Khalkoff, he intends to deport everyone who can protect you, until he has you here alone to deal with."

"But how absurd it is," she protested. "They are nothing, these letters. They are foolish. This man—this big rich man—he is dy-ing in his own dullness and he come all alive to fall in love with me. He write me so pretty, like a boy, and so happy, and he is so well. If I am a doctor, how much does he not pay me for that mira-cle, because I bring him back to life. And do I ask him for money? No. No, never. To me he offer it, and I am meek. I have learn how it is to be humble. I accept the helps for those others who need helps. Like Vladim, these poor children, they must have foods. And then I find it is an insult, this money. He has a fear of me. It is the price of this fear he pays. He sends a man to buy from me his letters and I am in a rage. I say, 'Very well. For that insult he shall pay. He shall pay, every month, so much.' And I keep the letters. And he send this man to spy—"

Duff stopped her by merely reaching out his hand again to tap a finger on his desk. "This sort of thing will land you all in Russia—or in jail. Bring those letters to me. We can do better than blackmail with them."

After regarding him a moment, in a clairvoyant silence, studying him, she said: "Very good. I bring them. Now. Right away."

And she went out, without another word, quickly, her hat in her hand.

Duff called up his friend in the local bureau. "All right, Clem," he said. "It worked. Much obliged. I'll be in to see you, in a couple of days, as counsel for Khalkoff. Leave it lay." He phoned his secretary in an inner office: "Get me an appointment to see Abe Enger as soon as you can. Within an hour, if possible. It's important." He filed Khalkoff's papers in a private drawer, and then he went to his bookshelves and got a digest of the law on contracts. With this he sat down as studiously at his desk as a lawyer working out a brief. "I'll have to take a chance," he said to himself. "Enger won't suspect me. He'll think I'm just a dumb detective." And he drew up a written agreement, between Enger and himself, on his official letterhead.

His secretary reported his engagement with Enger. "Good enough." He began to walk restlessly up and down his room. "Enger," he was thinking, "spent his youth fighting the world to defend his mother. That's the key to him. He was a crook for her. He made himself rich for her. And he's continued the holdup for his wife and his children. He's been a criminal because he's never had any sense of responsibility to anyone but them. All right. That's where we can get him."

He was in this mood of happy confidence when the Princess returned, as placid now as a little Buddha, and produced the letters from an inside pocket of her cloak. She gave them to him without asking any explanations and without exacting any promises. And he made none. "Sit down a minute," he said. "I'm on my way to see Enger."

She sat down like a fatalist, relaxed, defenseless, her head resting against the back of the leather chair, as if all her anxieties were suspended. She saw him put her letters in his pocket. She saw him get his hat and coat. "Wait for me here," he said. "I'll not be long."

She replied, merely, "I wait."

He turned at the door, as if to say good-by to her. "Maybe it's what they call being an aristocrat," he said. "I call it being a good sport."

She made a reassuring gesture of dismissal, in silence.

IV

He was not worried by the prospect of confronting Enger. In the first place, his client in the bankruptcy investigation had notified him to drop the case, and that could only be because Enger had found a way to frighten the client off. "Abe won't be afraid of me," Duff thought. "He'll think he's tripped me up from behind, and that'll make him feel superior." In the second place, he was going, as he would have said, "to con a crook." "You have to be careful," he had learned, "when you undertake to work any mental sleight-of-hand on an honest man, because he's quite open and free to watch you, but a crook has something up his sleeve himself, and he's always so busy hiding it that he doesn't half notice what *you're* up to."

He was not worried by the prospect of confronting Enger, but it was necessary for the part he had to play that he should appear worried, so, in the interval between opening the door of Enger's waiting-room and being ushered into the inner office, he worked himself into an anxious state of mind, like an actor, in the wings, hypnotizing himself into the emotion of his role before he makes his entrance on the stage. He followed the office boy, frowning over his thoughts. He entered among Enger's bouquets absent-mindedly, with that look of the eye turned inward which sees its surroundings without observing them. He nodded to Enger mechanically and put down his hat, evidently unaware that Enger was watching him with a keen and curious alertness.

Neither spoke. Duff sat down and rubbed the palms of his hands together nervously. Enger cleared his throat. "Well," Duff said, "that's a fine nest of copperheads."

Enger asked, "How so?"

"Why," he complained, "they've all been through the god-awfulest atrocities in Russia, and they think no more of murder than they do of cabbage soup. Furthermore, they run together like a pack of wolves. A detective has about as much chance among them as a sheepdog. They were wise to my men the moment they saw them." He raised his troubled eyes to Enger—but Enger was straightening a photograph on his desk. "They're wise to you, too. There must be a leak in your office. They knew you'd put me on this job."

"They did?" Enger just breathed it and no more. "Are you sure?"

"I got a man in among them and that was the first thing he found out. They'd been tipped off, and they were watching for me."

Enger asked softly: "Are you sure the information didn't come from your own office?"

"No," Duff admitted. "I'm not. That's what worries me."

Enger sighed.

"Well," Duff said, "that doesn't matter. I can take care of myself, but *you've* got to look out for trouble. These people have Oriental minds. They're kind of devilish. They've got it planned out that if you injure them, they're going to hit you where you live."

"Where I live?"

"Yes. They say you've got a grandchild, and they figure that sticking a knife in you wouldn't hurt you half as much as having something happen to that baby. They've got a servant in there, in your house. I don't know which one it is, but it's some one that can reach the nursery. One of their gang's a bacteriologist. He once helped wipe out a whole Bolshevist army by infecting their wells with typhoid. They say he knows more about the germs of spinal meningitis than any other man in America. If that baby died of infantile paralysis, you'd never prove it on any of them."

In the sleight-of-hand which Duff was practicing on Enger, this bit of deceit about the baby and the bacteriologist was the cover for the whole trick. It was the bright object on which the audience was to fix its eyes while the magician, unnoticed, did his palming. Enger fixed his eyes on it, fascinated, very still, very pale. "How did you get hold of this?" he asked, under his voice.

"I found that a newspaper woman named Dottie Parkins was working with Sipiagin, writing her autobiography for a magazine. I knew her during the war. I was a Major in Military Intelligence and she did some investigating for us. She introduced me to Sipiagin as a lawyer. One of the outfit, a young violinist, was having trouble about his passport, and I helped him out of it, as his attorney. That let me in, on the inside, and I found that they're going to use these blackmailing letters in her autobiography. It's an ingenious trick. They're not giving the name of your client. They're printing the letters in full without any name, but they're playing up the whole incident humorously, in a way to arouse public curiosity, so that if they ever give out the name, later, there'll be twice the kick to it."

This also was a pure invention but Enger was too preoccupied to question it. He listened, silent.

"Furthermore, this Parkins woman has got a playwright and a producer interested in getting up a play about the Princess's adventures in America, and they propose to use your client as a central character. They're making him a Cabinet member. They're writing the play to help sell the autobiography. They're doing it all just to make money. Sipiagin doesn't need it for herself but she needs it for these people that she's helping. They'd starve if it wasn't for her. The funny thing is that this damn fool client of yours started the whole business. She'd no idea of blackmailing him on his letters. She'd never asked him for a cent. He'd been sending her money and she'd been using it for these starving refugees, and then he tried to buy the letters back from her, and she considered this an insult that no decent woman could forgive. She started in to make him pay for it, and he went to you, and your detective tried to steal the letters. Then she turned the whole thing over to some of her brigands and they stuck up your man. They didn't intend to kill him. They were only trying to frighten him, but he put up such a fight that they lost their tempers and knifed him. They think it's a war to the death now. They think you'll probably get some of them in the long run, and they're prepared to take their revenge any way they can. That's where the bacteriologist comes in. He's half crazy, I should say. He'll do anything mad. He's trying to get a job as keeper in the Zoo, where he won't have to associate with anything but animals."

Enger had listened with his eyes on a framed photograph of his grandchild that stood on his desk; and still regarding that smiling infant, he asked: "Which servant is it?"

"I don't know," said Duff, truthfully enough. "You have six in your town house?"

"Yes."

"This is your only grandchild?"

"Yes."

"The mother and father are both dead?"

"They were killed in a motor accident."

"He was your only son?"

"Yes."

"You've two daughters, but this'll be the only child to carry on the name of Enger."

"Yes."

"Well," Duff said, "that's the way they dope it." He sat back with an air of having laid all his cards on the table. "Now, Mr. Enger, if you want to go ahead and fight these people, that's up to you, but I don't want to lose any of my operatives. It's too hard training new ones. I had to withdraw them from the case. It was too damn dangerous. And I had to take on the job myself, to see if I couldn't make some compromise that would let me back out safely. It appeared that this Sipiagin woman once had her life saved by a big deaf mute that looked like me. She fell for me easily. I got her to retain me as a lawyer in the passport case for her violinist, and then, as their lawyer, I persuaded these people that they probably wouldn't make any big money out of their autobiography, and I pointed out to them that ninety per cent of the plays produced in New York failed to make a penny for anybody. All they wanted was money, to keep them from starving till they got on their feet, and I argued that they could sell the letters back to you for more money than they could make in any other way, if they promised not to use them in a book or in a play, and not to keep any photographed copies of them. They gave me their word for that, as their lawyer." He produced a packet of letters from his hip pocket. "And they gave me the letters to turn over to you on these terms." He drew a paper from the package. "This is a contract between me and you to the effect that in return for services received from the Sipiagin woman, you'll pay me fifteen hundred dollars a month for her from now on. I guarantee that these are all the letters she had, that she's kept no copies of them, and she'll make no use of them or reference to them, or to your client, in any way whatever, either publicly or privately." He passed the letters and the contract to Enger. "That's the best solution I could find for the situation."

Enger showed nothing more in the expression of his face than a good poker player shows when his opponent suddenly throws down a better hand than his and says "All right. I quit. You can have it." He took the letters, glanced through the dates on the envelopes, opened a drawer of his desk, and dropped the package in it. He took Duff's contract, spread it on his blotter, drummed on it a moment with reflective fingers while he read it, dipped his pen and signed it. When he looked up, at last, at Duff, his lips were working in a twisted suppression of a smile. "You're a first-class detective."

Duff nodded grimly. "You don't know the half of it."

"Maybe not." He gave Duff his contract. "I have a case here—"

"Not for me," Duff said, as he rose. "Not till you find out where the leak is in your office. I've just been two jumps ahead of murder, with these Russians, for the past two weeks. I don't need any more of it."

~ ~ ~

When he opened his office door, on his return, the Princess was still sitting, motionless, in her chair, with her eyes closed, as peacefully as if she were asleep. And in fact she *was* asleep, as it appeared as soon as he took a step into the room, for she started up at once, staring, and "Oh, Baba," she cried, "I dreamed they kill you." (Only, of course, as she pronounced the words they sounded like "Oh, Bah-bah, aie dreamed tay kale yoo.")

"Not while I have my mouth free," Duff replied. "They'll never kill me unless they gag me first. I can always talk them out of it. Here. Put this in your safety deposit box."

He gave her Enger's contract to read while he hung up his hat and coat.

"What is it?" she asked when she had read it.

"Well," he said, "Enger probably considers it a scrap of paper. What's a contract between him and me to pay you money? Am I going to enforce such a contract? Why should I? What he has overlooked is this: It's the law in the state of New York that if two parties make a contract for the benefit of a third, the third party can enforce the contract even when the two contracting parties are unwilling to carry it out. Understand? This is no longer a question of blackmail. That document gives you a legal claim on Enger for fifteen hundred dollars a month. You can take him into court at any time and make him pay it. All this, of course, is something that never occurred to me. I'm as innocent as I am simple. When I gave you that contract, I'd no idea that it was anything but a con game. When I find that you've taken it to another lawyer, I'll be so surprised that I'll be funny. Run along, now, young woman. Your troubles are over—your passport troubles with all the rest. I've scared Enger with a wild tale of how you and your friends intend to kill his grandchild if he bothers you any more. He thinks you're a gang of professional cutthroats and blackmailers."

"Extroudinary!" She said it with her mouth as round in wonder as her eyes. "You do this for us? You make yourself a go-between for money that you think is wicked? You make yourself an enemy, perhaps, in this man who is so powerful?"

"Leave that to me," Duff said. "I can handle him."

"Not so," replied the Princess. She tore the contract into little pieces and tossed them into Duff's waste-basket with an imperial gesture. "We have finish with his money. He have back his letters. It is all." She straightened her hat as if it were a crown. She wrapped her cloak about her regally. "To-night, we make a fiesta. We dine, we have musics, we sing. You will honor us?"

"Princess," said Duff, "I will honor you as the gamest woman I ever met."

THE

FOGULL

MURDER

THE FOGULL MURDER

I

DUFF, AS A DETECTIVE, had a modern theory of crime on which to work. Any crime, he held, always happened in two places. It occurred physically, but it also occurred mentally. It took place in the mind of the criminal, even before it got itself expressed in his act; and it left a trail in his mind that was much more obvious—if one could get an eye on it—than any trail that the police followed.

Unfortunately, with the Fogull murder, it seemed impossible to find any mind whatever involved in the affair. It was an idiotic crime. Apparently, it began as a burglary, but why it began as a burglary no one could make out. There was nothing in the house to steal, and after turning everything upside down, elaborately, the burglars took nothing much away. What could they have been looking for in Fogull's little bungalow?—a summer shack of four rooms, rented furnished by the Fogulls for the season, at Whytesand Beach, in a summer colony of frame cottages that had nothing in any of them to attract a burglar unless he were hungry enough to dynamite an icebox.

Fogull—George Sylvanus Fogull—was on the staff of the department of English literature in Columbia University, and his salary for a year would have made any ambitious burglar blush. His wife was an East Side girl who had been working her way through college, when he married her. She insisted that the burglars had taken all her jewelry, but the only things that she could prove to be really missing were her purse and her wedding ring. The burglars had apparently pulled the ring from her finger when they were tying her hands behind her back, after they had knocked her unconscious with a blow on the head. They had also taken Fogull's watch, an old-fashioned silver watch, given Fogull by his parents when he entered Harvard University, with honors in Greek and Latin. On its silver hunting case, there was engraved a Bible text, chosen by his father, the Rev. Anson Fogull: "Watch, for ye know not the day nor the hour." What any sensible burglar could do with that incriminating relic no one could imagine.

Nevertheless, to acquire this loot, as the tabloids called it, two men had apparently cut their way in through the wire screen of a kitchen door, in Fogull's bungalow, shot Fogull in the head as he sprang out of bed at them, knocked his wife down with a blow on the forehead when she rushed in from the sleeping porch to aid him, tied her hands behind her with a cord cut from the telephone that stood on Fogull's desk in the living-room, bound her legs with a strap from the carry-all in which Fogull had brought steamer rugs to the beach, gagged her with a towel and a rubber sponge from the bathroom, and then hastily clawed through every closet and drawer in the bedroom, the living-room, the dining-room and the kitchen, tossing out clothes on the floor from the dresser, and searching through the table linen in the sideboard, and even emptying a drawer of knives and forks and spoons on the kitchen table and leaving them there.

What had they been looking for? No one could suspect Fogull of having money or jewels concealed, and there was no possibility that he was involved in any melodramatic mystery about stolen documents, military blue prints, missing wills, plans for a Red plot against Wall Street, blackmailers' letters, counterfeit money, or anything intriguing of that sort. True, he had been at work on a mystery, but it was the mystery of Shakespeare's "The Phoenix and the Turtle." Some years before, he had come on a passage from Emerson in which the Concord philosopher declared that the world of scholarship would be grateful to anyone who could explain what Shakespeare's cryptic poem really meant. Fogull believed that he had found out. He was writing a monograph on "The Phoenix and the Turtle" to show how it derived from Chaucer's "Parlement of Foules" and to display his own astounding knowledge of the Elizabethan literature of England, France and Italy. This monograph was to add new laurels to his academic fame. He had been an authority on Milton. He had written a thesis on the classical allusions in Tennyson. Now he was deserting the classics for the romance languages and he was nervous in his new field. He had come to Whytesand Beach with a trunkful of notes, quotations, cross-references and literary parallels, and he had dedicated his summer to the solitary labor of stewing down this hash of scholarship into the fluent extract of erudition which he was to pour out in his book.

The burglars had scattered his notes on the grass rug of the little living-room and left them there. They had left Mrs. Fogull lying on the floor of the bedroom, bound, gagged and unconscious, in the dark. And they had left Fogull sprawled on his back in bed, his pajamas torn open at the neck, his bedclothes disordered from the struggle, and a bullet in his brain. The bullet had entered through his right eye. Powder marks showed that the revolver had been held close to his face, and he had evidently closed his eyes at the last moment, for the bullet had gone through his right eyelid.

II

The murder was discovered by a neighbor, a lawyer, a New York lawyer named Walden—Henry Thoreau Walden, of the firm of Wirtz, McManus, Greenberg, Lasker, Walden and Cole, no less.

Walden was a friend of the Fogulls. He had arranged to take them on a motor jaunt from Whytesand Beach to the Delaware Water Gap, that day; and since it was Sunday and the roads would be crowded with joyriders, he wished to make an early start. So he telephoned to the Fogulls at seven o'clock in the morning to waken them and start them preparing breakfast. He expected to have breakfast with them. He was a widower, with no children, alone in his cottage, which he occupied only during week-ends, camping out there without servants.

When he could not make the Fogulls answer the telephone, it alarmed him. He dressed and drove over to their bungalow in his touring car. His cottage was on the beach; theirs was a half-mile further inland on some filled ground that had been made by a land development company at the edge of a New Jersey marsh. He arrived at their cement walk within half an hour of the time he telephoned.

No one answered his knocking on the front door, so he went around to the back and found the screen door cut and unhooked. He passed through the disorder of the kitchen into the little hall, and he saw Mrs. Fogull's bare feet protruding from the door of the bedroom. She was lying across the threshold, on her face, in her nightgown. He saw that her hands were tied behind her and a strap buckled around her knees. That frightened him. He peered into the room. It was dark; the blinds were drawn; but he could see Fogull sprawled motionless on the bed. He retreated, at once, to the kitchen, without investigating, afraid to touch either of them. In the kitchen he recovered sufficiently to run to the next-door neighbor's and telephone the police.

Fortunately, he was a lawyer. He called up the state police as well as the local constable, and he phoned to the County Prosecutor who was a friend of his, and to a private detective whom he knew in New York. Until the police arrived, he would let no one

enter the Fogull cottage. "Fingerprints," he explained. He was too
sick and upset to say more. He was having difficulty breathing. He
kept striking himself on the upper buttons of his Norfolk jacket
and coughing, very pale. He was a man of forty, at least, rather
fleshy and gray-faced, in a linen golf hat and plus fours; and he
stood on the veranda steps like an officer of the law, and waved
aside all questions. "Murder," he said hoarsely. "Wait for the police. Fingerprints."

That was how it happened that Mrs. Fogull was still lying,
bound and gagged, in the bedroom, when two state troopers arrived on motorcycles and took charge. Walden led them into the
house by the back way and pointed to Mrs. Fogull's feet—from
the kitchen doorway—and went no further. Even when they found
that she was alive, he kept in the background, only handing them a
steamer rug to cover her with, after they had carried her into the
living-room and laid her on a sofa there. Standing in the hall door,
he watched them examining Fogull's body. When they turned to
him, at last, he told them how he had come there and discovered
the murder. They went back with him to Mrs. Fogull.

She had regained consciousness on the sofa, but she was still
dazed from the blow on her forehead that had bruised the skin and
raised a swelling. She had difficulty recalling what had happened.
In the middle of the night—she did not know at what hour—she
had been wakened by the report of the pistol in her husband's bedroom. She rushed in to him from the sleeping porch on the side of
the house, through the living-room and the hallway, and she was
met by a blow on the head, in the dark, as she stumbled across the
threshold of his room. She remembered nothing more. She saw
nobody. She heard nothing. Sometime in the early dawn, she regained consciousness to find herself bound and gagged. She raised
her aching head, saw Fogull on the bed motionless, knew that he
had been murdered—and fainted. When she came to again, she
was on the sofa where the police had laid her.

Naturally, she was in a state of collapse, trembling with exhaustion, her teeth chattering, her arms and legs numb from the cord
and the strap with which she had been bound, groaning when she
raised a feeble hand to the bruise on her forehead. She was a hand-
some, foreign-looking, dark young woman, obviously high-strung
and rather neurotic. The two troopers showed that they were suspicious of her. They began to question her inimically, and Walden
interfered at once.

"Just a moment," he said. "I'm a friend of this young woman and her husband. If you suspect that she killed him—and then gagged herself, and bound her hands behind her back and knocked herself unconscious with a blow on the head—that's your privilege. You can suspect what you please. But she's in no condition to be put through a third degree. She's still so dazed that she's liable to say anything. I'm a lawyer. I intend to act for her. I intend to protect her. She has rights that you'll have to respect, because I'm going to see that you respect them."

He said it insultingly and the two policemen bristled. One of them, a heavy dark Irishman, asked "Who the hell are you?"

Walden explained who he was. "I was the last person with this young couple, last night. I brought Mrs. Fogull home about eleven o'clock and I sat and talked for half an hour with her and her husband. If you think she killed him—"

"Who said we think she—"

"You show it in your manner. Naturally, when a man's killed, you suspect his wife. That's the sort of people you are. But if you think you can use any third-degree methods on her, you don't know your vegetables. You attempt anything illegal with her, and I'll have you both thrown out of your jobs."

"What's eatin' you?" the trooper growled. "We ain't doin' anything to—"

"No," said Walden. "That's the whole point. You're doing nothing to get hold of any evidence in the case. You don't even look for fingerprints. I watched you handling that strap that she was tied with. Did you take any precautions not to destroy the prints that might be on it? You did not. Instead of that, you started right in to third-degree her—"

The trooper began to lose his temper. "Third degree my ear! If she's so damn innocent, what makes you so—"

"Don't you worry about her innocence. She doesn't have to prove her innocence to you. You're not the judge and the Grand Jury and the County Prosecutor and all the rest of it. You're just a fool cop. You think you can start in browbeating and accusing everyone in sight five minutes after you come into a case like this. It's not your business to be accusing her or anybody else." He threw his hat across the room, striding up and down the floor, waving his hands excitedly, red with anger. Mrs. Fogull wept on the sofa. "You've been bawling out motorists on the street corner so long, that's all you're fit for. This isn't a traffic violation. This's a murder. You can't walk in here and stick your paw up and start bawling her out for a murder before you take the trouble to find out the first damn thing about it—"

The arrival of the County Prosecutor interrupted the row, but did not end it. He and the local constable had a warm lack of sympathy for the state police, and they took Walden's side in the argument without hearing what the troopers had to say. The County Prosecutor summoned a county detective. Walden's private detective arrived with an operative from New York. An officer of the state police brought in a state detective. And the quarrel which Walden had started with the trooper widened to a definite split between the state officials and the county officials on the conduct of the case.

The County Prosecutor, Abraham Ammon, was a successful local politician who had happened to study law. Like all successful politicians, he knew that success in politics depended on being religiously loyal to one's friends. Walden and he were friends of long standing, and he took Walden's side without a moment's hesitation. "It don't look to me like an inside job," he said.

He was a slow, bulky man with a face like Thomas Edison, a strong face, with a rugged look of country wisdom, but behind his profoundly judicial manner, he was rather dim-witted. He admired Henry Thoreau Walden as a clever Broadway lawyer who had an income of some fifty thousand dollars a year. He felt safe on Walden's side of the argument, and standing with his hat on the back of his head, pursing up his lips and puckering up his eyes reflectively, he remained immovably opposed to any action that might show an official suspicion of Mrs. Fogull.

"It don't look to me like an inside job," he decided. "You'll have to show me some evidence if you want to convince me. Meanwhile, this lady'll remain in my charge. Mine and Mr. Walden's. He's her lawyer. Any day you show me anything against her, I'll produce her."

By this time, the little bungalow was full of officials, policemen and detectives. They prowled about from room to room, peering into everything, poking about everywhere, looking for fingerprints indoors and footprints outdoors, and drawing aside in little private consultations of twos and threes, every now and then, to mutter to each other in guarded undertones. State troopers on the lawn kept off a crowd of neighbors who had gathered to stare and comment. Policemen at the front door and the back held in check two groups of reporters and camera men who were compelled to wait till the preliminary investigations ended. Mrs. Fogull lay on the sofa, under her steamer rug, her face to the wall, her back to the detectives, a handkerchief to her eyes. Walden stood over her, at the foot of her couch, his arms folded, at bay. The County Prosecutor defended them.

"Go ahead," he said, "and get your evidence. This lady's in my custody. I'll take her statement and all that. Charlie, get that body out o' here. I'll issue the order for an autopsy. Nobody's going to be arrested till I see something we can hold them on. There's going to be no grandstanding in this case, and it isn't going to be tried in the newspapers. This county isn't going to start another Hall-Mills circus, not if *I* know it."

III

As the upshot of it all, Mrs. Fogull was not put through any third degree. She was taken to the County Hospital and isolated in a private room, with two nurses to take care of her, and one of Ammon's deputies at her door. Walden was allowed to return to his cottage on the beach, where he remained with a bodyguard of private detectives to protect him—and his servants from New York to make him comfortable. He refused to be interviewed. He gave out, through Ammon, a sworn statement of how he had discovered the murder; and Mrs. Fogull made a similar statement covering everything that she professed to know. That was all.

That was all from them, and from the County Prosecutor, but it did not end the matter. It did not more than begin it. The state troopers, and after them the newspaper men, regarded the evidence of burglary with suspicion. The drawers and closets had been emptied out too ostentatiously. The knives and forks and spoons on the kitchen table were absurd. If Fogull had been shot with his eyes closed, he might have been killed in his sleep; the torn pajamas and the tossed bedclothes might have been arranged to show signs of a struggle that had never occurred. Did the mild bruise and swelling on Mrs. Fogull's forehead indicate a blow sufficiently violent to leave her unconscious for a whole night? Or was her injury as amateur and "phoney" as the disorder of the rooms? Would real burglars carry off a wedding ring and an old silver watch? Or were these ridiculous thefts also phoney and contrived? Had Fogull been killed by burglars or by some one who had tried to set the scene to make it look like a burglary? Had Mrs. Fogull, and perhaps a lover, really committed the crime and plotted, in this way, to disguise it?

The papers were suffering from a summer shortage of exciting news and they began to play up the Fogull murder on the front page. They found that Fogull was a distinguished scholar, an authority on Shakespeare, engaged in original research and about to become world-famous by announcing an astonishing discovery which he had just made. Absorbed in his studies, he had rather neglected his young and beautiful wife. She had been dancing, flirting, joyriding, and enjoying herself on beach parties at night, while Fogull sat poring over his books and his manuscripts, alone, in the bare study of his little summer cottage. On the night of the murder, she had come home late, from a Saturday dance, with Henry Thoreau Walden, a rich widower, a clubman, a devotee of New York night life, in his high-powered car. Had her husband quarreled with them on their return? Had he denounced Walden? Had he refused to let them go together on the day-long joyride which they had planned for Sunday, instead of attending church? Had a wife and a lover murdered a jealous husband in a quarrel and then arranged the evidences of a burglary to hide their crime?

These were questions that could not be asked too openly in print, but they could be hinted at in reports that invented neighborhood gossip for the purpose, and gave "theories" on which the authorities were working, and quoted friends of Fogull who did not wish their names used. The reporters also interviewed anonymous friends of Walden who involved him in the case by defending him.

He and the Fogulls had dined together at the neighboring country club of Summerton on the night of the murder. When the dancing began, Walden motored Fogull back to his Shakespearean studies and then rejoined Mrs. Fogull at the dance. She and Walden left early. No one knew quite when. But they were heard returning to the Fogull bungalow about eleven-thirty, and a neighbor saw Walden drive away soon after twelve. The Fogull bungalow was isolated, and no one would have heard a quarrel if it had occurred, but there certainly had been no appearance of ill-feeling between the three at dinner, and if Fogull had been jealous of his wife would he have left her at the dance and let Walden motor him home?

There was nothing on which to base a suspicion of Walden, really, except the lack of an excuse for the burglary, and this lack was suddenly supplied by a newspaper story which rescued the whole case from suburban commonplace and put it into melodrama. Fogull had made a great Shakespearean discovery. He had been about to write a book concerning it. He had found a first edition of one of Shakespeare's plays, annotated and corrected by a contemporary, and he had proved that these notes were in Shakespeare's own handwriting. Such a volume was priceless. It was worth a fortune. It was so valuable that Fogull had kept his possession of it a guarded secret. He had concealed it even from his wife. It had worried him, like a Rajah's diamond, hidden in his bungalow, worth a million dollars if he could prove its authenticity.

And that was what the burglars had been looking for. And that was what they had found. They had turned the house upside down, in search of it. Having killed Fogull and gagged and bound his wife, they ransacked the place till they located the book, and then they carried off Fogull's watch and his wife's wedding ring so as to conceal the fact that it was the book they had been looking for.

This theory of the case was supposed to have come from the detective bureau that was investigating on Mrs. Fogull's behalf, but when the reporters interviewed the head of the bureau, he refused either to confirm or deny the story. "It's possible," he said. "Quite possible. It's more possible that the criminals had heard some such report about Prof. Fogull's studies and broke into the house for that reason. We've been working on the theory that there was some mistake of the kind—that the burglars broke into the wrong house. There's been a lot of bootlegging down that coast, around Whytesand, and two gangs of bootleggers have been quarreling about the territory. We're inclined to think that one of these gangs broke into Prof. Fogull's bungalow by mistake, in search of a bootlegger who had double-crossed them. We believe they shot Fogull, thinking he was this man, and then staged the burglary to cover their tracks."

In any event, these theories served to divert public suspicion from Walden and Mrs. Fogull, and when a Grand Jury failed to find any evidence against them, no one was indignant. The County Prosecutor announced that he would continue to pursue the case until the criminals were brought to justice. Meanwhile he allowed Mrs. Fogull to retire from public view, in the care of a married sister. Walden returned to his apartments in New York. The Fogull murder disappeared from the newspapers, and another unsolved murder mystery was added to the long list of them that had delighted and baffled the newspaper fans.

IV

It was at this point in the proceedings that Duff came into the case, under cover, and without ever making a public appearance in it. And it was at this point that he solved it, at his desk, by the application of his vague theory of the dual nature of crime.

He was called into the case by a telephone message from an attorney for the life insurance company with whom the murdered man had been insured for five thousand dollars. "Duff," he said, "you've read about this Fogull murder, over in Jersey? Well, I'm sending down to you a friend of Fogull's who seems to know something about it. I want you to follow it up for us if you will."

Duff asked: "When'll he be here?"

"Whenever you say."

"Within the next two hours?"

"Easily."

"All right. Tell him eleven-thirty. What's his name?"

"Theodore Hansen."

"Thanks. All right. Good-by."

He hung up, and dismissed the matter from his mind, and continued reading a file of operatives' reports on a bribery investigation. He knew nothing about the Fogull case except what he had read in the newspapers—that Fogull had been killed by burglars apparently, that his wife had been suspected because the details of the burglary were unconvincing, that the local gossip accused her of having a love affair with a New York lawyer named Walden. He knew who Walden was. He did not believe that Walden was fool enough to get himself implicated in a murder. Still, you could never tell; he might have been drinking.

He said, into his office phone, absent-mindedly, his eyes on the typewritten report: "A man named Theodore Hansen has an appointment with me at eleven-thirty. Send him right in."

There was only one thing about the murder that stuck in his mind: the bullet that killed Fogull had passed through his closed eyelid. That seemed to Duff sufficient proof that Fogull had been shot in his sleep. He would never have closed his eyes, in a struggle, to shut out the sight of a pistol at his head. Never. He would have been staring, wide-eyed with horror. Unless he had fainted? Would Fogull have fainted?

Well, perhaps this Theodore Hansen could tell him.

He rang for a stenographer and began to dictate a summary of his operatives' reports on the bribery investigation, like a lawyer preparing a brief from a transcript of testimony, humped over his papers studiously, working his heavy eyebrows, sucking in his lips. It was regular routine. He conducted most of his cases, in this way, from his seat at his desk, laying out the general strategy of an investigation with his office manager, assigning to his operatives their part in the campaign, plotting out their tactics with them individually, receiving their reports and directing their movements from day to day, and remaining as far from the scene of action usually as the commander-in-chief from the front-line trenches. And he was often the only person in the office who knew what the battle was about. He arranged with his detectives what they were to do, without explaining to them why they did it. They made their separate reports to him, unaware of what part they played in the general scheme of affairs. He summarized their findings in the end, fitting the pieces of the case together like a jigsaw puzzle of which only he knew the whole design. That reduced the danger of any office leak. By the time he came to dictate his summary to a stenographer, it was all over but the shouting.

He was still busy summarizing, when Hansen was announced by phone from the outer office. "Send him in," he said. He nodded to the girl. "Transcribe what you've got there and we'll finish later." He lay back in his chair and stretched enormously, as cramped as a caged bear. As he came out of a vast yawn, his door opened and he sat up to meet the Fogull murder.

It entered in the person of a near-sighted and scholastic-looking man, in rubbers and a faded mackintosh, carrying an unnecessary umbrella against a rain that had not arrived. He stood with his hand on the doorknob, till he saw Duff at the far end of the office behind his desk. Then he closed the door, his hand behind him, and with his eyes fixed on Duff through the thick lenses of his nose-glasses, he came forward slowly, as if he were feeling his way with his feet.

"He's a Swede," Duff thought. "A professor, I should say. Looks as if he'd just escaped from a library."

He was not an old man, though he stooped and shuffled a little as he walked. His hair was cut so close that his head looked as if it had been shaved. His necktie was awry under an obsolete wing-collar. But all that was unimportant. Obviously, he never gave a thought to his appearance. His whole mind was in his eyes, concentrated there, so that he was unaware of himself or his surroundings or anything else except the problem which he studied through his heavy lenses, thoughtfully intent.

That problem, at the moment, was Duff. And Duff, after his first quick glance at the man's indifferent clothes, was caught and held by the silent gaze of his protruding eyes. Magnified by his glasses, unblinking, in a set stare, they were as prominent as the eyes of a crab. They remained fixed on Duff while his hands laid his hat and his umbrella on Duff's desk, blindly, and drew a memo pad from his breast pocket. He brought the paper up swiftly to a close focus against his nose, withdrew it, stared at Duff a moment, and then said: "I'm a chemist."

Duff nodded. "Sit down."

There was a chair beside the desk. He drew it up nearer to Duff, sat down on the edge of it, and leaning forward, to bring himself still closer, he repeated: "I'm a chemist. In charge of the research department of Bender and Roth. By-products." He spoke almost in a whisper, moving his lips very little—pale lips in a pudgy pale face, without eyebrows, with colorless eyelashes, so that all his features looked as if they had been chemically bleached and devitalized. He glanced at his notes. He regarded Duff in silence. "I first met George Fogull in a lecture room, at Harvard, where he happened to sit beside me. We walked down the street together. He lived in my direction. Past the house where I boarded. Frequently thereafter. I got to know him very well."

He paused and waited. Duff said nothing. He consulted his notes. "I came to New York. To seek a position. In commercial chemistry. He came, too. He took a post-graduate course at Columbia University, on a scholarship. We roomed together. With a German family, up at Morningside. We were poor.

"We were there a long time. Five or six years. I found my work. Commercial chemistry. He became an instructor. In English literature. A lecturer. He had high ideals. Scientific ideals. He wished to apply the methods of pure science to research in English literature. He was making a name for himself."

He had finished the first page of his notes, and having laid it, face down, on the desk, he paused to gaze unblinkingly at Duff, as if he were considering the effect of his revelations on his audience. Duff nodded. "Go ahead."

He glanced at his notes. "Now," he said. He raised his hand, to make his point with an arresting forefinger. "He met a girl in his classes. One Ruby Anderson. It couldn't be her name. A translation perhaps. Her people, she said, were dead. She was working her way through college. A Russian. From the East Side. Liberal. Radical. Emancipated. She was living her own life. She came to consult him in his office. In his study. About obscurities in the scenes of Elizabethan drama. He was amused. Contemptuous."

He put down his notes. "I'm unable to give the details of their intimacy. I can give my interpretation of it."

"Go ahead."

"She opposed his ideal of scientific research in the study of literature. She argued that literature could be appreciated only by an understanding of life. Through experience. By living."

"I see."

"She presented herself as an emancipated woman. Living independently, like a man. She invited him into an adventure with her. In which he was to have no responsibility. An adventure in living. She was ambitious to become a writer. So she said. She wished to live, in order to have something to write about. She argued that *he* needed to live so as to appreciate what others had written about life."

"And he fell for that?" Duff asked.

"In time. This went on, you understand, over a long period. Without my knowledge. He didn't tell me. At first, yes. To begin with, he confided in me. We laughed together. He thought her absurd. Emotionally unstable. Russian. Then he talked no more about her. I wasn't aware that he continued seeing her. I had to leave town. To go West. For the firm. And when I came back, I found him worried."

"I see. Worried, eh?"

"Yes. She'd been very radical. She'd a theory that every woman had a right to be a mother. Whether she was married or not. An inalienable right. But now she argued that she didn't care about herself, but she couldn't let the child start disgraced. Illegitimate."

"Naturally."

"He would be destroyed, with the college authorities, if it were known. He'd lose his position. He had to marry her."

"Well," Duff said, "she's not the first emancipated foreigner who caught a good Nordic in that trap. So he married her, eh?"

"He married her."

"They never had any children, did they?"

"No. But don't misunderstand. He thought she'd just lost her head. Frightened. Temporarily. He was in love with her. She was a handsome girl. Vital. Temperamental. He was a gentleman. He had high ideals. Of responsibility to women. He didn't see it as a trick."

"You did?"

"Yes. I disliked her. She disliked me. I knew it was a trick. When I saw how he felt about her, I said nothing."

"And when they were married—then what happened?"

"She was ambitious. She set herself to destroy his ideals of scholarship. Of research. She wanted him to make money. To write for money. She never let him alone. With his work. Insidiously. Persistently. She kept at him."

"And this man Walden?"

"I don't know. She separated us. I didn't see them any more. She answered the telephone when I called up their apartment. She was brusque. I didn't wish—to intrude."

He waited a long time, watching Duff, as if he had come to the end of his story. "Well," Duff said at last, "and how about this murder?"

"I don't know." He put his hand to his breast pocket and drew out an envelope. "I hadn't seen them. Or heard of them. Not for months. I didn't even know that they'd rented this cottage. For the summer. At Whytesand Beach. Then he wrote me this note. That he was coming to town. For the day. And would I meet him? For luncheon? At the Faculty Club?"

Duff took the note from its envelope. It was scrawled in a spidery handwriting on a sheet of ordinary letter paper. He kept turning it over in his fingers while Hansen continued: "He said nothing at luncheon. We talked of everything else except her. Except his marriage. Except his life. But I knew there was something he wanted to tell me. And after luncheon I walked with him. Over toward Morningside Heights. Till we came to the railing overlooking the Park. Where he stopped."

He took off his glasses and began to polish them with a corner of his handkerchief, closing his eyes. "We could see the house. Below us there. Where we used to live. He began to cry. He'd been happy there. His life was wrecked. She'd destroyed his feeling for his work. His enthusiasm. His ambition. She'd deceived him about money. Pretending she earned it. She'd borrowed it. She'd taken it from this man Walden. Her lover. Even the rent for the bungalow they were living in. At Whytesand.

"He hadn't told her he knew. He discovered it, accidentally. He was afraid. A horrible feeling. Of impending tragedy hanging over him. Something awful was going to happen. He wanted to know. What could he do? He wanted help. He wanted me to help him."

He was struggling against tears, wiping his glasses instead of his eyes, forcing his voice through a choked throat, his head bowed, unable to look up at Duff. "He was still in love with her. He'd been hoping she'd find out that this man Walden—didn't love her. He didn't blame her. They'd been poor. She was ambitious. This man Walden—he was rich. She'd been using the money. Not on herself. She'd bought Fogull things. She'd been kinder. She'd worked hard around the bungalow. Fixing it up. Happy."

Duff interrupted coldly, "Just a minute. You say he thought something was going to happen. What did he think it was?"

He looked at Duff unseeingly, trying to focus his weak eyes, blinking. He swallowed. He said hoarsely, "Death."

"Did he think they were going to kill him?"

"I don't know. It was just—It was just—It was just a premonition. A dream."

"A dream?"

"Yes."

"You mean, in his sleep? A real dream?"

He nodded.

"Did he tell you what that dream was?"

"Yes."

"Can you remember it?"

He put on his glasses again and regarded Duff without seeing him. "Yes. He was being pursued by something. He didn't know what. It was something that would kill him. And he was himself pursuing something. Something that would save him. It seemed to him that it was his soul that he was pursuing. And he was surrounded by immense cylinders, revolving, and flashing lights. They made a deafening roar and a glare that blinded him.

"He escaped into a tunnel, underground. It led down into rooms. Elizabethan rooms that were hung with tapestries and furnished like palaces. Then he came to places that were like Greek and Roman temples. Further on, they were just caves. Prehistoric. And he hurried through them, pursued by something that would kill him and pursuing whatever it was that would save him if he could catch up to it. And then he saw it. It was a beautiful woman standing on the edge of an abyss. And he caught her in his arms and jumped into the—the chasm."

"Just a minute," Duff said. "Did he recognize this woman?"

"No. At first, he thought it was his wife. And then he saw it wasn't. It seemed to be his own soul."

"Good!" Duff chuckled. "Congratulations." He held out his hand. "You've solved the Fogull murder."

For the moment, evidently, Hansen suspected some jocular sarcasm, and he regarded Duff with all the doubtfulness of a literal-minded man who had no sense of humor himself and distrusted it in others. He did not take the hand outstretched across the desk to him. He asked, "How? How have I?"

Duff rose, beaming. "I'll tell you later. For the time being, not a word to anyone. Go back to your office. Don't say you've seen me. Keep absolutely quiet, you understand. I want to get this man Walden."

Hansen did not move. "But I haven't," he said, "I haven't finished."

"Yes, you have," Duff assured him. "You've finished. You've told the whole story." He gathered up Hansen's notes. "Don't forget these. Take them with you. Leave me the letter from Fogull. I want to use that." He all but put Hansen's notes in his pocket for him. He walked around the desk to give him his hat. "You've solved the whole mystery. You're wonderful. I'll explain it to you later." He patted Hansen on the back with a hand that urged him to his feet, and, as Hansen rose reluctantly, he gave him his umbrella. "You'd better go out this way." He led Hansen back to the door through which he had entered. "Be sure not to tell anyone you've consulted me. That's important, you understand. Most important. I'll get in touch with you in a day or two, as soon as I've seen this man Walden." He opened the door and encouraged the bewildered Hansen across the threshold. "In a day or two, you understand. In a day or two." The closing door caught Hansen, still hesitating, and gently propelled him into the outer office.

Duff hurried back to his desk phone. "Send Bennie in here," he ordered. "Right away."

Bennie was the bookkeeper, an old operative, too rheumatic for foot work, who had retired to a high stool. He came in softly, sniffling with a cold in the head, his spectacles in his hand. "Look at this handwriting, Bennie," Duff said. And Bennie, with an air of professional benevolence, took Fogull's note to Theodore Hansen and blinked at it silently.

"Can you do me a letter in that hand, d'you think? On paper like that? So I can say it came out of this envelope?"

Bennie studied it. "Yes," he said. "I think so, gov'ner. It's just reg'lar paper. 'Lowland Linen,' I should say. The kind you buy in a drug store. It's written with a fountain pen. I can do it."

"Good. Sit down and make a note. Here's what I want you to write." He took a few turns up and down the office, stood a moment looking out the window, and came back to his desk: " 'Dear Theo: This is to say good-by. It is the only way out of all this trouble. Everybody will be better off without me. You are the only person in the world whom I leave with regret, now that my mother is gone. Do not grieve for me. I am going happily. My work—my life—everything is destroyed. Ruby will be taken care of. She has found some one who can do it better than I. I am going to give her a chance to be happy.' And sign it the way that note's signed."

V

Some three days later, on what the poets call a cool September morn, Duff was waiting in the outer office of Wirtz, McManus, Greenberg, Lasker, Walden and Cole, with a leather portfolio on his lap, in the guise of a claim adjuster from the insurance company, waiting to see Henry Thoreau Walden as the lawyer of Mrs. Fogull. He had calculated that Walden would keep him waiting at least half an hour—to show that he was not alarmed by the visit—and he had brought with him all the records and reports that he had been able to gather about the Fogull murder, in the days that had passed since he had seen Hansen. He read them over, to refresh his memory, as patient as if he had come to try to sell a policy to Walden.

There was nothing in the outer office that he needed to notice. It was as stereotyped as a Broadway straw hat. It was the fashionable, the accepted, the required reception room of every big law firm in the Blackstone building or any other modern office building on Manhattan Island. It had its inevitable green carpet, and its padded leather chairs, and its indirect lighting, and its pictures of Lincoln and Chief Justice Fuller and Lord Shaftesbury, and the ruins of the Parthenon at Athens and the Coliseum at Rome. Some supply companies, he knew, must make a business of furnishing law offices, as a barber's supply company dictates the chairs and mirrors of the American barber shop. They had given Walden and his partners their best line of legal atmosphere in furnishings.

And there was nothing about the waiting clients to interest Duff. He was familiar with the business of these wholesale law firms in which a staff of a half-dozen partners, a score of assistants, and a hundred clerks, handle every conceivable sort of case as efficiently as a staff of doctors and internes and nurses in a hospital. He went on reading the papers from his portfolio till one of the office girls came to tell him that Walden was free to receive him, and he followed her into an inner corridor, his hat in his hand, his briefcase under his arm, busily absorbed and absent-minded.

Walden's office had also been furnished from a catalogue, but he had added to its conventional engravings a few impressionistic landscapes in oil of a modern school not too extreme. He did not rise to greet Duff. He sat in his padded swivel chair, grasping the arms firmly, backed by the dignity of his profession and his own taste in art as a man of the world.

Duff sat down meekly by the desk, put his hat on the floor and nursed the portfolio on his knees. "We're aware," he said without any preliminaries, "that your client, Mrs. Fogull, hasn't pressed her claim for the insurance on her husband's life, but we've been making an investigation of his so-called murder, in preparation for the day when the matter'll come up for adjustment, and I'm here to lay the result of our inquiry before you, Mr. Walden, as her lawyer, so that you'll understand exactly where we stand."

He gave it oratorically, as if it were a set speech which he had prepared, and, at the same time, in the pauses between his rotund phrases, he opened his portfolio and took out his papers. Walden listened, as silent as a judge, withdrawn, indifferent, inscrutable.

"The policy, as you know," said Duff, "is small, but it provides a double indemnity in case of accidental death—which would become operative if he were killed by burglars—and it contains a clause excepting suicide as a recoverable—er—cause of death." He drew out the letter, which Bennie had forged for him, from the envelope which Fogull had addressed. "The deceased had one intimate friend, named Theodore Hansen, whom he'd known in his college days—at Harvard—and with whom he'd roomed for years after he came to Columbia University, in this city. He wrote a letter to this man Hansen, some two days before his death—judging by the postmark on the envelope—but Mr. Hansen, at the time, was in the West, on business—he's a chemist, with the Bender and Roth Company here—and there was no one in his apartment to redirect his mail to him, so he didn't receive this letter until he returned to town, about six weeks later."

He passed the letter and the envelope to Walden, who took them grudgingly and read them both without remark.

"This letter," Duff continued suavely, "is pretty good evidence that Fogull killed himself, and if the claim for insurance is pressed, we intend to argue that he did in fact shoot himself on the night of the supposed burglary—that he lay down on his bed, put the revolver to his forehead, and closed his eyes and that his hand faltered after his eyes were closed so that the bullet passed through his closed eyelid instead of through his temple, as he intended. That, we shall maintain, is the only way in which anyone can account for this peculiar detail of his death."

Walden flicked the letter and the envelope across the desk to him without a word and settled back again in his chair.

"We shall then seek to prove that when Mrs. Fogull found him dead in bed, he had left a note beside him, similar perhaps to this, blaming her for his death and involving you in the scandal. We find that after you left the dance at the country club with her, you drove her to Foster's Gardens where you both had a number of drinks. We'll admit that she may have been somewhat intoxicated when she conceived and carried out a scheme to escape the scandal of her husband's suicide by pretending that he had been killed by burglars. We're aware that she was guilty of no crime in staging this pretense of murder, but it becomes a fraud if you attempt to collect insurance on his death, and we'll certainly resist it in court to the best of our ability."

Walden nodded grimly. "You've given yourself a lot of unnecessary trouble. No one's trying to collect insurance, that I know of."

Duff replaced the Fogull letter in his portfolio and rose briskly. "That's all I wished to know. Good day."

Walden watched him in silence. To Duff, it was the silence of accepted guilt, and he made no attempt to break it. He tucked his portfolio under his arm, took up his hat, and stood challenging Walden with an inquiring eye.

"Are you going to show that letter to the authorities?" Walden asked.

"Not if you say the case's closed."

"It's closed as far as we're concerned, and I don't want it reopened."

Duff put down his hat again. "Will you tell me one thing? What did she do with that other letter?"

"What other letter?"

"The letter he wrote to her, before he shot himself."

Walden sat tight a moment, still grasping the arms of his chair. Suddenly he threw out both hands in a gesture of convulsive impatience and disgust. "Damn her," he said, "she'd burned it. Now get out of here. Get to hell out of here."

Duff put on his hat. "Tell me one thing more. Why did you—?"

"I won't," he shouted hoarsely. "I won't. Go away. Go away." And jumping up from his chair, he hurried from the office through an inner door, and slammed it shut behind him.

~ ~ ~

"And you mean to tell me," said the lawyer for the insurance company, "that as shrewd a man as Walden let himself in for a charge of murder in order to escape the scandal of a suicide?"

"No," Duff answered, "I don't. I'm sure of only one thing, and that is, that Fogull killed himself. About the rest of it, you know as much as I do. It may have happened any one of several ways. My guess is this:

"Fogull wasn't dead that night, when they returned from the dance. He didn't kill himself until after Walden had left for home and she had gone to bed on the sleeping-porch. She was wakened, as she said she was, by the sound of a shot, and she ran to his bedroom and found him dying with some sort of letter beside him, accusing her and Walden. She saw she'd lose Walden if she got him involved in any such scandal, so the first damn fool thing she did was to destroy the letter. Then she realized that wasn't enough. She'd have to conceal that it was a suicide at all. And she'd have to conceal it from Walden, so as to take no chance of losing him. She must have felt that Fogull had tried to destroy her by committing hari-kari on her doorstep, and she went to work to outwit him by making it look like a murder and a burglary.

"She probably took the revolver and the watch and her wedding ring and her purse, and sank them all somewhere, in that salt marsh, out beside their bungalow. And she upset the house, and tore Fogull's pajamas at the neck, and banged up her head and strapped her legs—"

"And tied her hands behind her back?" the lawyer put in.

Duff laughed. "The human mind's funny, isn't it? That whole process gets run together some way, and the mind doesn't ever think to separate it. It's like sleight-of-hand."

"What do you mean?"

"Simply this: I believe Walden told the truth about the way he found those bodies. He was so scared he thought they were both dead. That's what he reported, over the phone, to everybody, including his own detective. But then, there's a hole in his story. He went back to the Fogull bungalow, and he was there for at least fifteen minutes before any of the neighbors got dressed enough to come and see what was going on. I believe that during this interval he saw that Mrs. Fogull wasn't dead, that her hands weren't properly tied, and that she had obviously faked the burglary.

"I take it he realized instantly what she'd let herself in for. The police were on their way. He hadn't time to turn around. The only thing he could do was what he *did* do. He saw he was in it, up to his neck. He had to go through with it and help save her. So he tied her hands—and he was so mad at her he tied them hard enough to cut her wrists—and he took her part against the police, and saved her from the third degree, and pulled her out of the hole."

"Well," the lawyer conceded, "that may be all true, but I still don't see what first made you think that Fogull had killed himself."

Duff grinned. "I'm ashamed to tell you it was a dream."

"You dreamed it?"

"No. Fogull did. Two days before his death, he had a dream that showed he was likely to kill himself."

"Are you trying to tell me you could know *that* from a dream?"

"Maybe I wouldn't have," Duff admitted, "if it hadn't been for a curious coincidence. I've an old friend, a doctor, a psychiatrist, and a few months ago he came to me for help with a patient. This patient, he said, was going to kill himself but didn't *know* it, and when I said, 'If he doesn't know it, how the devil do *you?*' he said he could tell it from the man's dreams.

"He was a landscape artist, it seemed, an impractical sort of guy. Life had been pretty difficult for him every way, and now he'd found out that his wife was unfaithful to him, and it had shot him all to pieces. 'If I warn him that he's in danger of suicide,' my doctor friend argued, 'I may be accused of giving him the suggestion. I want you to help me get up some little plot to convince him that his wife's all right—or something like that.' And while we were trying to work out some way to do it, the man shot himself."

"Aie! Aie!" the lawyer said. "There's a story."

"Yes," said Duff, "and the funny thing *is* that this dream of Fogull's was exactly the same kind of dream. It showed him kind of lost and bewildered among a lot of noisy machines and revolving lights—as if he saw our civilization that way, all noise and glare and machinery—and he escaped it by going into the past, into Elizabethan times and beyond that, through Roman and Greek days, into something prehistoric. It was what they call a regression. The thing looked as if he felt he had lost his soul and he was trying to find it. He was trying to find it in the love of his wife, and finally he thinks he sees her, a beautiful woman, standing on the edge of an abyss, but it isn't her. It's his soul. He grabs it in his arms and jumps into the abyss with it. Driven in on himself by this machine civilization of ours, and by the failure of his wife to meet him in the historical work into which he tries to escape, he ends by withdrawing from life entirely. He takes his soul in his arms and dies.

"I'm not a dream interpreter, but that's the way it looked to me. I took the chance that it meant Fogull had killed himself. And evidently that's just what it *did* mean, see?"

THE

HEFFLIN

FUND

THE HEFFLIN FUND

I

DUFF DID NOT TAKE the Hefflin case seriously, at first. It did not come to him through the proper door. One of his office staff, a Mrs. Cooley, brought it to him, on behalf of a friend of hers: and he listened to her as a doctor might listen to one of his nurses reporting a friend's symptoms. "Bring her in," he said cheerfully, "and let's look her over. She may be dreaming." But when Mrs. Cooley went back to the filing room and produced not only her friend Mollie Simpson—who was a stenographer—but Mollie Simpson's employer, who was Mary Bryant, Duff took a look at Mary Bryant and stood up at his desk to meet her, interested.

She was obviously no dreamer. She was a large and matronly young woman, quietly dressed in a mode of expensive simplicity. She entered Duff's office with an air of being the placid center of her surroundings. And she regarded Duff as if he were the most interesting object in those surroundings, but not permanently important to her way of thinking. Her gaze was direct but unconcerned. She greeted him in a polite murmur and gave him a firm hand. When she sat down, at his invitation, it was with a sort of old-fashioned dignity, completely self-possessed.

He expected Mollie Simpson to supply the voice in their consultation—for Miss Simpson was an alert and nervous young thing in bright colors, and she sat on the edge of her chair as if she were about to spring forward into the conversation at the first word. But when he said, on the rising inflection of a query, "I understand that you're worried about your aunt?" Miss Bryant answered quietly, "She's my great-aunt—my father's aunt. She's seventy-six years old." And, from that beginning, throughout the whole interview, it was she who answered Duff and explained the case to him, in an even flow of narrative, with scarcely a word from her eager secretary, who listened like an admiring younger sister.

The great-aunt, a Mrs. Newton P. Hefflin, was a wealthy and eccentric widow who had lived alone for many years in a Victorian brownstone "mansion" on Madison Avenue near Forty-second Street. "About five years ago," Mary Bryant said, "she sent for me, because she saw my picture in a newspaper—it was printed in connection with the campaign for woman suffrage—and she asked me if I'd live with her as a sort of a paid companion. My home is in Weehawken. I had already planned to come to New York on work of my own, and we agreed that I should live with her and be free to attend to my private affairs."

Mrs. Hefflin had quarreled with all her relatives. She had no friends. She was impatient and domineering and bad-tempered, even with her old servants. "I know that this is quite incredible," Mary Bryant said, "but she was so lonely in her home, before she sent for me, that she used to walk to the Grand Central Station, every morning after breakfast, and read her paper in the waiting-room, so as to have people around her."

It was there, in the Grand Central Station, that she first encountered a starving musician named Michael Raffaelli Coombs, who came into the waiting-room on a December morning to warm himself. "I don't know how they met," Mary Bryant said. "She never speaks to strangers. She's always very suspicious of people. And she never gives money to street beggars. She believes they're all impostors."

Soon after Mary Bryant came to live with Mrs. Hefflin, Michael Raffaelli Coombs was added to the establishment as a sort of secretary and court musician. He persuaded Mrs. Hefflin to found a "Hefflin Fund" for American music, under his management, and he had her employ Mollie Simpson as a stenographer on correspondence connected with the affairs of this Fund. Mollie Simpson and Mary Bryant at once became friends and confidantes, and among their confidences they shared a common suspicion of Michael Raffaelli Coombs.

"The other day," Mary Bryant said guardedly, "Miss Simpson found in his desk a book called 'Questioned Documents.' It's a book about forgeries and fraudulent wills—"

"Yes. I know it," Duff cut in, as if he were unaware of her implication that Coombs was perhaps preparing to forge a will for Mrs. Hefflin. "Tell me. Does Mrs. Hefflin go to church?"

"No," Mary Bryant said. "She's not orthodox."

"And she's very close in money matters?"

She replied, after a moment, reluctantly, "Yes."

"And conservative?"

"Conservative?"

"Yes. Does she use a motor car, for instance?"

"No. She still has horses and a coupe."

"Exactly. Then what is this man Coombs?—a spiritualist?"

Mary Bryant frowned, puzzled. Evidently, she did not see any connecting thread in the sequence of Duff's questions. Evidently, too, she did not wish to gossip with Duff about those personal peculiarities of her great-aunt which she considered outside the case. "When I heard about the book on wills and forgeries," she explained, "I was afraid that Mr. Coombs was either trying to persuade her to leave money for the Hefflin Fund in his hands, or that he was thinking of forging a will—"

"Quite so," Duff interrupted again, "but which? Which is he trying to do? That's why I ask you these questions. If she's not sustained by some religious conviction, she'll probably have a serious fear of death." He was using his most florid professional manner, rather pompous. "Of course, you know, the fear of death generally shows, at her age, as miserliness and conservatism; and I judge, from your description of her, that she has a fear of death and no religious faith to help her. The next question is this: Has Coombs any faith, such as spiritualism, to offer her? If he hasn't, he'll find it impossible, I should say, to talk to her about her will. Her fear of death will make the whole subject abhorrent to her. She'll fly into a rage at him for mentioning it. And if he's determined to have the Hefflin Fund continued after her death, he'll have to forge the provision himself. Do you follow me?"

"Yes." She nodded, thoughtfully. "He's not a spiritualist. He has no religion, so far as I know." She hesitated. "Mrs. Hefflin will not live with any one who expects to gain anything by her death. That is why she refuses to see her relatives. She warned me, when I agreed to come to her, that she would leave me nothing in her will."

"She probably warned Coombs in the same way."

"I imagine so." She glanced at her secretary. "Miss Simpson believes that he's been falsifying his accounts—his expenditures from the Hefflin Fund—so as to put by something for himself."

"Naturally. Who is he? Do you know?" She knew nothing about him except what he had volunteered. He said that he came originally from St. Louis, where his father had made a fortune as a railroad contractor. He did not remember his father. His parents had been divorced in his infancy, and his mother, who was artistic, had taken him abroad at an early age to study music. He was to have been a composer; and, when he returned to America, it was as a prospective young Chopin playing his own compositions on the piano, at public recitals. He had some success, particularly in Chicago, where he was taken up socially and applauded in the drawing-rooms. He did not suppose, then, that he would ever have to make his daily bread and butter out of music, because his mother apparently had a large income and they lived expensively; but when she died suddenly of an overdose of morphine—which she was using as a sleeping medicine—he found himself penniless. She had been living on her capital, and she left him nothing but debts. He borrowed enough money to escape from Chicago. He came to New York to teach music. He had no standing in New York. He was too poor to rent a proper studio and make an impressive appearance. He failed to obtain any pupils; and he might have starved on the streets if Mrs. Hefflin had not rescued him.

"His influence over her seems rather sinister, does it?" Duff asked.

No. She could hardly say that it seemed wholly sinister. By interesting Mrs. Hefflin in music and musicians, he had supplied her with an unselfish fad that filled her day and occupied her mind. She had become the flattered patron of a number of young singers and pianists and violinists who gave recitals in her home and paid in gratitude for the assistance they obtained from the Hefflin Fund. They sang or played to her, over the heads of the people in Carnegie Hall, when she sat in her box at the public concerts which she financed. "He's very clever," Mary Bryant said. "He never allows them to come to her with any of their little professional jealousies. He keeps all their quarrels and their back-bitings from her. He's quite ruthless in the way he manages them. I should never suspect the trouble he has with them if it weren't for what Miss Simpson tells me."

She turned to Mollie Simpson as she spoke, and that tense young woman said breathlessly: "He makes fun of Mrs. Hefflin behind her back!"

Duff ignored her. He had a purpose in ignoring her. "Her heirs are alarmed, of course?" he asked Miss Bryant. "And they've come to you?"

"Yes. They seem inclined to hold me responsible. I advised them to consult their lawyer, and the lawyer replied that it was a case for a detective."

"Do they know that you've come to me?"

"No. No one knows *that.*"

"Well." Duff had picked up a lead pencil from his desk. He began, absent-mindedly, to draw a design of squares and circles, on a scratch pad. "I could have one of my operatives rope Coombs," he said, as he drew the first circle, "and make friends with him," and find out if he's planning anything crooked; but it'd take a long time, and I'd have to use the cleverest detective I've got, and that'd cost you a lot of money." He put a square around the circle. "Or I could wire to Chicago and St. Louis, and have some of my people there pick up his trail and get his record. We might be able to judge from *that* whether he was on the level with you all; and, if he wasn't, we could blow him up with the information we got. But that would cost a lot of money, too, and it might be money thrown away. We might not find anything against him." He joined the corners of the square with diagonals that crossed each other in the center of the circle. "It would be better if we could make a little plant for him and try him out—a plant that wouldn't work if he was innocent and *would* work if he was planning anything crooked." He was drawing radial lines from the center of the circle to meet the circumference where it touched the sides of the square. "That wouldn't take so much time or cost so much money. It'd have to be arranged so as to clear him of any of your suspicions, if he was innocent, and scare him into running away if he was guilty." He was shading alternate segments of the circle in a pattern of black and white. "It ought to turn on the question of whether or not he was thinking of Mrs. Hefflin's will—either trying to get her to make a provision for him under the Hefflin Fund or flirting with the idea of forging a codicil, or something of that sort." He turned abruptly to Mollie Simpson. "Could you be called out of town for a day or two?"

"Out of town?"

"Yes. Have you any out-of-town friends or relatives who might send you a wire?"

She all but whispered her reply, in the gasping tenseness of excited conspiracy. "I have a married sister, in Schenectady."

"That will do." He dropped his pencil. "I'll phone you to say a telegram has come for you—as if I were speaking from your home, you understand. You'll tell me to open it. I'll say it's from your sister, that she's ill and wants you to come to her right away. You'll explain the situation to Coombs and leave at once—to be gone two or three days. You'll go home, then, and stay there till you hear from me. I'll try him out while you're gone. If he doesn't fall for me while you're away, I'll have a story ready for you when you get back. It'll explain everything innocently, of course. See? You don't have anything to do, *now*, but to take my message over the phone, tell Coombs you have to leave at once for Schenectady, and go quietly home. Do you understand?"

She understood, with eager alacrity. After being slighted and ignored by him, she found herself unexpectedly consulted and relied upon. It went to her head—as he intended it should. She asked, "What are you going to do?" as wide-eyed as a Joan of Arc prepared to accept her fate, no matter what it might be, with a devoted self-abnegation. "What are you going to do?"

"I'm not quite sure yet," he said, doubtfully. He thought a moment. "Could you borrow his book on 'Questioned Documents'?"

"Yes."

"And take it with you? Without letting him know?"

"Ye-e-es."

"If he's still here when you return, I'll find a way to give it an innocent appearance."

"Are you going to—to frighten him?"

"I'm going to try him out. I don't quite know how." He rose, preoccupied, and held out his hand to Mary Bryant. "I'll have to feel my way into it. You'll hear from me by telephone. And if you see me anywhere, just pretend that you don't know me. Good-by. I'll report to you in a day or two. You'd better go out through the file room."

He ushered them to the inner door of his office and handed them over to Mrs. Cooley again.

"I'll phone you late this afternoon, Miss Simpson," he said. "You'll leave for Schenectady to-night, and I'll call on Coombs to-morrow."

II

It was almost midday of a muggy, warm spring morning, when Duff arrived at Mrs. Hefflin's door, and he looked as hot as a big policeman in his winter suit of semi-official dark blue, a double-breasted jacket, a hard bowler hat, and the thick-soled shoes of a patrolman. He had left an operative in an automobile to wait for him at the corner of the street, and he advanced up Mrs. Hefflin's brownstone entrance steps as threateningly as if he had come to serve a summons. He reached out the relentless arm of the law to the bell. He did not merely press the button; he squashed it with his huge thumb. "Coombs," he said to the maid who opened the door. She fell back before him as he shouldered his way in.

"Who wants to see him?" she asked.

"I do," he said. He was standing with his hat on, looking around him in the manner of suspicious authority.

She asked timidly, "What's the name, please?"

He did not lower his eyes to her. "Hurry up," he growled. "Don't waste my time." He frowned at the closed doors of the drawing-room across the hall—double doors of dark walnut, inlaid with a marquetry of lighter wood—and without paying any further heed to her, he went to those doors as if he were making a raid on them, opened them officially, and walked into the drawing-room, still with his hat on.

She ran upstairs in a panic.

He knew, of course, that Coombs was in. He had learned *that* from Mary Bryant, by telephone, before he came. He could not tell the maid that he was a policeman; he would be liable under the law for impersonating an officer; but his pantomime was designed to send her, frightened, to Coombs, with the news that a policeman was downstairs; and, having achieved his effect, he took off his hat, and unbuttoned his coat, and hooked his thumb into his watch pocket.

He was on a carpet so thick and so padded that his big feet sank into it as though he were walking on a feather bed. He was facing a mirror over the mantelpiece—a high mirror, framed in tarnished gilt, over a marble mantelshelf that was full of the majolica and porcelain and Dresden china of a grandmother's esthetic impulse. Above him there glittered an old glass chandelier, all silver-frost and crystal, modernized with electric bulbs. There were gilt cornices at the tops of the window frames, and below them hung looped and tasseled layers of curtains and undercurtains and sash curtains, as many as the petticoats of a reigning belle in the days of crinoline. The room, in fact, was as old-fashioned as Mrs. Hefflin herself, and as well preserved—with a stuffy odor of rose-leaved decay, sweet and dry, and in the curtained gloom of that ancient magnificence, Duff's great muscled bulk made him an ominous figure.

It was with an air of very conscious rectitude that Coombs appeared suddenly in the doorway. "What's the matter?" he asked, and his voice was light and high.

Duff looked him over, without replying. Coombs was perhaps thirty-five years old, slight and boyish, in a cheerful spring suit, with a bow tie and a low collar. Sensitive-looking and obviously nervous, he confronted Duff's silent scrutiny, pale and staring. His eyes, large and dark as a girl's, were the eyes of a poet, but he was bald; and his cheeks were sunken and his face was lined and wrinkled.

Duff answered, at last, in a low voice: "Come in and shut that door."

After a moment of hesitation he came in defiantly but he did not shut the door. "What's the matter?" he demanded. "You can't force your way in here like this. This is a private house. What do you want?"

Duff passed him in silence and closed the door. "You've had a girl named Mollie Simpson working for you here," he said, "haven't you?" And when Coombs did not reply, he asked, "Where'd you get her?"

Coombs, relieved, thrust his hands deep into his trouser pockets. "She answered my advertisement."

"Did you know anything about her?"

"Certainly not."

"Where did she say she was going, when she left here yesterday?"

"To see a sick relative—a sister—in Schenectady."

"Sounds phoney," Duff grumbled. "Do you know whether she's really got a sister in Schenectady?"

"No." Coombs frowned. "What are you? A detective?"

"Yes." Duff eyed him balefully. "Did you know she took away a book of yours?"

"A book of *mine?*"

"Yes. A book called 'Questioned Documents.' "

"No! Did she? I missed it this morning. I wondered what—" He had begun by being surprised, not alarmed; but it was on some sudden thought, not merely of surprise, that he stopped in the middle of his sentence.

"That's a book about forged signatures and fraudulent wills, isn't it?"

"Yes," he answered, uneasily.

"Did you know that she's been taking scraps out of your wastebasket and piecing them together?"

He shook his head. "No," he said, rather hoarsely.

"Well, she *has.*" Duff was studying him as coolly as a chemist who adds a reagent to a solution in a test-tube and watches its effect. "She's been taking scraps out of your wastebasket and piecing them together."

Coombs did not speak; he cleared his throat, but he uttered no word.

"Signatures," Duff added and Coombs's eyes, that had been fixed in the stare of a scared girl, wavered in a horrid apprehension. He turned a sickly green.

Duff took him by the elbow. "Come over here."

He led the unwilling Coombs to a Victorian sofa by the window—a sofa as beautiful in its lines as the curves of a harp—and forced him to sit in the rounded corner of it. He sat down sideways himself, facing Coombs, still holding him firmly by the elbow and crowding him against the sofa arm with his immense knees.

"That's all right," he said, in a tone criminally low and confidential. "Mollie doesn't mean you any harm. And neither do *I*. We just want to get in on anything you make out of this game. And we'll help you *make* it. You can't pull it off alone. It takes experience. I'm not a detective; I'm a lawyer, see? I know more about wills than the guy that invented them. And I've got a clerk—see?—on my staff—a regular Jim the Penman. He can write the old girl's signature so she wouldn't know, *herself*, that it wasn't hers. You can make a lot more money out of this Hefflin Fund than you've been making. We can help you there. You tell the old lady you want your accounts audited, and I'll get you an accountant that'll always give you a clean bill, no matter what your books look like. Then you work me in as your legal adviser for the Fund—see?—and get me next to Mrs. Hefflin, so's people'll get used to seeing me around, and when she croaks I'll have a will all signed, sealed and delivered, making you and me executors for a Hefflin Fund as big as the Rockefeller Foundation. You won't have to do anything but sit back and take the money. We'll work up all the documents. *You* can't do it. You don't know how. It's no job for an amateur. You need a professional. That's me."

Coombs, held helpless in the corner of the sofa, had listened, hypnotized. "I don't," he gasped. "I haven't—"

"No, of course," Duff soothed him. "I understand. You've just been playing with the idea. You haven't been planning seriously to carry it out. I understand that. You've nicked a few dollars off your accounts, but that's as far as you've gone. When you ran across this book exposing forgeries and fake wills, you just tried a few signatures to see if you could make the grade better than the guys in the book. I understand all that. The point is that I need the money. So does Mollie. She's my little prospector. She goes out and locates the pay-dirt and I come along later and pan it out. This's a good claim you've got here, but you can't work it without taking us in on it, see? We've got your book and your signatures and a line on the accounts that you've been padding. We don't want to make any trouble for you, but you've either got to play with us or take a tumble. If you turn us down"—Duff chuckled, with a loathsome geniality—"we'll turn you up. If you want any more of the old dame's money, you've got to share it with *us*, see?"

Coombs looked around him wildly, in search of some way of escape. That was an impulse which Duff did not wish to check.

"All right," he said, "think it over. I don't need to crowd you. Take your own time. I'll come in and see you again, this afternoon. There's no hurry, see? The old girl's good for a few years yet—unless you make up your mind to bump her off. That's up to you." He patted Coombs on the knee and rose cheerfully. "Think it over. The more you think about it, the more you'll realize why you've got to take us in on it. You need us as much as we need you. I'll see you later." He put on his hat. "I'll drop in, again, this afternoon."

He glanced back as he opened the door. Coombs sat, crowded into his corner of the sofa, watching him go, so paralyzed with the encounter that he was unable to move as long as Duff was still in sight. Duff nodded good-by to him—a sinister nod that was a threat and a confirmation.

There was no one in the hall. He let himself out the front door and sauntered back to his operative in the automobile. "We'll wait here a minute or two, Jack," he said, as he climbed into the closed car. "I've lit a fire under a lad in there and I think he's going to bolt."

The operative had been sitting at the steering wheel, like a waiting chauffeur, reading his morning paper. "What's he up to, Chief?" he asked idly.

"I don't think he knows," Duff said. "I suggested several things to him that he might run into if he went ahead along the road he's on—several things, including murder—and he looked as if he'd climb the fence and take to the fields as soon as I was out of the way. I want to see which way he goes, in case he carries off anything that we'll have to bring back."

The man went on reading his paper. Duff settled himself comfortably in his seat, took up a book from the cushions beside him, and began to turn over the leaves while he waited. The book was Coombs's copy of "Questioned Documents." Duff had obtained it from Mollie Simpson in the hope that he might find on its margins some definite indication of what aspect of fraud and forgery

Coombs had been most interested in. He had found nothing. He found nothing now. He turned the pages, in a sort of absent-minded muse, preoccupied with the memory of Coombs's frightened expression of face when he saw himself involved in a conspiracy to steal and forge and perhaps murder.

Duff smiled to himself—a smile of contemptuous pity—with an eye on Mrs. Hefflin's entrance steps.

"Here he comes!"

Coombs hesitated a moment at the door, a suitcase in his hand, an overcoat on his arm. He looked up and down the street, to make sure that Duff was nowhere in sight. "Going traveling, I guess," Duff concluded. "Follow him up to the station, Jack, and see where he buys a ticket for."

Coombs was walking rapidly away from them, in the direction of the Grand Central Station. The operative started the car and began to follow slowly at a safe distance. "Wait a minute," Duff said. "Drop me at the house, and as soon as you find out where he's heading for, phone me here. Mrs. Newton P. Hefflin. You'll find the number in the book. I want to talk to them before he gets too far on his way."

"All right, Chief."

"Wait till he's around the corner."

As soon as Coombs had disappeared, Duff dropped off, with "Questioned Documents" in his hand, and the car darted ahead again. Duff mounted Mrs. Hefflin's steps for the second time, but now he was as carelessly cheerful as a book agent. He rang a staccato passage on the bell. "Good morning!" he greeted the maid, with a broad conspiring smile. "Miss Bryant's waiting to see me. Tell her I'm here, will you? The name's Duff."

"Well!" she cried, in indignant surprise at this change of manner.

"Yes. Thanks," he said. "Quite well." He bowed his way past her, with a burlesque politeness. "Don't keep Miss Bryant waiting," he added, over his shoulder, as he entered the drawing-room.

"Well!" he heard her say again as she started up the stairs.

He put his copy of "Questioned Documents" on an old "clover leaf" table between the windows, and covered the book with his hat. He began to pace thoughtfully up and down the room, pursing his lips. After all it was not a satisfactory solution of the case—to drive Coombs out on the streets again, and end his charitable administration of the Hefflin Fund, and leave Mrs. Hefflin without the innocent fad that Coombs had found for her.

"I'm afraid I've gone too far," he said, at once to Mary Bryant, as soon as she appeared in the doorway. "I've frightened Coombs into running away. He's up at the Grand Central, now, buying a railroad ticket. One of my men is watching him. He'll phone me in a few minutes. I want to talk the thing over with you, and decide what to do."

"How did you frighten him?"

She seated herself placidly on the sofa where Duff had put the screws on Coombs. She folded her hands in her lap. Duff, still pacing up and down the room, gave her a carefully expurgated account of his interview with Coombs. "He's a dreamer," he concluded. "He's been a mama's boy. His mother took all the practical business of life out of his hands and left him to his imagination. He's what we call a Narcissan—in love with himself—and he can't take punishment any better than a girl. As soon as he saw himself in danger, he beat it. Now, here's the point. He's capable of dreaming about forging a will for Mrs. Hefflin but he couldn't possibly carry it out, and now that I've turned his dream into a nightmare for him, he'll never think of it again except with horror. I'll guarantee that. He's safer than if he'd never thought of it in the first place, you understand."

"Yes," she said. "I see."

"Well, then," he argued, "it'd be wiser to keep him here than to let him go—better for Mrs. Hefflin, and himself, and these young musicians. We can get the Fund properly administered, so he'll not be tempted to juggle his accounts—"

"But I thought you said he'd run away?"

"I've got an operative with him. He's going to phone me here. I'll have him bring Coombs back, if the poor mut hasn't jumped the first train for Nowhere."

She rose at once. "The telephone's upstairs," she said, "in the library."

III

Within a quarter of an hour, Duff, at the drawing-room window saw his operative drive up with Coombs in the car and help him out—as weak and unsteady as if he were being brought home, a feeble convalescent, after a month in the hospital. Coombs had bought a ticket for Toronto, Canada, but his train was not to start for an hour, and he had gone to sit in the waiting-room while the operative phoned the news to Duff. "Trot him back here," Duff had said, "right away. I want to see him." And the operative had brought him back by merely taking him firmly by the upper arm, picking up his suitcase, and saying, "Bo, you're wanted. Come along."

It was so that he led Coombs, now, from the automobile to the Hefflin steps, as dumb and as dazed as if he were being marched from Murderers' Row to the death house and the electric chair. He looked glassily at Duff when Duff opened the door—without waiting for them to ring—and if he recognized the detective, he showed no recognition in his blank stare. He allowed himself to be passed across the threshold to Duff, stiffly trembling. "All right, Jack," Duff said, "put his coat and his bag in the hall here and wait out in the car. Come along, Coombs. I want to talk to you."

Coombs allowed himself to be taken into the drawing-room and led to the sofa. "Sit down," Duff turned him round. He sat down as if his knees were jerked out from under him. He had his hat on. His hands lay, palms up, limp in his lap. Duff put the hat on them. He drew a long shuddering breath.

"Come out of it," Duff said. "You're all right. Nobody's going to hurt you. I just wanted to throw a scare into you. Some of Mrs. Hefflin's heirs have been worried about what you were doing here, and they paid me to find out. You haven't done anything to go to jail for. Come out of it. Don't be a damn fool."

It was like trying to talk a semiconscious man out of a faint.

"I'm not a crook," Duff explained. "I'm a detective. I sent a decoy telegram to your secretary, last night, to get her out of the way, and then I slipped a man in here to go through your desk. *He* stole your copy of 'Questioned Documents'—not the Simpson girl. We figured out that you had probably been trying your hand at the old lady's signature, so we cooked up that story about piecing together scraps from your waste-basket. And we suspected that you'd probably been making something out of the Hefflin Fund, on the side, so we added *that* to our little plant." Some color had begun to return to Coombs's cheeks. He breathed a trembling sigh as his lungs relaxed. "I just wanted to throw a scare into you. I wanted to show you the road you were on, and where it'd probably lead you to, if you didn't jerk yourself up. Nobody knows about it but me. You behave yourself, from now on, and the whole thing'll go no further."

Tears of relief had gathered in Coombs's dazed eyes. His lips began to tremble. He wept silently, staring ahead of him, with his face distorted, as shameless as a whimpering child.

Duff reached the copy of "Questioned Documents" from the table. "Here," he said. "Put that back where it belongs and we'll say no more about it."

Coombs could not touch the book. Duff laid it on his knees and it fell to the floor.

"You go to Mrs. Hefflin and tell her that you want a board of trustees to handle her Fund—a board composed of yourself, and her lawyer and Miss Bryant. You understand? Then you'll not be able to juggle your accounts. I'll report that I've investigated you and found you all to the good. If you're ever tempted to try any monkey tricks, remember that I'm laying for you and sure to trip you up. Go to it now, and keep your mouth shut." He put on his hat. "When the Simpson girl gets back here, she'll tell you that the telegram from her sister was a fake. That's all right. You don't know anything about it, see? Keep your mouth shut and watch your step. Good-by. I hope I never see you again as long as I live. You make me sick."

He paused in the doorway to give the abject Coombs one last disgusted look. Then he hurried out to his motor car. "Step on it, Jack," he said. "I've got to get back to the office. We're done with this case."

~ ~ ~

When the Hefflin Fund was incorporated under the administration of Mary Bryant and Michael Raffaelli Coombs, the newspapers made Mrs. Newton P. Hefflin famous as a patron of American music and its native composers. There is talk of crowning Coombs before the Academy of Arts and Letters for his services to culture. "Well," Duff says, "it's better than shaving his head and giving him a pair of handcuffs."

THE END

RAMBLE HOUSE's

HARRY STEPHEN KEELER WEBWORK MYSTERIES

(RH) indicates the title is available ONLY in the RAMBLE HOUSE edition

The Ace of Spades Murder
The Affair of the Bottled Deuce (RH)
The Amazing Web
The Barking Clock
Behind That Mask
The Book with the Orange Leaves
The Bottle with the Green Wax Seal
The Box from Japan
The Case of the Canny Killer
The Case of the Crazy Corpse (RH)
The Case of the Flying Hands (RH)
The Case of the Ivory Arrow
The Case of the Jeweled Ragpicker
The Case of the Lavender Gripsack
The Case of the Mysterious Moll
The Case of the 16 Beans
The Case of the Transparent Nude (RH)
The Case of the Transposed Legs
The Case of the Two-Headed Idiot (RH)
The Case of the Two Strange Ladies
The Circus Stealers (RH)
Cleopatra's Tears
A Copy of Beowulf (RH)
The Crimson Cube (RH)
The Face of the Man From Saturn
Find the Clock
The Five Silver Buddhas
The 4th King
The Gallows Waits, My Lord! (RH)
The Green Jade Hand
Finger! Finger!
Hangman's Nights (RH)
I, Chameleon (RH)
I Killed Lincoln at 10:13! (RH)
The Iron Ring
The Man Who Changed His Skin (RH)
The Man with the Crimson Box
The Man with the Magic Eardrums
The Man with the Wooden Spectacles
The Marceau Case
The Matilda Hunter Murder
The Monocled Monster

The Murder of London Lew
The Murdered Mathematician
The Mysterious Card (RH)
The Mysterious Ivory Ball of Wong Shing Li (RH)
The Mystery of the Fiddling Cracksman
The Peacock Fan
The Photo of Lady X (RH)
The Portrait of Jirjohn Cobb
Report on Vanessa Hewstone (RH)
Riddle of the Travelling Skull
Riddle of the Wooden Parrakeet (RH)
The Scarlet Mummy (RH)
The Search for X-Y-Z
The Sharkskin Book
Sing Sing Nights
The Six From Nowhere (RH)
The Skull of the Waltzing Clown
The Spectacles of Mr. Cagliostro
Stand By—London Calling!
The Steeltown Strangler
The Stolen Gravestone (RH)
Strange Journey (RH)
The Strange Will
The Straw Hat Murders (RH)
The Street of 1000 Eyes (RH)
Thieves' Nights
Three Novellos (RH)
The Tiger Snake
The Trap (RH)
Vagabond Nights (Defrauded Yeggman)
Vagabond Nights 2 (10 Hours)
The Vanishing Gold Truck
The Voice of the Seven Sparrows
The Washington Square Enigma
When Thief Meets Thief
The White Circle (RH)
The Wonderful Scheme of Mr. Christopher Thorne
X. Jones—of Scotland Yard
Y. Cheung, Business Detective

Keeler Related Works

A To Izzard: A Harry Stephen Keeler Companion by Fender Tucker — Articles and stories about Harry, by Harry, and in his style. Included is a compleat bibliography.

Wild About Harry: Reviews of Keeler Novels — Edited by Richard Polt & Fender Tucker — 22 reviews of works by Harry Stephen Keeler from *Keeler News*. A perfect introduction to the author.

The Keeler Keyhole Collection: Annotated newsletter rants from Harry Stephen Keeler, edited by Francis M. Nevins. Over 400 pages of incredibly personal Keeleriana.

Fakealoo — Pastiches of the style of Harry Stephen Keeler by selected demented members of the HSK Society. Updated every year with the new winner.

RAMBLE HOUSE's OTHER LOONS

Mysterious Martin, the Master of Murder — Two versions of a strange 1912 novel by Tod Robbins about a man who writes books that can kill.

The Master of Mysteries — 1912 novel of supernatural sleuthing by Gelett Burgess

Dago Red — 22 tales of dark suspense by Bill Pronzini

The Night Remembers — A 1991 Jack Walsh mystery from Ed Gorman

Rough Cut & New, Improved Murder — Ed Gorman's first two novels

Four Gelett Burgess Novels — *The Master of Mysteries, The White Cat, Two O'Clock Courage, Ladies in Boxes,* with more to come from Surinam Turtle Press

The Organ Reader — A huge compilation of just about everything published in the 1971-1972 radical bay-area newspaper, *THE ORGAN.*

A Clear Path to Cross — Sharon Knowles short mystery stories by Ed Lynskey

Old Times' Sake — Short stories by James Reasoner from Mike Shayne Magazine

Freaks and Fantasies — Eerie tales by Tod Robbins, collaborator of Tod Browning on the film FREAKS.

Four Jim Harmon Sleaze Double Novels — *Vixen Hollow/Celluloid Scandal, The Man Who Made Maniacs/Silent Siren, Ape Rape/Wanton Witch* and *Sex Burns Like Fire/Twist Session.* More doubles to come!

Marblehead: A Novel of H.P. Lovecraft — A long-lost masterpiece from Richard A. Lupoff. Published for the first time!

The Compleat Ova Hamlet — Parodies of SF authors by Richard A. Lupoff – New edition!

The Secret Adventures of Sherlock Holmes — Three Sherlockian pastiches by the Brooklyn author/publisher, Gary Lovisi.

The Universal Holmes — Richard A. Lupoff's 2007 collection of five Holmesian pastiches and a recipe for giant rat stew.

Four Joel Townsley Rogers Novels — By the author of *The Red Right Hand: Once In a Red Moon, Lady With the Dice, The Stopped Clock, Never Leave My Bed*

Two Joel Townsley Rogers Story Collections — *Night of Horror* and *Killing Time*

Twenty Norman Berrow Novels — *The Bishop's Sword, Ghost House, Don't Go Out After Dark, Claws of the Cougar, The Smokers of Hashish, The Secret Dancer, Don't Jump Mr. Boland!, The Footprints of Satan, Fingers for Ransom, The Three Tiers of Fantasy, The Spaniard's Thumb, The Eleventh Plague, Words Have Wings, One Thrilling Night, The Lady's in Danger, It Howls at Night, The Terror in the Fog, Oil Under the Window, Murder in the Melody, The Singing Room*

The N. R. De Mexico Novels — Robert Bragg presents *Marijuana Girl, Madman on a Drum, Private Chauffeur* in one volume.

Four Chelsea Quinn Yarbro Novels featuring Charlie Moon — *Ogilvie, Tallant and Moon, Music When the Sweet Voice Dies, Poisonous Fruit* and *Dead Mice*

The Green Toad — Impossible mysteries by Walter S. Masterman – More to come!

Two Hake Talbot Novels — *Rim of the Pit, The Hangman's Handyman.* Classic locked room mysteries.

Two Alexander Laing Novels — *The Motives of Nicholas Holtz* and *Dr. Scarlett,* stories of medical mayhem and intrigue from the 30s.

Four David Hume Novels — *Corpses Never Argue, Cemetery First Stop, Make Way for the Mourners, Eternity Here I Come,* and more to come.

Three Wade Wright Novels — *Echo of Fear, Death At Nostalgia Street* and *It Leads to Murder,* with more to come!

Four Rupert Penny Novels — *Policeman's Holiday, Policeman's Evidence, Lucky Policeman* and *Sealed Room Murder,* classic impossible mysteries.

Five Jack Mann Novels — Strange murder in the English countryside. *Gees' First Case, Nightmare Farm, Grey Shapes, The Ninth Life, The Glass Too Many.*

Six Max Afford Novels — *Owl of Darkness, Death's Mannikins, Blood on His Hands, The Dead Are Blind, The Sheep and the Wolves* and *Sinners in Paradise* by One of Australia's finest novelists.

Five Joseph Shallit Novels — *The Case of the Billion Dollar Body, Lady Don't Die on My Doorstep, Kiss the Killer, Yell Bloody Murder, Take Your Last Look.* One of America's best 50's authors.

Two Crimson Clown Novels — By Johnston McCulley, author of the Zorro novels, *The Crimson Clown* and *The Crimson Clown Again.*

The Best of 10-Story Book — edited by Chris Mikul, over 35 stories from the literary magazine Harry Stephen Keeler edited.

A Young Man's Heart — A forgotten early classic by Cornell Woolrich

The Anthony Boucher Chronicles — edited by Francis M. Nevins
Book reviews by Anthony Boucher written for the *San Francisco Chronicle, 1942 – 1947.* Essential and fascinating reading.

Muddled Mind: Complete Works of Ed Wood, Jr. — David Hayes and Hayden Davis deconstruct the life and works of a mad genius.

Gadsby — A lipogram (a novel without the letter E). Ernest Vincent Wright's last work, published in 1939 right before his death.

My First Time: The One Experience You Never Forget — Michael Birchwood — 64 true first-person narratives of how they lost it.

The Black Box — Stylish 1908 classic by M. P. Shiel. Very hard to find.

The Incredible Adventures of Rowland Hern — Rousing 1928 impossible crimes by Nicholas Olde.

Slammer Days — Two full-length prison memoirs: *Men into Beasts* (1952) by George Sylvester Viereck and *Home Away From Home* (1962) by Jack Woodford

Beat Books #1 — Two beatnik classics, *A Sea of Thighs* by Ray Kainen and *Village Hipster* by J.X. Williams

Ruled By Radio — 1925 futuristic novel by Robert L. Hadfield & Frank E. Farncombe

Murder in Silk — A 1937 Yellow Peril novel of the silk trade by Ralph Trevor

The Case of the Withered Hand — 1936 potboiler by John G. Brandon

Inclination to Murder — 1966 thriller by New Zealand's Harriet Hunter

Invaders from the Dark — Classic werewolf tale from Greye La Spina

Fatal Accident — Murder by automobile, a 1936 mystery by Cecil M. Wills

The Devil Drives — A prison and lost treasure novel by Virgil Markham

Dr. Odin — Douglas Newton's 1933 potboiler comes back to life.

The Chinese Jar Mystery — Murder in the manor by John Stephen Strange, 1934

The Julius Caesar Murder Case — A classic 1935 re-telling of the assassination by Wallace Irwin that's much more fun than the Shakespeare version

West Texas War and Other Western Stories — by Gary Lovisi

The Contested Earth and Other SF Stories — A never-before published space opera and seven short stories by Jim Harmon.

Tales of the Macabre and Ordinary — Modern twisted horror by Chris Mikul, author of the *Bizarrism* series.

The Gold Star Line — Seaboard adventure from L.T. Reade and Robert Eustace.

The Werewolf vs the Vampire Woman — Hard to believe ultraviolence by either Arthur M. Scarm or Arthur M. Scram.

Black Hogan Strikes Again — Australia's Peter Renwick pens a tale of the outback.

Don Diablo: Book of a Lost Film — Two-volume treatment of a western by Paul Landres, with diagrams. Intro by Francis M. Nevins.

The Charlie Chaplin Murder Mystery — Movie hijinks by Wes D. Gehring

The Koky Comics — A collection of all of the 1978-1981 Sunday and daily comic strips by Richard O'Brien and Mort Gerberg, in two volumes.

Suzy — Another collection of comic strips from Richard O'Brien and Bob Vojtko

Dime Novels: Ramble House's 10-Cent Books — *Knife in the Dark* by Robert Leslie Bellem, *Hot Lead* and *Song of Death* by Ed Earl Repp, *A Hashish House in New York* by H.H. Kane, and five more.

Blood in a Snap — The *Finnegan's Wake* of the 21st century, by Jim Weiler and Al Gorithm

Stakeout on Millennium Drive — Award-winning Indianapolis Noir — Ian Woollen.

Dope Tales #1 — Two dope-riddled classics; *Dope Runners* by Gerald Grantham and *Death Takes the Joystick* by Phillip Condé.

Dope Tales #2 — Two more narco-classics; *The Invisible Hand* by Rex Dark and *The Smokers of Hashish* by Norman Berrow.

Dope Tales #3 — Two enchanting novels of opium by the master, Sax Rohmer. *Dope* and *The Yellow Claw.*

Tenebrae — Ernest G. Henham's 1898 horror tale brought back.

The Singular Problem of the Stygian House-Boat — Two classic tales by John Kendrick Bangs about the denizens of Hades.

Tiresias — Psychotic modern horror novel by Jonathan M. Sweet.

The One After Snelling — Kickass modern noir from Richard O'Brien.

The Sign of the Scorpion — 1935 Edmund Snell tale of oriental evil.

The House of the Vampire — 1907 poetic thriller by George S. Viereck.

An Angel in the Street — Modern hardboiled noir by Peter Genovese.

The Devil's Mistress — Scottish gothic tale by J. W. Brodie-Innes.

The Lord of Terror — 1925 mystery with master-criminal, Fantômas.

The Lady of the Terraces — 1925 adventure by E. Charles Vivian.

My Deadly Angel — 1955 Cold War drama by John Chelton

Prose Bowl — Futuristic satire — Bill Pronzini & Barry N. Malzberg .

Satan's Den Exposed — True crime in Truth or Consequences New Mexico — Award-winning journalism by the *Desert Journal*.

The Amorous Intrigues & Adventures of Aaron Burr — by Anonymous — Hot historical action.

I Stole $16,000,000 — A true story by cracksman Herbert E. Wilson.

The Black Dark Murders — Vintage 50s college murder yarn by Milt Ozaki, writing as Robert O. Saber.

Sex Slave — Potboiler of lust in the days of Cleopatra — Dion Leclerq.

You'll Die Laughing — Bruce Elliott's 1945 novel of murder at a practical joker's English countryside manor.

The Private Journal & Diary of John H. Surratt — The memoirs of the man who conspired to assassinate President Lincoln.

Dead Man Talks Too Much — Hollywood boozer by Weed Dickenson

Red Light — History of legal prostitution in Shreveport Louisiana by Eric Brock. Includes wonderful photos of the houses and the ladies.

A Snark Selection — Lewis Carroll's *The Hunting of the Snark* with two Snarkian chapters by Harry Stephen Keeler — Illustrated by Gavin L. O'Keefe.

Ripped from the Headlines! — The Jack the Ripper story as told in the newspaper articles in the *New York* and *London Times*.

Geronimo — S. M. Barrett's 1905 autobiography of a noble American.

The White Peril in the Far East — Sidney Lewis Gulick's 1905 indictment of the West and assurance that Japan would never attack the U.S.

The Compleat Calhoon — All of Fender Tucker's works: Includes *The Totah Trilogy, Weed, Women and Song* and *Tales from the Tower,* plus a CD of all of his songs.

RAMBLE HOUSE
Fender Tucker, Prop.
www.ramblehouse.com   fender@ramblehouse.com
318-455-6847   443 Gladstone Blvd.   Shreveport LA 71104